The Author would like to acknowledge the use of lines from a traditional Appalachian folk ballad *Down in the Willow Garden* and the use of lines from Sir Harold Boulton's *The Skye Boat Song*, a Scottish Folk song.

Paperback ISBN: 978-1-62251-039-9

Summary: A young woman caught between two worlds fights a deep anxiety while searching for the truth.

For my family,
with gratitude and love.

Dragon song

Jennifer Carson

Prologue

Sophie, age 6

Sophie poked her finger into the thin-skinned air bubble in the bread dough. She liked the pop it made when the trapped yeasty air burst out. Her mom giggled with her and pushed the dough over Sophie's hands, trapping them in the warmth. Making bread with Momma on Monday mornings after Daddy went to work was her favorite thing.

Mom screwed up her face and held her finger in the air like she was making an important announcement. Wisps of light brown hair stuck to her damp forehead. "I declare this loaf of bread will be the best in all the kingdom."

Sophie giggled and slid her hands out of her dough jail.

A loud rap on the apartment door broke through their giggles. Before Sophie's mom could wipe her hands, the door was forced open, the metal knob crunching into the wall. Sprinkles of plaster littered the wood floor.

Her mother whisked her off the stepstool. "Hide Sophie," she hissed and pushed her toward the bedroom. The high-pitched note in her mother's voice told Sophie not to argue.

She raced down the hall and climbed into the wardrobe and huddled in the corner of the wooden closet. Her chest was tight under her sweater, beads of sweat dampening her forehead. She pulled the doors closed from the inside. The small click of the latch might as well have been an explosion. The cabinet had been in her mother's family for a very long time, passed from mother to daughter for centuries. It wasn't the first time she'd hidden in it, and usually her heart sped from the excitement of the game. But this time, it didn't feel like a game.

She crushed her knees into her forehead, her breath pooling hot and damp in her face. An image of the witch cooking little children from Gran's storybook sprang to mind.

A rush of prickly heat spread down Sophie's arms and made her fingers tingle. What was happening? Who had pushed their door open? She unfolded herself, and on shaky legs she rose to peek into the room, one eye pressed against the keyhole.

Her mom stumbled backward through the bedroom door. A wide-chested man followed. His chin thrust forward, his heavy black boots crushed the cream carpet.

"Where is she?" His lips curled like a snarling dog. "Where is the little chit?"

Her mom shook her head, eyes wide. The man's hand connected with Mom's cheek. The slap echoed in the room like the lid of an alley dumpster slammed shut by the wind.

Sophie ground her teeth so hard they ached. She longed to fly out of the cabinet and punch that man in the stomach. She curled her fingers into fists. She raised her hand to push the door open when the man snarled. "Tell me where the girl is!"

"She's too young to have gone far on her own."

Sophie's mouth fell open. A sudden chill took hold. Was the man looking for her? A warm head pushed under her arm and Sophie wrapped her arms around the long neck of her friend, Bailean. Usually she only saw him at Gran's house, but she was glad he'd come. She buried her head into his chest.

~Stay hidden. That is what your mom would want you to do, Bailean's voice whispered in her mind. They always talked to

each other like that, in their minds, where no one else could hear them.

Sophie didn't know the man in the room, but she did know that he wasn't a nice person. Bailean's scales were warm and the comforting beat of his heart drummed her cheek.

"The girl!"

"I don't know who you're talking about." Her mom's whisper was hoarse and tight. "I'm the only one here."

Sophie trembled, wanting to obey her mom's orders, but hating that her mom was being hurt. She bit her bottom lip until the taste of blood filled her mouth. Another slap echoed through the room and Sophie cringed. Her mother gasped but did not cry out.

Bailean wrapped his tail around Sophie and pulled her close. *~Don't worry. We'll protect you.*

Gathering courage from the dragon, Sophie drew a deep breath. She peeked back into the bedroom.

Droplets of red splattered across her mom's apron as the man struck her again. Her mom touched her split lip with a shaking hand. She straightened, muscles stiff as boards. "Hit me all you want. I will not yield."

A small smile grew on Sophie's face and she sagged against Bailean. It would be all right. Her mom was brave. She would get the man to leave.

Footsteps thundered in the stairwell, loud as a gang of elephants marching through a forest. Someone was coming to help! Sophie struggled in Bailean's grip. Why did he still have such a strong grip on her?

~We don't know that it's someone coming to help, Sophie. Be quiet!

An older man marched into the bedroom followed by four others. "Have you not broken her silence yet?"

The lilt of his voice was familiar, like someone Sophie had once known, but the tone was chilling. She promised Bailean she'd be quiet. He loosened his tail-grip on her just enough that she could press her eye against the keyhole once more. The man stepped further into the room.

He was dressed strangely—nothing like how her dad dressed when he went to work. His pants were baggy and held up at his waist by a thick belt. His shirt had poufy sleeves with lace on the cuffs. A large black key hung from his belt, and a green jewel shone from its perch on his finger. And then Sophie remembered; she knew this man.

Her parents had taken her to the Renaissance festival at the Cloister's museum a few weeks ago. He had sung a ballad to the queen in a voice her mother had called *velvet*. She remembered the way his hair stuck up, like a cornered alley cat. He'd taken a photo with her and mom. It was pegged to the refrigerator door with a magnet from the museum. The king had pretended to be amazed at the camera, even calling it a magic artist box and asking Dad where he had found such a tiny being to paint the portraits. Sophie had thought he was funny and after seeing the intertwined dragons carved into his belt buckle, she confided in him about her friend, Bailean.

Her gaze traveled to his belt buckle. The intertwined dragons made her insides freeze. The king-man cleared his throat as the other men shuffled about, crowding into the small space. His hands clasped around Mom's upper arms, gently at first, and with an open smile.

Then the man's grip suddenly tightened. "Maria…"

Sophie's mother gasped. Her eyes burned bright.

The king-man's smile turned into a smirk. "Pity you did not recognize me at the festival. I knew you as soon as I saw you, though you've darkened your hair and put on a man's wardrobe. And the child, she is the mirror image of her mother. No?"

Her mom looked away, her shoulders curling in. The man picked up her chin with his hand and forced her to look at him. His voice was soft. "Tell me where she is."

Tears stung Sophie's eyes as her mom's gaze wavered toward the wardrobe. "You must be mistaking me for someone else."

"Come now, there's no need to pretend," the man said, his voice low and even. His thumb stroked the bruise starting to color Mom's cheek.

A gleam lit her mother's eyes and she stood straight and stiff again. "Your caring pretense will not work with me. You will never find her."

The man shoved her mom into the wall, where she curled in the corner, just like Sophie, except her mom didn't have Bailean to protect her. That's it. Bailean should protect Mom.

~No. I have to stay with you.

A loud thud reverberated throughout the room. A moment later the mirror above her mom's dresser shattered. The vase the king-man had thrown at it tumbled to the floor. The other men in the room snickered. Sophie's mind raced. Bailean's tail coiled tight again. Her heart warred as the dragon restrained her. As if Bailean could read her mind, his tail-grip pulled her further into the closet. She struggled, wanting to go to her mom, especially since Bailean wouldn't help. Her foot bumped the paneled door.

"NO!" her mom screamed.

~What have you done, Sophie?

The hair on Sophie's body stood up. She squeezed her eyes tight and her arms close.

The king-man turned an ice-cold glare at her hiding spot. "Come out, come out wherever you are. Sophie, I'm your friend. Don't you remember? You told me about your dragon."

Sophie bit her lip. She'd learned to obey her elders. To respect their wishes…

~No, Sophie. He must not find you. It's the only way to save her.

~But I met him at the festival. He has dragons on his belt.

~He is not our friend.

Sophie curled into Bailean, making herself as small as a mouse. Her bottom lip trembled and her ears grew hot. Beads of sweat trickled down her neck. "You can't see me, you can't see me, you can't see me," Sophie whispered over and over, hands tight over her eyes. She cringed as footsteps approached.

The door of the wardrobe flung open.

Sophie's heart jumped into her throat; her stomach threatened to be sick. The king-man tore the clothing from the hangers above her. Mom's silky shirts and cozy sweaters swept over her head.

Sophie repeated the mantra in her mind: *You can't see me. You can't see me.*

The man's ragged breathing brushed her neck and she stiffened. His hands scuffed along the wooden base by her feet. He was searching; his fingers picked at cracks in the wardrobe's floor and slid over the painted walls. The now empty hangers swayed and squeaked against the rod, and clanged into each other. Sophie struggled to hold her breath. Her lungs cried out for air, but she thrust her face deep into Bailean's chest, fighting the overwhelming panic.

The king-man cursed and slammed the wardrobe doors. They cracked like thunder as they bounced off the frame. "Search the other chambers! Leave nothing unturned. There's no telling what other powers she has. Look everywhere. Even if only a mouse would fit."

With a sob, Sophie gasped and turned on wobbly legs. She couldn't believe it had worked—the man really couldn't see her. Just like a spell in a fairy tale.

The lock did not catch, and one of the wardrobe doors hung open, allowing her to see into the room. The bed sheets were in a pile on the floor, the mattress hung half off the bed frame. Dresser drawers were overturned, their contents scattered across the floor.

She had to make it stop. She had to save her mom. She bit her lip. What could she do that would matter in a room full of men?

~*Stay here.* Bailean's voice was firm but soft.

Drawing the dagger from his belt, the king-man cornered her mom. "You think you're clever hiding her from me, don't you?" Sunlight glared on the metal biting at Mom's throat. A drop of crimson slid down her neck. The butt of the knife struck her mom's temple. With a whimper, she crumpled to the floor.

The coils of Bailean's tail did not relax. Sophie's cheeks were wet and sticky. Her body grew limp in Bailean's grasp. She stared at her hands as if she was accusing them for not being able to stop the man from hurting her mom.

The king-man hadn't seen Sophie. She stayed hidden like she was told, but that hadn't saved her mom. Nothing could.

Sophie couldn't bear to watch the men drag Mom from the room. She flinched each time her mom's body made a thud as the men made their way down the stairwell. Sophie imagined the purple bruises that would color her skin. Why weren't the neighbors coming to help? Where was everybody? Why wasn't anyone helping her?

~Your mother loves you. She says help will come soon. Stay hidden. Don't follow. Remember the stories always.

Sophie barely breathed for fear the men would come back. As the day passed, every sound made her muscles tense. Police sirens wailed. Mr. Finck's flat-faced dog barked. The garbage trucks roared in the alley. Mrs. Ling's high-pitched voice floated down with the smell of sweet and sour chicken from the floor above. Sophie's mouth watered. She hadn't even gotten to eat the bread she and mom had been making.

Her legs ached from the weight of the dragon's tail curled over them. Her fingers cramped from her grip on his neck, but she didn't move. The calming drum of Bailean's heart and the lullaby he sang lulled Sophie into a trance-like state.

As the shadows in the room grew long and her eyelids fluttered closed, a familiar whistled tune floated up the stairs. Her blood rushed in her ears, drowning out the sounds of city traffic and Bailean's lullaby. The dragon loosened his tail grip. Her legs tingled as the feeling returned. Heart racing, she peered around the wardrobe door. The apartment door opened and the whistle faltered. A familiar, but frightened, voice called out, "Maria? Sophie! Where are you?"

She scrambled out of the wardrobe, no longer holding back the sobs. She stumbled from the bedroom and collapsed into the arms of her dad.

He brushed her hair from her damp forehead with a shaking hand. "Where's your mom?"

Sophie's lip quivered. She shook her head. "The men took her."

chapter one

the memories of my grandmother's house were a tangled mess of happiness and grief. I remembered being curled up in the window seat reading fairy tales with Mom and Gran, the rays of sun streaming through the tall panes. Gran's voice always changed: deep and gruff when the troll demanded a toll to cross the bridge, soft and lilting when the princess spoke to the frog. Without my mother beside me, the house's triangular gothic peaks cast a foreboding presence. The dull wrought iron fence with its speared finials looked more like medieval instruments of death. From the back left corner, a narrow spire seemed to pierce the clouds.

Everything about the house screamed *heartache*. The pale paint peeled away from the wood siding in thick curls like a birch shedding its outer bark. The once-neat paths leading to the fairy garden were now overrun with weeds. If the windows of the house reflected its soul, then these eyes had cataracts.

It wasn't much, but it was mine now. And it suited me.

I reminded myself that I had time to bring it back to its former beauty before the tough Vermont winter laid a blanket of snow at our feet. Smoothing the travel wrinkles from my shirt I smiled at my dad. "Home, sweet home."

The heavy weight of his arm lay across my shoulders. "Are you sure you want to do this?"

His eyebrows drew together over his wire frames. He was worried, but I was sure. I had made up my mind a long time ago.

I nodded. "A fresh start. Thanks to Gran."

Dad's brow smoothed, though worry still tinged the corners of his mouth. After a quick squeeze, he walked to the back of his car. The trunk lid gave a pop as it opened. A moment later he walked past me, arms wrapped around a box labeled Office.

A rush of excitement laced with anxiety gave me goosebumps. Rubbing my hands over my shirtsleeves to get rid of the raised skin, I followed my dad up the brick paved walk. I hadn't seen my grandmother since those first drug-hazed days in the hospital after the accident. She'd patted my shoulder. Told me I was stronger than I knew, that dragons always brought fire to the fight. That when I was ready I should come to her. For two years I'd been wracking my brain for a part of the conversation that the drugs had blocked out. A piece that would make her whole puzzling pep talk come together. But I'd never found the keystone. The next month Gran had died leaving this house, and everything in it, to me. Only two years ago, yet it felt like a lifetime.

Stepping through the front door felt like coming home after a long absence. Hints of lavender and vanilla hovered in the air. I dropped my backpack and pushed it out of the way with my foot. Wanting to postpone the inevitable labor for a few minutes, I wandered down the narrow hallway and into the kitchen. I could almost smell the apple oatmeal muffins baking in the oven, hear the whistle of the kettle. I leaned on the door casing. An enormous stone fireplace took up much of the wall in the far room, the same gilded, time-worn mirror I remembered was centered above it. My reflection was small and hazy from this distance—my scars unnoticeable. I pulled my braids forward, a habit I'd developed to cover my neck, even though it was just me and Dad in the house.

Dad came around the corner, beads of sweat already building on his forehead. "That's the living room."

I raised my eyebrows and smirked. "Yeah, I remember the overgrown fireplace. Our whole apartment in the city would fit in this one room."

"I'm surprised you remember it. You were still very young the last time we visited. You must have been around five, I guess, before your mom…"

I finished the sentence for him in my head. *Before your mom left us.*

I'd stopped correcting him a long time ago.

He cleared his throat and walked across the kitchen, flinging open another door to reveal a small but well-lit room with a warm oak desk. "This will be my office for a while, if it's okay with you?"

"Dad, just because Gran left the house to me doesn't mean you have to ask me questions like that."

I was glad he was staying with me for the summer. Deep down, I wasn't sure if I was ready to be on my own.

My dad's shoulder hitched. "I'm trying to be respectful. It is your house."

I sighed. "It's your house too—for as long as you want to stay."

He nodded. "It will just be for a little while. Until I can get settled at the college. Then I'll find an apartment in town."

He was trying to let go, trying to let me be an adult, but the last few years had been hard on both of us. First the accident, then the multiple surgeries and psych visits. Even though my external wounds had healed, Dad and I were still healing on the inside; we still needed each other, and I was okay with that.

He gestured to the archway on his left. "There is the dining room and a formal parlor."

I crossed the kitchen and peeked through the painted arch. "The formal parlor. I was never allowed in here. What are we going to do with a formal parlor?"

Dad wiped his brow and rested his hands on his hips. "Perhaps we'll have a party. Who knows? We might decide to get crazy!"

I laughed. "You're already crazy." I didn't need Dad to tell me *I* was crazy. Years of therapy had convinced me of it. I'd gotten good at hiding the crazy though, having figured out pretty quickly that even though people like to pretend they do, the general public doesn't *really* believe in dragons and other mythological creatures. To them, they were just symbols of abstract thoughts and ideas. A way to understand the unseen forces in the universe.

"The bathroom is at the top of the stairs. Since it's legally *your* house, I left the big bedroom for you." He pushed his glasses up his long nose and smiled. "And there's a surprise for you in there. Go check it out."

Smiling, I jogged up the creaky stairs. Why did no one *ever* fix stairs in an old house? Did they like the creepy haunted feeling or were they just making sure it was hard for their kids to sneak out in the middle of the night? I'd bet on the latter.

I swung around the newel post at the top of the stairs. There were five doors: two on the right, and two on the left, and one in the middle. The middle door was the bathroom. Light poured into the hallway from one of the bedrooms on the left. The door was ajar. It was my room, the one I'd slept in when I came to visit so long ago. My insides tightened. I longed to open the door, to see the things my grandmother had left behind, to find the surprise Dad had for me, but I decided to hold on to the excitement for a bit longer and check out the other bedrooms first.

An old, iron-framed bed with a sagging mattress was pushed under the peaked roofline of one of the bedrooms to my right. I recognized the bed frame from my dad's room in our old apartment. Two windows faced south and let the bright sunshine stream through. Dust motes danced in the golden rays. The room was cozy, the walls painted a light gray.

It was perfect for my scholarly, calm, never-a-hair-out-of-place dad. I turned away, my footsteps resounding on the painted wooden floor, and pushed open a second door.

A plain room, painted a soft yellow, welcomed me. There wasn't much to it besides a chipped white iron bed. A trunk stood guard at the foot of the bed, and a small table with a dusty vase of dried lavender perched near the head. Bittersweet memories filled the hollows of my heart. I sat on the bed and ran my hand over the patchwork quilt. How I had loved my time in this house with Mom and Gran. I could still hear Mom shrieking when I put my cold feet on her legs, feel her arms around me as she tried to warm me up. I remembered hiding under the blankets while she told me and Bailean stories about Sophie the Brave and Bailean the Gallant. I wondered what she would think of me now. Brave didn't really come to mind as an adjective to describe myself. I smiled wistfully as I rose, closed the door, and opened the next.

The bathroom had rows of pink tile halfway up the wall. The top half was still semi-covered in a faded flowery wallpaper. An oval mirror hung over the pedestal sink. Chrome pipes curved behind it. The toilet was the old-fashioned kind where the water tank hung on the wall above. Gran had called it Moby, like the whale, because when you flushed it, the toilet whistled and spurted water all over the seat. I smiled. The bathroom hadn't changed a bit.

I closed the door so I could pee in peace.

After pulling the chain that would flush the ancient gurgling toilet, I re-smudged my charcoal eyeliner and pulled my braids forward again. In the low light, my scars were barely noticeable. I ran my fingers over the rough patch at my collarbone. It was less leathery looking thanks to the coconut oil I'd been slathering on it. I'd often thought of getting tattoos to hide the scarring, but I always chickened out. Maybe this year I'd find the courage. I unlatched the bathroom door and stepped back into the hallway.

Two years ago, I would've drawn out my cell phone and texted Liz, my so-called best friend, to complain about the hick town or the fact that there was so much work to do to bring the house back from the brink of death. But after the accident, Liz had disappeared like a puff of smoke. Life had become very small for a while—our apartment, the hospital, the Cloisters museum where my dad worked. I'd spent countless hours sketching the building, studying the illuminated manuscripts, wishing I could melt through one of the paintings and be in another world. I'd left behind everyone and everything I'd known, but it hadn't been enough to rid me of the terrible nightmares. That's when I decided to move. To truly leave everyone and everything behind. Including my mobile, which I might regret sooner than later.

My fingers reached out for the doorknob of the third bedroom. It had been my Gran's bedroom. I tried to turn the knob, but it was locked. I jiggled the door just in case. Finally coming to grips with the fact that I needed to find a key, I dropped to my knees and peered through the antique keyhole. The room was shrouded in darkness; the furniture, draped in sheets, looked like misshapen ghosts. I could kind of make out the shape by following the edge of the floor where it met the wall. This was the room with the spire. I didn't remember ever being in it. What had Gran locked up in there?

Something sparkled under one of the chairs. I strained forward, pushing against the door as if I could force myself under it. The sheets fluttered like linens on a clothesline. Had a breeze pushed through an open window? But all the windows had been locked and secured two years ago. At least, that's what I'd been told by the estate lawyer—a wiry guy in a wool suit that had seen better days. A finger of hot air poked my eye. It was a small puff, but like the machine at the optometrist, there was some force behind it. I blinked the dryness away and strained to see past the limitations of the narrow opening. Suddenly the doorknob rattled. I scrambled away like I'd been branded, and ran my fingers over my cheekbone. No harm had been done, yet prickles of heat spread down my spine.

"It's just your imagination. Nothing is there. Old houses do funny things." My chest tightened as I struggled to keep my breathing even and the anxiety monster at bay. "Everything is normal. Nothing to hurt you." I talked myself down, drew in a long breath, and held it. I gripped the locket I always wore dangling from my neck. Slowly, I exhaled like Dr. Parket taught me—to the count of seven. Sometimes I didn't always make it to seven. The anxiety I'd suffered nearly my whole life reared and kicked its feet, but after a minute of controlled breathing, the hair on my neck relaxed and the urge to flee dissipated. My kneecaps still bounced with nervous activity, but I could ignore that. It was the dangerous thoughts about Bailean flustering my head like a swarm of bees that was harder to disregard.

Of course it had all been in my imagination. The windows had been locked for two years. I was just overwhelmed by the emotions the house had stirred up. And thirsty from the long drive. I swallowed, trying to get rid of the dryness in my mouth and throat. My knees felt too weak to stand, so I stayed at the top of the stairs and studied the etching on my locket. It was a good distraction. The knotted design ended in a dragon's head biting its own tail. I didn't even know where my mother had gotten it, but I wore it every day. I popped the locket open.

A small flake of gold-colored mica shone out. With a twist of my hand, the light undulated over the flake and the color changed from gold to a fiery orange. I'd always wondered about the significance of the mica. Most people put a curl of hair or photos of their loved ones in a locket. So why had my mother kept a flake of stone in hers instead of a picture of me or Dad?

I snapped it shut and tucked the locket under my shirt. It was another mystery to add to my collection. Dad's shoes clunked on the sidewalk out front. He came through the front door with another box—this one was labeled Kitchen.

When he saw me sitting at the top of the steps, his eyebrows drew together. "Everything all right?"

"One of the rooms is locked. Did the lawyer give you any keys besides the front door?"

"Nope." He shook his head and continued down the hall.

Another mystery. My heart fluttered, but I squelched a cough, took a breath, and stood up. I approached the final door—the bedroom slated to be mine—and turned the knob. I cringed with anticipation. Kept time by the beat of my heart.

I counted to five. When nothing happened, relief flooded my limbs. My imagination liked to run free sometimes, like a wild mustang. The house had been closed up for so long, it was probably just the propped open front door that had drawn the hot air out of the other bedroom.

I scanned the room and anxiety took hold. It laughed maniacally while the part of me that hung on to realty retreated like a cornered mouse. On the far wall of the room sat a large wardrobe. I cleared my throat, then clenched my hands into fists to keep from trembling. Distant music filtered across the room as the wardrobe door creaked open. I swallowed, eyes darting into every corner, but no one was there. Hesitantly, I crossed the empty space. I could do this. I didn't need to freak. It was just a piece of furniture. As my hands touched the wood panels to shut the door, my stomach clenched. The screech of wire hangers moving down a metal rod, and a man's deep, insistent voice filled my ears.

Where is the girl?

The room faded away. I was a little girl again, curled up in the wardrobe, squeezed so tightly by the dragon's tail that my toes tingled. Quick breaths turned into shallow gasps. My ears rang with the sound of things hitting the floor.

Search the chamber again! The girl is here. Leave nothing unturned.

"You can't see me, you can't see me, you can't see me." I pushed my fists tight against my eyes.

"Sophie!"

I whimpered and slid down the wardrobe door, knees tucking under my chin. My ribs squeezed my heart. My throat seemed too narrow for even air to pass yet I screamed as a hand curled around my shoulder.

"Sophie." Dad pulled me into his embrace, his whisper damp on my temple. "Breathe. It's all right. Everything is fine."

"Wh-where did it come from?" I sniffed and ran my wrist under my nose. Tears welled in my eyes and I blinked to keep them away. My heart hammered so hard I was surprised Dad couldn't feel it. Or maybe he could.

He smoothed my hair. His motions slow and gentle. Caresses meant to soothe the monster inside me. "Sophie, you always played in the wardrobe when you were little. It was your favorite place to hide. After Mom left, I shipped it up here—I couldn't bear to look at it every day. But, I thought someday you'd want it."

"Mom didn't leave." I drew a deep breath.

Dad stroked my hair again. "I know…I know. My choice of words was wrong. But the police never found her…I suppose it's easier for me to think that she left of her own volition." He pulled away, held me at arm's length. "Maybe we should call your doctor."

"No." I extricated myself from his embrace and crossed my arms over my stomach. Doctors were always his first response. Did he still not believe that I could manage myself? "No. I can handle this."

I plopped onto the hard wooden window seat; the brightly colored pillows I remembered were long ago faded and dull. I held my breath. He'd promised. Once we'd moved to the country, no more doctors. He couldn't take that away now. It was just one small panic attack. I could get it under control— it's just the move, the heat. I wanted to stay here. I wanted to belong to this house, to this place.

The tall windows looked out over the fenced yard and the half-circle driveway. It would be so easy to impale myself on one of those sharp fence points. Just be done with it. No more arguing. No more anxiety. No more doubts. I squeezed my eyes shut and pictured myself in my head. I acknowledged the destructive thought, thanked it for coming, and then told it to go away. "You promised."

"I promised I wouldn't push the doctors if your anxiety stayed under control."

"It is."

"You were doing so well before." Dad ran his hand through his sandy-blond hair. "Maybe I shouldn't have agreed to bring you here so soon."

"It's been two years! I'm fine." I pulled my knees into my chest and rested my forehead against the window frame. The tall windows were reminiscent of the view from our apartment, but in the city, I could see the Hudson River and skyscrapers lining the horizon. Here, the trees were the skyscrapers, and a distant church tower jutted into the sky. My everything-is-going-to-be-great attitude was slipping away. I groped for it like a mountain climber reaching for a ledge.

A glint, like a reflection of sunshine on metal, flashed in the distance. My heart raced for a moment as a spark of recognition made me so joyful that I soared above the clouds, weightless. Then the little voice in my head told me it was just my old friend Imagination, up to its tricks again. My stomach clenched and brought me spiraling back down to earth. But there was something moving in the tree line. A pale flash. Antlers. A deer stepped forward warily. The stag looked both ways before coming out of the woods completely. He blinked in the bright light before bounding off across the lawn.

Dad walked over and squeezed my shoulder. "I'm sure some of my new colleagues at the college will know a good psychologist."

"No doctors." I tugged on my hair, white-hot anger ready to leap out and take over. Mentally, I leashed it. Dad had said it would be better here in the country—a slower pace of life, more time to heal—yet he was already talking about doctors. We hadn't even been here for an hour yet. He hadn't given me a chance. The monster inside told me he'd never planned to.

"We'll see how you do, but we might have to find someone—just in case."

"No!" I screamed. My limbs flushed and my temples pounded. I tried to silence the voice inside my head, to keep the angry in check, but when Dad mentioned doctors I wanted to strangle him. "I've had enough doctors poking into my mind for two lifetimes." I shrugged his hand off my shoulder. My muscles twitched as the tension built in my throat and clenched jaw.

"You're overreacting, Sophie. Even though you are an adult, as your father, I still have to do what's best for you."

"That's right, Dad, I'm an *adult*. And unless you plan on committing me against my will, I suggest you start listening." Tears threatened, burning the back of my eyes, but I glared at him as if I could make him burst into flames. "I said I'm fine."

I turned on my heel and stomped out of the room.

chapter two

The tall weeds sliced at my ankles like knives and tangled between my legs, but I had to get out of the house before I did or said something I'd regret. I yanked the thick climbing vines that twisted through the iron gate separating the yard from the gently rolling field, and, further on, the forest. Beads of sweat rolled down my back as I shoved and pulled at the black metal. The vine refused to give.

"Stupid, stupid vine. Let go so I can get through," I ground the words out through my clenched teeth and yanked on the thickest vine. I felt it give a little, so with another hard shove of the gate, I broke through. The hinges protested with bawling cries, mocking my unspent tears. I didn't bother to open it all the way, but squeezed through. My journey took me down the hill and into the shade of the trees, my tears finally finding some release as I ran. Water gurgled somewhere close by and I followed the sound to a creek. I collapsed on the rocky surface near the edge. The roughness poked through my cotton shorts, but I didn't care. The feeling reminded me of sitting on Umpire Rock after a day at the Central Park Zoo. The garden had been Mom's favorite spot.

This little place at the edge of the creek was less tame, but no less beautiful. Felled trees covered in emerald moss crisscrossed the stream. Dragonflies hovered near, as if they were checking out a strange new beast. I flapped a hand at them and they flew away, only to circle back a moment later. A breeze lifted the ends of the loose hairs that had escaped my braids and made them twist around my face like the snakes on Medusa's head.

An unmistakable urge to hiss slid over my tongue.

I wanted to rage against life—to hate it—to hate this place that was so far from everything I'd ever known—but I couldn't. I was determined to make this work. Strangling the air from the monster inside me, I gave him the boot. My foot kicked out as if it could really make contact.

The blinding rays of the sun softened, dappling the forest with shifting spots of filtered light. The trills of birdsong helped my mind fly away from its damaging thought pattern. The trickle of the stream soothed the rampant beast still lingering close to the surface. This little spot of tranquility I'd stumbled upon was like another world—and I wanted desperately to stay here forever.

A younger version of myself might've thought the gurgle of the stream was the singing of water nymphs. I smiled at the thought and swiped the wet tracks from my cheeks. I didn't recognize that little girl anymore. It was the version of me before I'd convinced myself that magic, and magical beings, weren't real. I sniffed and ran my wrist under my nose. Then I unlaced my sneakers, kicked them off, and stepped into the water. My toes gripped the rounded stones as a numbing current rushed past.

I relaxed, letting my head fall back. I breathed in the deep, earthy smell of the forest. I uncurled my hands, giving permission to the fear and anger I'd held on to for so long to leave. I imagined it dripping from my fingertips and into the water. I visualized the stream carrying it away. I really didn't want to hang on to it any longer, but the fiery grip on my heart had been with me for far too long to simply permit it to all go at once.

I sighed and turned my attention to the forest surrounding the creek. I hated to admit it, but the trees in Central Park were nothing compared to this. The aroma of a thick forest was something so distant I'd thought I'd imagined it, but I vaguely remembered my grandmother bringing me here. We'd caught minnows, Gran holding up her skirt to keep the hem from getting soaked. A long braid hung down her back, the ends tickling the surface of the water as she bent. Her rose-scented perfume wafted about us.

I missed her.

The air was wet and heavy—like the botanical gardens I'd visited as a child. And it was quiet. Maybe too quiet. Deafeningly quiet. Would I actually miss the screech of the public bus brakes, the beep of the garbage truck at four in the morning, and the people talking on their cell phones as they rushed by? Yes. And no. It was peaceful here in this little patch of forest. I could see this becoming one of my favorite spots to get away from the bone-crushing expectations of the world.

All tightness gone from my chest, I snatched my shoes and splashed over the creek, trotting deeper into the woods. It was at least ten degrees cooler under the leafy canopy. I unbuttoned my over shirt and pulled the clinging tank top away from my body, fanning the skin of my stomach and chest with the cooler air. I bent, pushed my wet feet back into my sneakers, and pulled the laces tight. On this side of the stream, there was a trail wide enough for two people to walk side by side. From the hard packed ground, it seemed like it was used often.

I followed it, imagining where it might lead. Then I stopped. Maybe I shouldn't follow it. I rolled my bottom lip under my teeth as I weighed my options. What was the worst that could happen? It was a well-marked trail, so I wouldn't get lost. And I wasn't in the city where attacks on single women walking in Central Park were common…but I was in a strange forest, alone. My decision to get rid of my cell phone might not have been the best idea. Still, I pocketed my worries and pressed forward like Sophie the Brave in one of my mom's stories.

A few minutes later, the trail joined a set of stairs made of wooden beams and packed dirt. I hesitated for just a moment, but then jogged up the steep climb. My calf muscles were just beginning to burn when the stairs ended in a well-manicured lawn. As I caught my breath, I noted the large flowerbeds all a-bloom. A small reflecting pool, the surface languid on this hot summer day, rested in the center.

The house on the property looked like a cottage from a fairytale, minus the thatched roof. It was obvious the inhabitant was a talented gardener. Purple flowers burst out of small window boxes and trailed over the sides. Dark leafy vines crept from the side of a chimney, constructed from round stones.

"My neighbors must be the seven dwarves." I giggled at the thought of seven little men filing out of the house. Well, at least I'd found a master gardener's cottage at the end of the trail and not the house of the gingerbread witch.

A hot pink flower beckoned me over with a wave of its leaves. It had five large petals and one long pistil that ended in a cloud of pollen sacs. I stepped forward and stroked the soft petals.

The bloom deepened in color, from pink to bright fuchsia. It started at the center of the flower and spread to the pointed tips like I'd caressed it into a blush. A gust of wind swirled the fresh grass clippings around my feet.

~You have the magic touch.

Bailean? *No! No! No!* I yanked my hand away, my heart leaping into my throat. I squinched my eyes shut and tried to calm the racing of my heart. Hours of therapy, countless medications that gave me stomachaches or had me seeing ghosts, the nightmares of my mom being dragged down the stairs. I wasn't going back there again. I refused. *Magic isn't real. Dragons aren't real. The voice in my head isn't real. The color shift was just a trick of the light…a trick of my mind…* Slowly my breathing evened. The rush of adrenaline had wakened the beast, but I put him back to bed, tucked the sheets tight under his chin. When I opened my eyes again there was no hint of color in the pale white petals.

I slowly drew my fingers away. Hadn't the flower been pink before?

"It's a hibiscus."

I jumped, startled by the voice. Immediately my cheeks blazed with embarrassment. I backed away.

"Pretty, isn't it?" The old woman's voice hung in the air like the echo of a bell. She was a vision from a bygone era with her long hair piled on top of her head and pristine white apron.

I nodded. "Y-yes." *Great*. Dad was going to be pissed that I'd trespassed in the neighbor's garden. I rubbed the back of my neck and blew out a breath of air.

"No worries, my dear. You are a welcome guest." The woman snapped off the blossom I had been admiring. "You *are* Sophie Lincoln, are you not?"

The old lady turned and walked to the reflecting pool. I scratched at a mosquito bite on my ankle, words feeling like peanut butter stuck to the roof of my mouth. I stared at the grass. How did she know my name? "I'm sorry. I shouldn't have trespassed. I'll go."

"Nonsense." She waved her hand in a dismissive gesture. "My name is Anna."

"S-Sophie." Nervously I drew my locket back and forth on the chain. "But you already knew that."

Anna smiled. "I haven't seen that locket in years."

I stopped so suddenly it felt like someone had pushed an off button. "You…you've seen it before?"

"Yes." Anna chuckled and patted the bench seat beside her. "It belonged to your mother."

"You knew my mother?" I strode forward and sat next to the old woman as she bent to place the flower in the pool.

"I know your mother," Anna said.

I know your mother. My mind immediately went to that crazy place where I knew my mother was still alive. The world reeled and I threw out a hand to steady myself on the rough surface of the bench. "My mother was taken away when I was six."

"Ah, yes. You must forgive an old lady and her bad memory." Anna brushed my worries away with the wave of her hand, as if she was swatting a fly. My thoughts were fuzzy for a moment, but they cleared as Anna spoke again. "Do you know anything about what's inside the locket?"

I shrugged nonchalantly, as if having a piece of stone in a locket was a normal thing. I peered at Anna through my eyelashes. "I know the stories my mom used to tell me, but it's just a piece of mica."

"Oh, that's not mica, dear." Anna clicked her tongue. "I may be old, but I know a dragon's scale when I see one."

chapter three

I stood abruptly and a forced laugh burst from my mouth. Who the hell did this woman think she was? My mother's stories were just that—stories. Tales told to a wide-eyed five-year-old with an active imagination. "Okay. Nice to meet you, Anna, but I-I've got to go." I bolted for the stairs at the edge of the path trying to put as much distance between me and the eccentric woman as possible.

"You shouldn't run from the truth, Sophie!"

My mind whirled as my feet propelled me forward. The truth. What did some weird old lady know about the truth? Dragons weren't real. Magic didn't exist. Life was not a fairytale. And my mother wasn't hauled away by men from the Renaissance Faire. Those were the truths pounded into me year after year by my dad and the doctors. But the little voice in my head said they were someone else's truths. That dragons *did* exist. That Bailean *was* real. That all the proof I needed was right there in the locket my mother left for me.

Thunder rumbled in the distance and the shadows of the forest melded together. A burst of wind made the tree leaves rattle. I spun on my heel and scowled, sure that my glare would've turned the old woman to stone if I were capable of it. "What do you know about the truth?"

Anna stood and strolled toward me. Her hair floated about her face; her gray eyes flashed like lightning in a storm cloud. Was she the one bringing in the storm? "I know you were born in the grasp of a dragon, and that's why you can see him."

My kneecaps bounced. I locked my legs and clenched my fingers. No one knew that story but me and Mom. "Him?"

"You call him Bailean."

The pit of my stomach dropped into my feet. I hadn't said his name out loud in so long. It was almost as if I'd only dreamed it all. But here was someone else validating my experience. Here was someone else who knew his name... Could the memories I'd repressed be true?

Anna smiled. "For too long, you have been told that magic doesn't exist. That dragons aren't real."

The tightness in my chest threatened to suffocate me. "Because dragons *aren't* real!" I whispered. The lie weighted my tongue. I tried to swallow, but my throat was so dry it wouldn't work. My lungs labored. If I couldn't talk myself down, I'd be in full anxiety mode in a matter of seconds. The air buzzed like I'd stuck a finger in an electric socket. I bolted for the stairs, but Anna's last words stalked me like a hunter on the trail of a wounded deer.

"Trust yourself, Sophie. Listen to the quiet voice inside you. Only you know the truth!"

The old woman's statement pounded in my ears. *Only you know the truth.* It became my mantra as I took the stairs at breakneck speed. Stumbling, I collapsed at the edge of the river. My fingers dug into the cool soil, my knees grated against the gravelly shore. A wave of nausea and dizziness rolled over me. I closed my eyes, concentrated on my breathing. I felt the cool damp air expand my lungs, controlled the rate at which I exhaled. I listed the things I could physically touch: soil, rocks, sand, ferns. It brought me back to earth, fixed me in one spot. The world stopped spinning and I slowly opened my eyes. I couldn't go to the house and face Dad. Not yet—not until I'd worked things out in my head.

I dropped to my stomach and dipped my shaking hands into a shallow pool that had formed at the edge of the water.

The dirt on my fingertips washed away. I splashed my face, the cool water working its calming magic.

The Truth. What was the truth? Was the truth a whisper from deep inside when you were alone? Was the truth what your dad or your doctors insisted? Was the truth different for me than it was for other people, or was the truth the same for everyone? A universal truth to be held up as the one certainty for every being on the planet. Tiny glints of light flashed just under the surface of the stream like sparks of magic, but it was only a school of minnows. I plunged my hands in again and the fish scattered.

I took a deep, cleansing breath, the tightness in my shoulders easing as I smoothed my wet hands over my forehead. The ripples I'd created in the pool settled and I stared at my wavy reflection. I lay there, counting breaths and heartbeats, until I could hear nothing else. In a calming trance I saw nothing but the bright white clouds reflected in the moving water beneath me. As I came back into the world, I searched for silly shapes in the clouds reflected in the water like Mom and I used to do in Sheep Meadow. I traced the outline of a long-eared rabbit and a fat bird as I reawakened every muscle in my body starting with my toes. Just as my heart rate was returning to normal, a pointy snout came into focus above my right shoulder. Bright gold eyes blinked open slowly, as if the light was too bright. Slanted nostrils flared wide.

Goosebumps flashed up the back of my legs. The hair on my neck stood painfully at attention. I strained my ears. The birds were silent; even the rush of the river was muted. I dared not blink in case he disappeared. I stared into those gold eyes. I hadn't seen him in so long, but it couldn't be, he'd been gone for years…but he looked so much like…

"Bailean?" I whispered.

A rush of hot wind caressed my neck. At once familiar and yet foreign. We'd changed. We'd grown up. I turned, raising my hand to him to stroke his long neck. He was a friend too long gone.

The snap of a twig broke the spell; my heart instantly ached as Bailean vanished.

"Hey, are you all right?"

Lungs gripped in fear, I gulped for air. My fists clenched and I scrambled to stand up, my teeth gritted in frustration. "Didn't anyone ever teach you not to sneak up on people?"

"Sorry," the guy said. His grin was a bit lopsided, as if he was holding back a laugh. "I thought you heard me come up the path...but I guess not. I'm Lawrence."

I immediately regretted my waspish reaction...but he had surprised me, coming out of thin air...or what felt like thin air. And he'd scared Bailean away.

He stuck out his hand. My heart rattled hard in my chest. Hesitantly I grasped his long fingers. His grip was firm, but not in that superior way some men had. The ones who make the handshake more about letting you know who is stronger—more in control. When you have no control over your own body, it's very irritating. The only thing that's worse is someone rubbing your nose in it. Thankfully, Lawrence's grip just said, *I'm sure of my place in the world.* I was instantly jealous, but that was better than being frightened of him.

"I'm sorry—you scared me. I wasn't expecting—" A ray of sunlight broke through the canopy, lighting up the guy's face. His eyes gleamed gold in the sunlight.

He shook his head. "Nope. No apologies necessary. It was completely my fault. Are you all right?"

His expression was so genuine and warm that I instantly knew I liked him—whoever he was. The charming crinkles on his forehead faded as his worried brow smoothed. His eyes had dulled into a copper brown as the tree canopy shaded the creek once again.

I nodded, smoothing my hair away from my face. I liked the tone of his voice.

"What's your name?" Lawrence dropped my hand and flipped his bangs away from his eyes with a toss of his head.

"Sophie." I pulled my hair forward to cover the scars, then took a step back so I could really look into his face. He was at least eight inches taller than my average five foot four.

Black hair curled up at his collar and swept over his slightly tilted eyes. I couldn't quite put my finger on it, but there was something about him that intrigued me. He was attractive, in that boy-next-door way, but that wasn't it. I was instantly comforted by his voice, yet his manner was contradictory--my gut said he was full of mischief.

He grinned and then squatted at the edge of the creek. I watched him track something under the water with his eyes. "You must be Constance's granddaughter."

How did he know who I was? My stomach flip-flopped. I picked at the loose skin on the side of my nail. "What makes you think that?"

"She always talked about how pretty you were."

A seed of warmth planted in my stomach but I quickly squelched it. I didn't need a man complicating my life, no matter how handsome he was. I needed to care about me and only me for a while. And, he'd said my grandmother said I was pretty—he didn't necessarily agree.

He stood and grinned at me. "Plus, we've been expecting you."

I avoided eye contact as I tried to figure him out. Why had he been expecting me? And who was *we*?

Lawrence tossed his bangs. He smiled. "I mean, the house was left to you, so we knew you'd eventually make it up here."

"Who's we?" I gave him a skeptical eyebrow raise.

"Oh, I live with my great aunt."

"Who is…" I pressed one hand against my stomach as the flutters rose.

"My great aunt was your grandma's best friend."

I brushed a stray hair from my face with a shaky hand and tucked it behind my ear. Of course. They knew the house had been left to me. Probably heard rumors that we were moving in. It was a small town. It made sense. Still, it made me a little nervous.

Lawrence crouched low over the rushing water. His hand flashed into the creek and came out gripping a giant frog.

Imagining the slimy skin, I couldn't help but make a face. I didn't know much about boys, but I was pretty sure they grew out of their frog catching stage when they were like ten. "What are you doing?"

"What? You don't eat frog legs in the city?" Lawrence grinned. "Darn, and I thought my speed and accuracy would impress you." He flipped the bullfrog on its back and ran his finger down its pale underbelly.

Was he really catching frogs to eat them? Or was he testing my reaction? Trying to see how much of a prissy city girl I was?

A dimple puckered his cheek as he tried to keep a straight face. "They're actually pretty good. Some people say they taste like—"

"Chicken?" I finished for him with a smirk. "That's disgusting."

I couldn't keep a grin from sneaking out though.

Lawrence laughed. A breeze pushed through the trees, making the leaves rattle. It seemed the forest laughed with him.

"I was actually checking for markers of the river being polluted. Frogs are an indicator species. They can be the first to show signs. I'm working with the college biology department this summer."

So that's how he knew. He worked at the college where Dad was going to work. His intense gaze made me feel like a worm on a hook. It was almost as if he could see into the marrow of my bones or pick out the markers in my DNA that made me different. His eyebrows rose in a tick of surprise as he noticed the scars along my neck.

Quickly, I pulled the collar of my camp shirt closed. I hated people staring at me. I hated it more when they asked how it happened. Cheeks flush with embarrassment, I turned to leave.

"See you around, then?"

Involuntarily, my heart leapt a little with joy.

"Maybe." I glanced over my shoulder, a small smile tugging at my mouth. I pushed away the earlier thoughts about men and complications and just enjoyed the view. The light streamed through the trees behind Lawrence, silhouetting his lanky form. A greenish mist, full of glowing orbs, twinkled around him and made him look like a magical being. I knew it was just a trick of the light above the moving water, or my imagination acting out again, but it was beautiful. I turned and walked back to the house wondering about Lawrence the whole way.

chapter four

"Just call me Cinderella," I mumbled. Unfortunately, I didn't have any little mice to help me wipe down the trim boards, or birds to whistle while we worked. I dunked the rag into the deep gray water and wrung it out. I wouldn't be surprised if I was putting more dirt on the things I was trying to clean. In the last three days, I had tackled the whole house from top to bottom—except for the bedrooms upstairs and the locked room with the spire. I still hadn't found the key, but I wasn't giving up.

I'd been sleeping on the floor in the living room by the massive fireplace and away from the wardrobe. The memories of the last time I'd hid in it freaked me out. The wire hangers creaking against the steel rod, and the close, hot space—it was hard to think of anything else when I was near it. But today was the day. I was determined to face down the fear. If I didn't, Dad would drag me back to the doctor, regardless of his promise. I pushed open the door, walked in, and set the bucket down on the window seat.

Dad had only been able to open one window in the room. That had been my first excuse to not sleep in here. Then I'd said I hadn't gotten to cleaning it yet. With the rest of the house clean and in order, I was quickly running out of excuses, and Dad had promised to work on the other windows today. An engine revved as a large truck rumbled up the driveway. I crossed the room and stuck my head out the open window.

The words *Milligan's Home and Garden Store* blazed across the side of a truck in bold blue letters. The screen slammed against the frame as my dad ran out of the front door. He let out a joyful whoop. "Finally! My lawn mower!"

I rolled my eyes and called down to him. "You're stoked about mowing the grass?"

"Heck, yeah!" Dad ran to meet the truck in the half-circle drive, grinning like a little boy on Christmas morning.

A big guy in a navy blue uniform shook my dad's hand and lifted the rear door of the vehicle. He had a head full of spiky hair that looked like an albino porcupine was nesting there. A quick tingle of recognition, like déjà vu, swept through me. *Weird.* The delivery guy couldn't be someone I knew. I hadn't met anyone yet—just Lawrence and his strange old aunt. I conjured up a picture of Lawrence in my mind. Dark hair sweeping over his forehead, long tanned legs, eyes the color of...well, I guess I could call it amber until the light hit them. I shook my head. He couldn't have been as hot as I remembered.

The whine of a motor pulled me from my daydream. A large sloping platform eased down from the back of the truck. Another guy hopped out of the cab and jumped into the rear. Soon, an engine started and Dad's new toy rolled onto the driveway. I grinned. He was smiling from ear to ear as he hopped into the driver's seat and drove the mower into the yard. Boys were weird.

The delivery guys pulled a long box from the back of the truck and headed toward the house, one man on each end. It looked heavy. I dropped the rag in the bucket and went to meet them at the door, holding it open.

"Looks like your husband is having fun, eh?" the spiky-haired delivery guy said. The oval nametag embroidered on his shirt said Wilhelm. A dimple puckered his cheek when he grinned.

Despite his friendly nature, I was instantly uneasy. I dropped my gaze to his waist, but he was wearing coveralls—

no belt buckle. It had to just be coincidence, right? Sometimes people look like other people. Doppelgangers was the word for it. I took a shaky breath and answered as casually as I could. "That's my dad."

Wilhelm at least had the decency to blush. "Oh, sorry, I just…you uh…I just assumed you were newlyweds."

"Where do you want this, miss?" the other man interrupted. He gave Wilhelm a withering look.

I shrugged. "What is it?"

"It's one of those fancy beds with the canopies all around."

I swallowed hard and cleared my suddenly tight throat. I'd wanted a princess bed when I was, like, eight. Okay, I still wanted one, but my room in the apartment had been too small. And now I was too old for princess stuff. But it had to be for me. Now I had no excuse not to sleep in my new room.

Wilhelm shifted his end of the box, readjusting his grip. "You got a little sister?"

Squeezing past the two men, I trotted up the stairs two at a time. "Follow me."

They followed, huffing up the stairs with their heavy load and set the box on my bedroom floor. Then they set to work cutting the box open and pulling out the antiqued iron pieces of the bed frame. They were packed in enough bubble wrap to fill a city dumpster.

"So, you moved from New York, did'jya?" Wilhelm asked.

"New York." I shifted uneasily in the doorway. I didn't really want to leave two strange men alone with my belongings, but I didn't want to talk to them either.

"You'll like it here," Wilhelm said. "Fresh air, nice people, soft grass under your feet. You can't go barefoot in the city, that's for sure!"

The older man stood up with a groan. "Forgot to grab the wrench from the tool box." He shuffled from the room, past me, and halted in the hallway, turning back to the other guy.

"Since I'm going down you might as well come with me and bring in the mattress."

A dark look crossed Wilhelm's face, but he sighed and nodded. "I'm coming."

He squeezed past me in the hallway his arm brushing against mine. Revulsion slinked through my body. The stairs creaked as the two men descended.

I crossed to the bay window. I should do something productive while I waited for them to finish. And if I was busy, maybe the creepy one wouldn't feel obligated to talk to me. I grabbed the bucket of wash water and went into the bathroom. The black water swirled down the drain of the sink. I rinsed out the bucket and filled it back up, dumping in a liberal amount of lemony cleanser.

Since I didn't want to be in the same room as the creepy guy, I walked into Mom's old bedroom. I'd been putting it off after my first visit since her presence was so strong here. I remembered how she used to sit in the window seat and read while I fell asleep. How her hair had shone like a halo in the golden light of the setting sun.

I felt close to her sitting in this room. Her presence so strong it felt like she might come through the door at any moment. With a deep sigh I stood. There was work to be done. Strolling down memory lane would not clean the dust off the dresser or sweep the spiders out of the corners.

I tossed the faded pillows from the window seat onto the floor. Under the pillows, a set of hinges had been hiding. I didn't remember, or maybe I'd never known, that the top lifted up. Grabbing the edge, I raised the panel slowly, wary of what might be lying in wait, disguised by the darkness. There could be a nest of mice. I squinted just in case of an onslaught of vermin tried to escape.

But there was only a rolled up carpet squashed into the storage space. Dust floated into the room like fog rolls into a harbor. With a cough, I waved it away, then wrapped my arms around the end of the carpet and yanked.

It was heavy and I strained against it, bracing my feet on the front of the bookshelves, careful not to push on any of the books Gran had left there. I wiggled and pulled with all my might, swearing under my breath, sweat rolling down the middle of my back. Why had Gran stuffed this carpet under the window seat, anyway?

"You want me to help you with that?" a voice asked.

I'd been so intent on getting the rug out I didn't hear the delivery guys come back up the stairs. Shaking my head at Wilhelm, I growled and tugged harder. My body temperature rose as his eyes burned a hole through my backside. I was about to snap and tell him to stare at something besides my ass when the carpet released, dropping me on my aforementioned body part. Wiping the sweat from my forehead, I swore again, and kicked the rolled carpet.

An antique key spilled out and clanged on the wood floor.

My heart raced. Was this the key to unlock Gran's room? My hands shook as I reached for it, but the blackened metal was cool as my fingers curled around it. I bit my lip. What was so important in that room that Gran had kept it locked up and hid the key?

I felt Wilhelm's hot stare and glared at him over my shoulder.

He made a gesture with his head. "What'cha find?"

"Nothing." I tucked the key in my shorts pocket and stood up, arms crossed over my breasts. "Is the bed put together already? Wow, you're fast!"

Wilhelm sucked on his teeth and gave me a once over. "Nah. We're still working on it."

He sidled across the hall like a snake looking for cover. I hoped after today, I would never see him again.

Turning back to the carpet, I flung my arms around it again, ready to wrestle it free. With a little more struggle and a few choice words, it came out of the window box completely. I unrolled it as the two delivery guys, arms full of cardboard and bubble wrap, traipsed back down the stairwell.

The carpet was worn, even threadbare in spots, and it looked ancient. In fact, it wasn't a carpet at all, but a tapestry. It wasn't as big as any of the tapestries in the Cloisters museum where Dad used to work—more like the size of an area rug, about six feet long and eight feet wide. The colors had faded into muted tones of mauve, forest green, and gray. I wondered how brilliant the colors were originally. An intertwined ribbon pattern formed the border while the main part of the tapestry was a blooming glade surrounded by trees. A tall, dark reindeer stood in the middle of the scene, and it reminded me of the deer I'd seen the other day. His head turned toward me, ears alert, antlers catching the sun. It was almost like I'd interrupted his grazing. A tense energy grew between us. I was sure if I moved a muscle he'd dart off into the forest.

The heavy scent of wet leaves made my nose tingle. It reminded me of the visit to the creek. A light breeze caressed the damp skin at the back of my neck. Goosebumps welted my arms. I rolled the tapestry back up and pushed it out of the way as Wilhelm shuffled one end of a thick mattress from the hallway into my room.

I slipped into the hallway while he was busy and paused at the locked door. I curled my hand around the key in my pocket. I felt Wilhelm's eyes on me again and looked over my shoulder. He *was* staring at me. *Creep.* I darted down the stairs and out the front door. The storm door slammed against the wood siding and I cringed as it squeaked back into place.

My dad bounced along on his mower, happier than I'd seen him in a long while. I wished a lawn mower were all it took to make me happy. He made a tight turn around a tree, and then, out of the corner of my eye, I caught movement by the front gate. My palms grew clammy as I turned my head. Four people stood at the gate. Two I recognized.

What would Anna say to my dad about my visit the other day? It seemed logical that Gran would've told Anna about me, but she seemed to know about things she'd had no right to know and that made me nervous.

I scanned the line of bodies standing next to Anna. A young couple waved. At the end stood Lawrence, grinning from ear to ear. My stomach leapt a little at the sight of him. He was as hot as I remembered. Inside, I groaned. I didn't need a mirror to tell me I was sweaty, dirty, and had hair sticking out in every direction. My struggle with the tapestry had probably left me stinking like a pig, too. I resisted the urge to lift my arms and smell my armpits. My head said a social call with frog boy was not what I needed right now, but my body wasn't listening.

I brushed the dust off my shirt, but that just made it worse. Tucking a few stray hairs that had fallen out of my braids behind my ears, I sent a silent prayer to the universe that my deodorant was still working and called it good.

I waved my arms at Dad. Once I caught his eye, I pointed to the front gate, and then cupped a hand to my mouth and yelled, even though I knew he probably couldn't hear me over the mower engine. "Visitors!"

He didn't answer, but nodded and waved then turned the mower back toward the house. I dried my palms on my shorts and loped down the driveway, trying to put on an air of carelessness, but I was anything but. Nervous energy was already making me shaky.

Anna's brown skin wrinkled around her smiling eyes. Her hair was loose and flowed over her shoulders like a veil, just like it had the other day. The young couple that stood next to her, too young and fair-skinned to be related, looked friendly enough. They were probably in their mid-thirties. The woman was pregnant, her stomach round and distended.

"You must be the neighborhood welcome brigade." I opened the gate and gestured them in.

The roar of the mower motor sputtered to a stop. My dad wiped his forehead with the hem of his shirt, swung his leg over the seat, and joined us. He extended his hand to the older man, and they shook hands vigorously. "Hello. Nice to meet you. I'm Jack Lincoln. This is my daughter Sophie."

He wasn't as tall as my dad, but his shoulders were impressively broad. He had strawberry blond hair and blue eyes. He reminded me of a stereotypical Viking, sans beard. I nodded and clasped my hands behind my back to keep from chewing on a ragged fingernail. One of many that had broken during the marathon cleaning.

The viking beckoned to me. "Come, say hello."

I walked over, almost as if my feet were propelling me forward of their own volition, and offered my hand. He took it, and after inspecting my dirty fingernails, shook it politely. "Nice to meet you, Sophie."

Lawrence chuckled and I peeked at him from under my eyelashes. He had this smirk on his face, and he winked at me. My neck and cheeks flared with heat. He'd caught me, but I was determined to put my finger on what it was about him that was so intriguing. Maybe it was long, tight muscles in his arms, or the dark fringe of hair across his forehead.

The pregnant woman's voice interrupted my musings. "My name is Samantha. I'm Henry's wife." She laid her hand on her husband's arm and he dropped my hand. I nodded in greeting. Samantha gestured to Lawrence. "This is Lawrence, but I heard you two already met, and his great aunt Anna."

Lawrence shook my dad's hand with a sideways glance at me. "Nice to meet you, Mr. Lincoln. Any relationship to Abraham?"

"No." Dad chuckled. "Uh, not that I know of, anyway." He turned to Lawrence's aunt and gently took her hand, raising it to his lips. "Anna, it's been too long."

My mouth dropped open in surprise, but I quickly clamped it shut. Dad knew Anna? Had it been Dad who'd told her all those things about me?

"Always a gentleman," Anna said, patting the hand still gripping hers. "It's a pity we haven't seen each other again before now. What's it been—fifteen years?"

My dad's cheeks flushed. "I'm ashamed to say it's been longer than that."

"Oh, no matter. You're here now." Anna let go of his hand and moved to greet me. "Sophie and I met the other day." Anna took my hand and patted the back of it with her cool palm.

"Oh?" Dad raised his eyebrows. "She didn't tell me."

Guilt tapped on my shoulder. I probably should've told him about my little adventure, but I wasn't a kid anymore. I hadn't kept our meeting a secret on purpose—it just hadn't come up in conversation. Plus, if the last few years had taught me anything, it was that it was better not to tell Dad I'd gone off and met a weird lady who talked about dragons being real.

"Constance, your grandmother, was my best friend." Anna wrapped her arm around my shoulders. Behind her, Lawrence winked at me as if we shared an inside joke. I wished he'd let me in on it.

Anna pointed to a patch of weeds surrounded by a layer of stones. "She had the most beautiful pink cone flowers here in this bed. Do you remember?" The elderly lady looped her arm around mine and led me to one of the flowerbeds.

"I don't remember much about the gardens—except the stories Gran told." I didn't elaborate. Gran's stories had been full of magic: flowers that purred like cats, weeds that pulled themselves and ran away, tiny beings that appeared in the dew drops on summer mornings. Exactly the kind of stories of which my dad disapproved.

Anna's weight pulled on my arm as she bent and removed some of the weeds from around a plant, tossing them onto the cobblestone path. "Of course. You were so young, but with just a little love from you, dear, the yard could be beautiful again. Pull those weeds and thin out the lilies. Lawrence can help you spread some new topsoil."

"I think I can handle spreading a bit of soil myself." I rolled my eyes. Why did the older generation always think a woman needed help from a man? Though it might be entertaining to watch Lawrence's muscles strain with the work. I pictured him with no shirt on, tanned skin glistening with sweat...

Anna ran her fingers down the soft flower petals. "It won't take much work to bring it back once you get started. You have the magic touch," Anna whispered. "Just like I do."

The bloom blushed from pale pink to a bright fuchsia. A gust of wind swirled the fresh grass clippings around my feet.

I squinched my eyes shut and got lost in the beat of my racing heart. *It was just a trick of your mind... a trick...* The rush of adrenaline fed the beast inside. I talked my heart into slowing it's racing beat. Commanded my brain to stop the spinning. The rise of anxiety only made the beast crave more, but he wasn't needed right now. I could handle this. When I opened my eyes again, the petals had returned to their former pale pink.

"I'm so sorry," Anna breathed. Her face had gone as white as her hair. Her hand shook when she reached for my shoulder. "I didn't know it was this bad..."

I clenched my teeth. My heart skipped a beat. I tried to keep my face emotionless, like a stone statue, but my eyebrow ticked. How much had Dad told Anna?

The pregnant woman waddled toward us, hand cradled under her stomach. "Anna is the best gardener in the town of Castleton. You want to know something about plants, she's the one to ask."

"Great." The word barely made it past my swollen tongue. I breathed deep and swallowed, convincing myself that it was normal size—that nothing was out of the ordinary. Behind

Samantha Dad talked animatedly to Lawrence and Henry. I uttered a soft thank you, as relief filled my limbs; Dad hadn't seen me freak out.

"Anna helped me with my garden. Henry and I live in the next house down the road, about half a mile around the bend."

"That's nice." Half a mile? My closest neighbor in the city was less than twenty feet away. I chanced a glance at Anna, who still had a somewhat stricken expression on her face.

Samantha flashed a warm smile at me and tossed her curly hair over her shoulder. "The baby is due sometime in the beginning of August. Though to look at me, you wouldn't think I had four days to go, let alone four weeks. Do you think it's a girl or a boy?"

I shrugged, but a niggling sensation in my gut said it was a boy. I answered in a small, questioning voice, "A boy?"

"Anna says it's a boy, too, and I guess you two would know…" Samantha didn't wait for me to pick up the conversation, but linked her arm through Anna's and took in the French braids hanging over my shoulders. "Did you braid your hair yourself? I've always wanted to wear my hair in braids, but never learned how to do it. Would be cooler in the summer, that's for sure."

"It's not hard to learn." I smoothed down my hair, suddenly aware that both women had probably seen my scars. I stepped away before one of them could pull me into their little huddle, and wondered if Samantha was always a motor mouth or if at some point she might let someone else get in a word. Not that I was bursting with ambition for conversation. Small talk was not my forte.

Finally, Dad started toward the house. "I made some iced tea this morning. Would you ladies like a glass?"

"Oh, that sounds wonderful!" The chatterbox pulled Anna along to the front door.

Dad caught my gaze and grinned. "Are you coming in?"

I smiled. "Of course. A glass of iced tea sounds great."

And Samantha couldn't talk while she was swallowing.

chapter five

I whispered in Dad's ear as we climbed the front steps. "This isn't really how I thought I'd spend my afternoon."

"Get used to it," he whispered back. "We live in a small town now. Everyone knows everyone and everybody's business."

"What secrets would you need to keep anyway?" Anna chuckled. The color had returned to her face.

My dad held his hands up in the air and feigned innocence. "Don't look at me. What you see is what you get." He walked into the kitchen and pulled open the freezer door. "Have a seat at the table and we'll get you all refreshed."

I stepped out of the hallway and into the kitchen. Everyone's eyes were on me. They were like hungry lions waiting for the killing pounce. They wanted my secrets. Wanted to tear them from me like wild cats ripping the flesh from a lame zebra they'd taken down. I ducked their gaze and grabbed glasses out of the cupboard. The ice cubes clinked out a clumsy tune as Dad dumped them into the glasses. When I poured the warm tea over the cold ice, a crackle filled the room.

"It's not that I don't enjoy company, I just like to be prepared. Maybe, take a shower before I entertain." I brought over a couple of glasses and set them on the table, a plastered on smile. "I probably stink to high heaven. I've been slaving away all morning."

Anna reached for a glass and lifted it in a salute. "A fine job you've done. Your grandmother would be proud."

Faces beamed at me all around the table. A warmth grew in the room. It was an odd feeling, being amongst strangers who didn't feel like strangers but old friends. I relaxed a little; maybe everything was going to be okay after all.

I turned to Lawrence, still feeling a bit too much in the spotlight, even if it was a friendly spotlight. "Do you want to go upstairs? We could listen to some music."

Lawrence looked a bit startled at the suggestion but recovered nicely. He flipped his hair casually off his forehead and shrugged. A crooked grin sat on his lips. "Yeah, sure."

"Great." I grabbed two glasses from the counter and handed one to him. "Let's go then." I led the way up the creaky stairs, sipping my iced tea and trying not to spill it everywhere. I was a little relieved to be out of the range of scrutiny, even if it wasn't with bad intentions. I pushed open the bedroom door and froze.

Wilhelm was hanging the last curtain on the bed and it looked like something right out of Tinker Bell's house. In all of the hubbub I'd forgotten they were even here. A big grin pulled at my mouth. My own fairy bower.

"What do you think?" Wilhelm asked.

I set my glass on a box and fingered the iridescent green curtains. When I was little, I used to set up a faerie hole by tossing a green blanket over a card table. Dad had called it a hobbit hole and pretended he was a troll looking for Bilbo Baggins. He would dance around, the sun streaming through the living room window and I would try and catch him stepping in the light puddles. If I did, he would turn to stone and I could make a break for it. It made me smile just to think of it. Life was happy before Mom was taken away, when Dad still played make believe and had faith in fairy tales. My chest tightened, tears pricked behind my eyes. I blinked furiously to get them to go away. "It's cool, I guess."

"You guess?" Wilhelm asked.

"We just have to bring in the couch and TV and we're out of here, miss." The other delivery guy tipped his hat and trotted down the stairs. "Let's go, Wilhelm."

Wilhelm sauntered across the room and stopped next to me. As he raised his hand the hair on the back of my neck rose. He pulled one of my braids playfully, and then whisked it over my shoulder. I shivered at his touch, even though it was brief, crossed my arms over my chest, and glared at him.

"Sweet dreams," he whispered.

He winked at Lawrence and moved into the hallway. He tried to catch my gaze from the stairs, but I ignored him. He whistled on the way downstairs, the steps creaking under his weight. Nausea rolled in waves over me, crashing like the ocean surges onto the shore.

"Do you know him?" I whispered to Lawrence.

He closed his eyes and shook his head. "Not really, just from around town. What a weirdo."

My guts churned but I shrugged and swallowed the sick feeling. "I'm used to weirdos. There's tons of them in the city, but he's different...creepier somehow." I licked my lips, my mouth suddenly feeling dry. Wilhelm totally made me uneasy. He knew where I lived. And which bedroom was mine. I'd have to check the locks on the doors. *Make sure all the window locks work too*, the little voice in my head added. *Maybe have Dad cut the ivy vine that grows up the side of the house under my window. Would it hold the weight of a grown man? Stop! Stop it.* I sipped from my glass, tried to mask the shaking in my hands, and boxed up the disturbing thoughts in my mind.

"Don't worry about him. He's just a creepy old guy." Lawrence broke the awkward silence that had permeated the room.

I nodded and took another drink from my glass.

"Where's your CD collection?"

I nearly blew tea across the room. "Really? CD's?" I shook my head and knelt in front of a pile of boxes near the wall, opening one. "Don't you have a laptop? Cell phone? iPod?"

Lawrence blushed. "I've got a computer." He rubbed the back of his neck.

"Well, welcome to the twenty-first century."

"Hey! You can't rag on me about a cell phone, because I haven't seen you with one either."

I laughed and pulled my laptop from the box. Unplugging the earphones, I turned up the volume. "What kind of music do you like?"

He shrugged. "I dunno. I like lots of music. Forestland, The Oracle, some other more popular stuff."

I'd never heard of either of those bands. It must have shown on my face because Lawrence shoved his free hand in his pocket and curled his shoulders. "Well, what kind of music do you listen to?"

"Flyleaf, The Used, Blue October, Five Finger Death Punch…" I searched his countenance for signs of recognition. "You've never heard of any of those bands, have you?"

"Sure I have," Lawrence said, but his eyes traveled off to the left. He wasn't telling me the truth. He finished his tea in a long, gulping swallow and set the empty glass on my dresser. I scrolled through my favorite playlist and clicked on a good song. I grabbed the two pillows I'd thrown onto the floor earlier from Mom's window seat and tossed one at Lawrence before flopping to the floor.

He followed my lead, but rolled on his back and cushioned his head, staring at the ceiling as a husky voice rang out of the speakers. The twang of an electric guitar joined in and then drums.

I must have picked a good song, because when the chorus came in Lawrence sang along. It was terrible. I joined in hoping that if I sang, maybe he'd stop. He rolled onto his side and stared at me. I pretended not to notice by staring out the windows.

What I could see of the sky had turned from a bright blue to a dull gray. The sun strained through the gathering clouds. The windowpanes shivered in their casings as a stiff breeze picked up. Small drops of rain hummed on the roof.

When the music faded into the next song on the playlist, I rolled to my stomach, pulling the pillow under my chest. Lawrence had this really strange look on his face, a look somewhere between awe and confusion. I couldn't quite figure him out. At the river he'd acted like a little boy, catching frogs and making jokes, but sitting across from me now, he was different. More somber. His face was full of deep thoughts.

"Did you like that song?" I scrolled through the list so I wouldn't have to meet his questioning eyes, then flinched as a loud roll of thunder boomed overhead.

Lawrence folded his long legs underneath him and stuffed the pillow in his lap. He cleared his throat. "Yeah, that's a good one, but..."

I raised my eyebrows and looked up at him. "But?"

"Your voice..."

"Mine?" I laughed. "You were the one caterwauling like a stray cat."

Lawrence grinned. "I meant your voice was beautiful, but, yeah, Aunt Brunella always says my voice has a 'unique quality'."

I clicked on another song. As the intro rolled in, I smiled at Lawrence. He liked my voice. "Having a unique quality isn't a bad thing…but being tone deaf is."

"Touché." Lawrence chuckled and stared at the wood floor, his finger tapped out the beat of the music on his knee.

The tapestry reminded me of the key in my pocket. I ran my fingers over the shape of it. Then I pointed out my door and across the hall. The corner of the tapestry was poking out behind the bed in Mom's room. "See that tapestry over there?

I found it stuffed under the window seat this morning. Took me forever to get it out."

"Can I see it?" His hands ran excitedly down the front of his shorts.

I shrugged. "I don't care."

Lawrence rolled up off the floor and strode across the hall. I followed as he bent to unroll it. He dropped to his knees and studied the scene, long fingers tracing the black coat of the reindeer. I knelt beside him. Lightning flashed through the windows and made the trees in the rug look as if their leaves were gently waving. The wind picked up. The rain fell hard and fast against the windowpanes. The smell of damp forest seemed to emanate from the tapestry; goosebumps rose on my arms. The window in my room overlooking the driveway was still open, and the wind blew through as the storm rolled in. The scent must be carrying on the wind.

"What do you think about the tapestry?" I asked.

"It's beautiful." Lawrence's voice was husky when he finally spoke. It struck me as a little weird. He seemed rather emotional. Did he know something about it? Was it a long lost family heirloom? Had it been stolen and stashed here in an empty house, the thieves biding their time to pick it up later? I shook my head. My imagination was running away again. There was probably a very simple explanation if I just asked.

"Have you seen it before?"

He nodded and a long rumble accompanied his words. "A long time ago, when I was just a boy. Where did you say you found it?"

"Stuffed under the window seat."

"You should hang it on the wall instead of walking on it."

"I wouldn't walk on it," I scoffed. "It's a tapestry, not a carpet." Did he think I was some stupid city girl?

Lawrence smiled. "I nearly forgot. Your dad is an art history professor. Of course you know its value."

I gave him a little smirk. "Will you help me hang it?"

As lightning lit up the room, Lawrence raised his eyes. They shone like polished gemstones, the same burnished gold I'd seen the other day. He cleared his throat and nodded. "Sure. Do you have the hardware we need?"

I shook my head. My throat had tightened with the change of color in his eyes. They reminded me so much of Bailean, my childhood friend, that it caught me off guard. I wasn't ready for the strong emotional reaction I was having.

"Not a big deal. We can get the hangers we need at the hardware store in town."

I sat up straight, surprised again. "Right now?"

"Or tomorrow. Or Thursday. Whatever works." He ran his hands nervously down the front of his shorts.

I smiled. "You mean Cinderella gets to leave the castle? Yeah, well, I'll have to run it by my dad, but it should be fine."

"You still have to ask permission? I thought you were like, twenty."

I looked away, unable to meet his gaze. I scratched my neck and hitched a shoulder. The iced tea turned sour in my stomach. "I am. He's just over-protective."

"What happened?" Lawrence asked.

The storm grumbled and murmured. It seemed to have come in quick and fierce and was now petering out. Even though in this moment it felt like I'd known Lawrence my whole life, I wasn't sure if I could trust him with my secrets yet. I picked at the hem of my shorts. New beginnings meant making new friends, and new friends couldn't be made if I hid behind my past. I took a deep breath. "I was in science class, senior year, and my partner was this guy who thought he knew everything and wouldn't listen to anybody…especially me. He pissed me off regularly but the teacher wouldn't let me switch partners. She said we 'needed to learn to work together despite our differences'."

Lawrence snorted. "I know just the kind of guy you're talking about."

I looked up, saw the slight disgust in Lawrence's expression. He *did* know. I could talk about this. "One day he was about to add the chemicals to our experiment in the wrong order and blow up the whole school. So, I grabbed for his hand to stop him and our Bunsen burner flared. Some of the chemical spilled into the fire, I guess."

"Did you get hurt?" Lawrence's eyebrows arched.

I nodded and swallowed, the sound of my fingers pick-pick-picking at the hem on my shorts loud in my ears. "Yes, and I burned his hand and part of his face. He was a star football player and he lost his scholarship because he couldn't throw a football anymore. The worst part was that no one wanted to listen to my side of the story. They all just assumed I did it on purpose because I didn't like him." I yanked my hair away and showed him my scars. "Why would I do this to myself on purpose? Why would I do it to anyone?"

Lawrence cleared his throat. He bit his lip. I could see the gears in his mind rotating a million miles a minute. He raised his hand, hesitated, and then touched the scarred tissue on my neck. I was so startled that I froze. Only the doctors had ever touched me there.

I averted my gaze, closed my eyes. His hand was warm against my skin. "I should never have lost my temper, but it would've been at lot worse if I'd let him add the wrong thing. It was an accident that the flame flared up like it did." Tears burned at the edge of my lashes. "Even though I know it wasn't my fault, deep down I still feel guilty about it."

Lawrence cleared his throat. "I'm sorry that guy got hurt, but it sounds like he was the jerk, not you."

I glanced at him out of the corner of my eye as he withdrew his hand. I could still feel the heat of his palm on my skin. A tear wobbled out and streaked down my face. I swiped at it and twisted the end of my braid around my finger. "Sometimes I have a hard time controlling my feelings. Things just bubble under the surface until I can't contain them anymore. Then they leap out and…"

Lawrence gave me a tight-lipped smile. "Everyone gets angry and scared. It's important to know why you have those feelings though. Instead of being angry at the whole world, and letting that anger swallow you. You have to direct that anger at the person who deserves it."

A weight lifted from my shoulders. My hands grew warm as I looked at him. I had to pinch myself—surely he wasn't real. I must be dreaming. A tingling sensation spread through my body making me uncomfortable in my own skin. Abruptly, I stood and reached for the cleaning rag in the bucket, wringing out the excess water. I hoped Lawrence didn't think I was rude. I just wasn't used to the feelings that were zipping through me right now. He was the first person who actually understood where I was coming from—the first person who listened to me without dismissing the feelings behind the words.

"Come on." I beckoned him with a toss of my head. "I've got to get my room clean today. I've been sleeping on the floor in the living room."

"Want help? I could unpack some boxes." Lawrence hopped to his feet and followed me back across the hall. He grabbed a box before I could decline the offer. I bit my lip in anticipation, knowing exactly what was in the box he held.

The look on his face was worth the wait. I couldn't help but burst out laughing at his shocked expression as he realized he'd grabbed a box of my underwear. I held out the rag to him. "Perhaps it's safer if you wipe the bookshelves."

We exchanged places and embarrassed smiles. He pulled out the storybooks Gran had left for me then wiped the dust from the shelves. I placed my belongings into the tall dresser. I tried not to laugh, imagining what thoughts had run through Lawrence's mind as he'd opened the box. How could such a handsome guy be so embarrassed by lacey underwear? Was he one of those weird guys who pledged to stay virgins until they were married?

"I'm not, um…" Lawrence started, then cleared his throat.

I whipped my head around. Prickles ran down my spine.

"I'm not strange, that is." He wiped his brow with the back of his wrist. "My upbringing was just…*different* than yours." He smiled, then returned to his task.

I wondered what he meant by that. "Didn't you grow up next door?" How could his upbringing have been that different? I mean, okay, I really couldn't see Anna wearing lacey underwear, but you never know. She did seem like kind of a rebel.

Lawrence shrugged. "I didn't spend much time here. Most of my growing up has been with my other great aunt Brunella."

I cocked my head. "How many great aunts do you have?"

"Just Anna and Brunella, but my grandmother had a brother, too. He-he's passed though."

We cleaned in companionable silence for a few minutes. I pondered his family tree while I piled socks into a drawer. "Where did you say you grew up?"

Lawrence smirked. "I didn't."

My retort was cut off by Henry's voice echoing up the stairwell. "Lawrence! The storm has passed. We're leaving now."

Lawrence dropped the rag in the bucket with a tiny splash. "So, how about Thursday then?" His eyebrows arched and he shoved his hands in his pockets.

"All right." I bit my lip, suddenly unsure. I hadn't been on a date since before the accident.

The dimple in his cheek puckered. "I'll pick you up around twelve thirty. Sound okay?"

I nodded and he turned to leave.

"Wait!" I put my hand on his arm.

"Change your mind already?" Mischief danced across his face.

"No, I uh…I just need to ask you something before you leave." I didn't know why I wanted to ask him, but something deep inside told me that he knew more than he was saying, just like his aunt. "Do you know why the other bedroom is locked? I mean, since Anna was my gran's best friend and all…I thought maybe you'd been in it before?"

Lawrence shrugged. "I'm not sure. Are you positive the door isn't just jammed up a bit?"

"Yeah. It's definitely locked."

"Do you have the key?"

I shoved my hand in my pocket and gripped the key in my palm. I hadn't had a chance to try it, and I wasn't sure if I wanted to open it the first time with Lawrence here. If I told him I had found it, he'd want to unlock the door before he left. What happened if there was something in there that made me freak out? I wasn't ready to show him that side of me yet. A lump formed in my throat. I swallowed. "No luck finding it yet."

chapter six

"Down in the Willow garden
Where me and my love did meet
As we sat a-courtin'
My love fell off to sleep..."

I searched the sky, the song fading from my lips. Thunder had rumbled in the distance all morning, but now it sounded like a giant crashing down the beanstalk. Great gray clouds rolled and glided over each other, like a flock of woolly sheep, each vying to be the leader. I leaned further into the flowerbed I'd been cleaning out since just after breakfast. I had been so intent on yanking all the weeds before the predicted rain hit that I'd lost track of time, but it must have been close to two. Ripping the unruly weeds out of the soil had brought immense satisfaction.

The front door opened and Dad stepped out, apple in hand. "Wow. You do have the magic touch." He crunched through the red skin, wiping his mouth on his sleeve.

I tucked my hair behind my ears, weighing my answer carefully. It wasn't fair that he could casually toss metaphors around like that without other people second-guessing his sanity the way he would second-guess mine. "I just pulled all the weeds. Nothing magical about it."

"Well, magic or not, the flowerbeds look fabulous." Lightning zigzagged through the sky to the west, and Dad and

I watched it warily. "Can I help you finish before the storm rolls in?"

I patted the soil around the latest cleaned out area. "I just need to rake up the weeds."

"And put the tools in the shed," Dad added. "We don't want them to rust."

"Sure." I gathered the garden claw and spade and stood up. My knees ached from kneeling all morning, but finally the flagstone path that wound its way to Gran's fairy garden looked inviting instead of creepy. I smiled at the now weed-free flowerbeds.

Dad tossed the apple core to the far edges of the lawn and held out his hand.

"Litterbug," I teased.

Dad smiled. "It's not littering if the animals can safely eat it."

I laughed at the old joke between us and dropped the tools in his palm. A deep rumble shook overhead. The storm was closing in fast now.

"I'm really proud of you, Sophie. I wasn't sure you'd stick with it."

"Yeah, well, don't be too proud. It's just a flowerbed." I stretched and clenched my fingers, working out the stiffness. I had lost myself in the toil this morning. The beast inside seemed to hibernate as I sang. And I had sung like Mom and Gran and I used to—with all my heart and without shame. I sang like no one was listening but the flowers. I hadn't let myself go like that in a really long time. I started thinking that maybe that was part of my problem—I couldn't let go. I had this deep need to control everything around me in order to control my anxiety—to control the slumbering beast.

Once upon a time my imagination had connected me with a deeper current of truth that ran beneath the surface of everyday life. Most people don't pay attention to the hidden energy that unites us all like the roots of trees entwined beneath the soil.

The tangles we couldn't see led a life all their own, and yet they were connected to the tree above. They nurtured it, and nourished it, and made it strong. Ever since I met Lawrence, I felt something changing inside me, like I'd found a kernel of strength that I'd hidden away long ago. It was like my roots had found water.

As if the storm could read my thoughts, it let out a low grumble, and then a blinding flash. The thunderclouds split and abandoned their heavy load. Quickly, I raked and scraped the scattered weeds into a pile. I gathered them from the sidewalk and tossed them in the wheelbarrow as the raindrops rang against the bucket like a steel drum. Dad grabbed the wooden handles, pushing the wheelbarrow as fast as he could to the little shed in the backyard. I ran behind him with the rake in hand, taking cover under the shed's tin roof.

"Mother Nature isn't holding anything back, is she?" Dad said.

I laid the rake alongside the wall, took off my gloves, and shook the dirt from them. I wiped the sweat from my brow as another deafening crack sounded. It was followed by streaks of lightning that arced over the house. I was soaking wet. "You making a run for it or waiting it out?"

A look of surprise crossed my dad's face. Then a grin lit it up. "Definitely running."

I nodded and grinned back, then jumped as the loudest clap of thunder yet made my bones vibrate. Leaves flashed their silver underbellies in a roar of wind. The sound of the rain on the roof turned into a steady ring.

"That's not rain anymore. That's hail!" Dad looked wary, brows furrowing. "It's now or never. You ready?" He shifted his weight from foot to foot.

As the next strike of lightning hit the ground, and a crack of thunder echoed, I made a break for it. "Last one in's a rotten egg!"

Dad was on my heels. The ice balls pelted against our skin. I could almost imagine giants in the sky counting the number of hits they made and yelling "five points" every time a ball of hail landed on my head. The rain soaked through my jean shorts. I flung open the back door and we tumbled into the kitchen. The clock on the microwave was dark. I flicked the light switch. "Electricity is out," I panted.

"Shut the windows so the rain doesn't blow in." Dad pushed down the window sash over the kitchen sink. He left a crack and the cold wind seeped through. "Not all the way though, just in case there is a tornado."

"Tornado?" Those were something we'd never had to worry about in the city. I trotted into the dining room and pushed down the window sashes. There was a flash at the edge of the trees and I froze. Through the rain-laden pane I saw a dark shadow creep near the iron fence. Adrenaline rushed into my veins. My throat went dry. My heart stumbled over itself, thumping irregularly against my ribs. Whatever was casting that shadow was big. Like, *elephant* big. I leaned so far forward trying to see if I was really seeing something at the edge of the trees that the window steamed up. Dad tromped upstairs. I should follow. Instead, I wiped away the fog with a fist and pressed my nose upon the glass again. I begged for another strike of lighting to illuminate the darkness.

"Sophie!" Dad yelled.

Scared by the tone of his voice, I turned from the window and ran, taking the stairs two at a time. Around the newel post I swung, breathless as I entered Dad's room. I didn't know what to expect.

The wind, hail, and rain blew through the small square opening. Ice balls littered the floor. Shiny puddles gathered in the worn away areas of the wood floor. The hail must have broken the window.

Dad was holding a towel over the jagged pane, but the storm still blew in with a vengeance. I didn't know what to do, but then I saw a still unpacked box.

I ripped the tape off the box and dumped its contents. Photos and old thirty-five millimeter negatives slid onto the floor. Faded faces peered up at me—a smiling woman with long hair and toffee-brown eyes. I knelt, forgetting about the box, and the rain, and the hail blowing into the room. My fingers brushed over the photograph of my mother.

"Sophie! The box!" Dad yelled.

But his words didn't register. I could think of nothing but those toffee-brown eyes.

"Sophie!" Dad roared.

Startled, I dropped the photo and stood. Stars formed in my eyes from the sudden change in position. I handed the cardboard to Dad. He broke out the remaining jagged edges of glass and shoved the box into the opening. When it was secure, he leaned on the wall, catching his breath. The room was a mess of rain and glass shards. He laughed nervously and flicked the rain out of his hair with a shaking hand. "That was quite an adventure. What would I do without you, Soph?"

I shrugged. "Well, the bedroom would probably be floating away if it wasn't for my quick, decisive action." Who was I kidding? I'd frozen up like a computer infected with malware. I bent and plucked up a piece of hail the size of a golf ball. It pinched my palm with its frigid bite and I dropped it with a gasp. Shards of glass were scattered over the painted slats and in the shimmery pools of rain.

"Ah, don't worry about it." Dad waved his hand in a dismissive gesture. "Everyone finds themselves in situations where they aren't sure what to do. It's not like hail breaking a window is an everyday occurrence."

The room lit up, the quick flash of lightning throwing shadows. A long rumble of thunder shook the house. The sound of hail pounding the roof softened back into rain.

I shrugged. "Well, at least I know how to clean the mess up. You'll be in charge of fixing the window though."

I made my way down the dark stairwell and toward the kitchen to grab towels, the broom, and dustpan. I was nearly to the kitchen when a knock on the front door made me jump.

I peered back down the narrow hallway, searching the long windows on each side of the front door. Who would be out in a storm like this? Lightning lit the front porch and I recognized the tall silhouette beating at the entrance. Lawrence! What was he doing here? I wasn't expecting him until tomorrow. I ran to open the door.

He stumbled in, rainwater rushing off his yellow slicker. "I was getting worried. Didn't you hear me knocking?"

"Sorry. We were upstairs." I shut the door.

"I brought these over." He held out a bunch of candles tied with a ribbon. They were smooth and fat and smelled like flowers. Lawrence shifted, his wet slicker squeaking. He cleared his throat and reached for the doorknob.

"Wait!" I held up a hand. When he looked at me, words stuck in my throat. "Uh…Thanks for the candles. Come in the kitchen. Dad made some oatmeal cookies this morning while I was working in the garden. I've been dying for a taste."

Lawrence looked surprised. "Are you sure? We don't have to hang out just because I brought candles."

I gave him a smirk. "Like I'd only want to hang out because candles are involved." I turned and walked down the hallway to the kitchen. The snaps on his coat ripped open. I couldn't help but smile at the sound.

I set the candles on the table and dug the matches from the utility drawer, hearing the crumple of the stiff fabric as Lawrence hung his coat on the rack before following me.

Dad strolled into the kitchen behind him. "Don't worry—not crashing the party, just getting the paper towels since Sophie forgot."

I shook my head. "I didn't forget, Dad." Actually, I hadn't thought about it once since Lawrence walked into the house.

"Did Anna make those?" Dad pointed to the candles.

I struck a match, the smell of sulfur hanging in the humid air. The flame flickered and then grew as the wick caught. Dad rummaged around in a cabinet and pulled out a pair of candleholders. I stuffed in the fat end of one candle and took it from him.

"Yeah." Lawrence crossed his arms, tucking his hands under his armpits. "She sells them at the farm supply store in town and Henry takes them to the local Renaissance festivals, too."

Prickles ran up my spine at the mention of the Renaissance festival. I blew the match out and gave it a good shake to gain a few moments to pull myself back together. "Do you go and help out?"

A little smile pulled at the corner of his mouth. "Sometimes."

I tossed the match in the sink and ran some water over it.

"Do you dress up?" My dad asked.

I turned as Lawrence's cheeks flushed. "You kinda have to. It's festival policy for merchants."

"But you like it, don't you?" I teased as I pulled cookies out of the jar, three for each of us.

"It's fun to live in a different time and place, pretend to be someone else, if only for a day or two." Lawrence took the cookies I offered and bit into one.

"My parents took me to the festival at the Cloisters when I was six. Have you been to that one?" A sudden crack of thunder made goosebumps prickle down my arms.

"Yeah, I've been to that one," Lawrence said through a mouthful of cookie. "The tapestries in the museum are amazing."

My dad nodded. "The museum is full of lots of fabulous artifacts."

"Yes, sir." Lawrence held up the last bite of cookie before popping it in his mouth. "You're a good baker, Mr. Lincoln."

I set the lit candle on the small plate with my cookies on it and grabbed Lawrence's arm. "Is it okay if Lawrence hangs out for a bit?"

Dad nodded. "Sure…just leave the door open."

Oh my God. He didn't just say that, did he? My face grew hot. "Really, Dad?"

My dad shook his head and twisted his mouth. "I'm sorry. Sometimes I forget that my little girl is an independent adult. Rewind!"

I rolled my eyes. "Let's just put you on pause for a minute. Okay?"

Dad nodded, his lips stiff as if they were sealed. "Deal." He skirted around us and pulled open the pantry door. A roll of paper towels flipped through the air and landed in his hand. "Please tell Anna thank you for the candles."

"I will, Mr. Lincoln."

"C'mon!" I dragged Lawrence out of the kitchen, up the stairs, and into my room. I set the plate on the window seat and curled up in the corner.

"Your room looks great. Well, what I can see of it." Lawrence's white teeth flashed in a grin as he sat cross-legged in the opposite side of the window seat. He stared at me for a hot second. "And I understand what all those romance books mean about candlelight now."

"*You* read romance books?" I couldn't keep a smirk from forming on my lips. What was he doing reading romance?

Lawrence laughed and shrugged, but he didn't exactly admit to reading the smut novels. His face relaxed and then lengthened. His hands trembled before he clasped them in his lap. His chest visually rose and then fell with a deep breath. "I live with my aunts because my dad died when I was little…and my mom, she's in no position to raise me."

I moved the candle off to the side and scooted forward until my knees were so close to his that an energy buzzed between us. My heart thumped in my throat, but if anyone could understand what I was going through, it would be Lawrence. His mom was still alive but he couldn't be with her, and as far as I knew, my mother was still alive, too… somewhere. "My mom…went away when I was little. I've never found out what happened to her or where she went. All I have left of her are bits of disjointed memories that don't make sense anymore, and a fear that creeps into my head when I least expect it." I twisted a length of hair around my finger and peeked at Lawrence through my lashes, trying to gauge his reaction. "I used to be certain that I knew exactly what happened to her, but no one ever believed me. As I got older, I started disbelieving myself."

He nodded but wouldn't meet my gaze.

I shrugged. "But I don't know who to be angry at. Should I be angry at Dad and the doctors for not believing me? Or should I be mad at Mom for…going away? Or should I be mad at myself?"

My hands grew warm as I looked at him, his angular jaw softened by the candlelight. His eyes softly glowing as if they were full of unshed tears. He seemed to genuinely care. How could I have almost written him off as a weird frog boy?

Silence filled the space between us, the waning thunder a symphony underscoring our whispered confessions. "Someday I'm going to find her, and I'm going to prove to my dad that I wasn't making up stories. That she didn't just walk out on us."

My mother's face bloomed in my memory, and I suddenly remembered the photos that had spilled out of the box. I hopped up. "I'll be right back."

I slipped into my dad's room. The pools of water no longer shone on the floor. All the photos had been scooped into a pile in the corner, except one. The one I'd seen earlier of Mom propped on the table by Dad's bed.

My breath caught in my throat and my heart fluttered. I'd leave that one there. Slowly, I bent and picked up the photos.

"What have you got?" Lawrence leaned forward as I returned to my room and let the photos flutter to the floor. He knelt on the floor next to the pile and flipped over a photo. A deep chuckle filled the room. He'd grabbed a photo of a pig-tailed version of me with ice cream smeared across my nose.

I yanked it from his hand and held it close to my chest. "Don't laugh at me."

"Oh come on! You were like three," Lawrence said.

"So? It's still embarrassing." I set it aside and rummaged through the pictures, flipping over the ones that were upside down. A photo of a much younger Mrs. Ling smiled back at me.

Lawrence pointed to the Asian woman. "Who's that?"

I fondly remembered the afternoons in our old neighbor's kitchen making dumplings. A pang of sadness gripped me unexpectedly. "That's Mrs. Ling. She was like my grandmother. I spent a lot of time with her when my dad was at work." She had passed away last year and her daughter had taken over the apartment. The daughter was nowhere near as nice as her mother. I put the photo aside. Later, I'd pin it next to my mirror.

A pair of brown eyes stared out from under the pile. I grabbed the photo of my mom and me posing with the man dressed as a medieval king. A shiver pulsed through my body. The delivery guy looked so much like the man in the photo that it was startling. But it had to be a coincidence. He *couldn't* be the same man. It was impossible.

Lawrence hesitantly reached for the photo. "Where was this picture taken?"

"That was the day my parents took me to the festival at the Cloisters. I was six."

"And that's…your mom?" His finger stroked my mom's long hair.

I nodded. "She's been gone for fifteen years now."

"You're lucky to have these pictures."

I cocked my head. "Do you have any memories of your mom?"

Lawrence ran his hands through his hair and let out a sharp laugh. "Some. Not too many from when I was little, and the ones I do have are pretty horrifying. My aunties used to tell me stories about her antics when she was young...before things changed."

The wind gusted, throwing rain and leaf debris on the window. The glass trembled in the frame. Something caught the candlelight and shimmered at the corner. I rolled to my feet and peered at it through the window. A piece of mica was stuck to the pane. How would a flake of mica get all the way up here?

I pressed my fingers against the smooth glass.

I didn't notice that Lawrence had risen to see what I was looking at. Nor the fact that he was so close to me I could feel his warm breath on my neck as he whispered, "Looks like a dragon scale."

Gooseflesh prickled my whole body. Did Lawrence believe in dragons, too? My psychiatrist's voice went off in my head: *Sophie suffers from a delusional disorder called* bizarre delusions— *things that are so far from reality that they just could not be true*. I straightened and spun on my heel. Lawrence was standing close and I could feel the warmth radiating from his body. We couldn't both be delusional—could we? The photo of Mom and me was still in his hand. "Why does everyone keep saying that?"

Lawrence cocked an eyebrow. "Everyone?"

I pulled the locket out from under my tank top, cradled it in my palm, and gently pried it open. The mica sparkled in its silver casing. "I've had this locket ever since I can remember. It was my mother's. When I asked your aunt about what I thought was a flake of mica, she said it wasn't mica—but a dragon's scale."

"Really? Huh." He smiled and rubbed the nape of his neck. He didn't meet my gaze, but looked over my shoulder out the tall windows. The wind still tossed through the trees, but the storm had moved on and the sun was struggling to find its way through the overcast sky. "Since the worst of the storm has passed, I should probably head back home, before Anna starts worrying about me." He held out the photo to me. "It's a nice picture."

I snapped the locket closed and tucked it back under my top. Was he avoiding my question or did he think there was something weird about me? I pulled the photo from his grasp.

He slowly wiped his hands on his shorts. "I'll come by tomorrow after lunch if that's okay?"

"For what?" I asked. Wasn't he just trying to get away as fast as he could?

"Uh…do you still want to go to town with me?" Lawrence shoved his hands in his pockets and then yanked them back out again. "I mean, um, it's…uh, it's okay if you…if you don't."

I slapped my palm against my forehead. I was so stupid. "Sorry. Yes, I want to go."

A smile lit up Lawrence's face. The sun broke through the clouds filtering into the room and making his eyes shine that golden color. "Great. I'll see you tomorrow then."

"Yeah, tomorrow." I smiled back at him. Maybe he wasn't trying to get away from me after all.

Lawrence pointed at me. "That's the first time."

"What's the first time?"

"The first time I've seen you really smile. It looks beautiful on you." Lawrence turned and walked out of my room. I followed him, pausing in the doorway, feeling as if my feet weren't touching the ground.

He started down the stairs, but stopped and looked at me over his shoulder. "By the way, you should ask Anna about the dragon scale thing again."

I leaned over the railing. "Why?"

Lawrence skipped down the last of the stairs and grabbed his raincoat. He shrugged it on and looked back up at me, his amber eyes flashing in the low light. "Because I think you're ready, and she knows a lot of dragons." He grinned and pulled open the front door, and with a final wave was gone.

I think you're ready….she knows a lot of dragons. Lawrence's words repeated in my head. He didn't say she knows a lot *about* dragons. He'd said she knows a lot *of* dragons. Did he misspeak? Or did he mean *real* dragons, like Bailean? The locket suddenly felt warm against my skin. I wrapped my fingers around it as a melody popped into my head. I started humming. I couldn't quite remember the lyrics but I'd known the tune forever. Down the steps I skipped.

"Looks like we're grilling for dinner and eating by candlelight!" My dad rubbed his hands together eagerly and then grimaced. "Man, my hand hurts. Maybe you should take a look at it. I might've gotten stuck by a piece of glass when I was cleaning up the rain." He plopped into a chair.

I sat next to him. "Okay, let me see." I prodded the small cut on his palm. Something shiny caught the bits of sun pushing through the kitchen windows. "You're right." I brushed at the shiny bit, pulling it away from the cut and pinching it between my fingers.

"Did you get it?" Dad asked.

I squinted at the sliver of green mica. My throat tightened. "Yeah, Dad. Just a little sliver, nothing to get all woozy about."

But my stomach clenched like a noose had been thrown around it and pulled tight.

chapter seven

the cold stones of the castle wall pressed into my back. The door at the end of the narrow hall inched open and an elegant lady looked out. She had piercing blue eyes and a locket hanging from her neck. It swung forward, catching the light. Etched into the gold locket was a knotted dragon biting its own tail.

"My Queen," a gruff voice said. The knight's bushy white brows knit together as he turned into the alcove. The silver bears embroidered on his faded green surcoat swatted at each other with every step. His expression held suspicion and concern. I didn't know this man, but there was something about his determined walk that made me feel I could trust him. "Gafford has been taken to the dungeons."

"Please, Edward, come in." The queen's gaze traveled past the knight's shoulder and met mine. My stomach flip-flopped. "Quickly now, are you sure no one has followed?"

I shook my head, stunned by the beautiful waves of thick dark hair that cascaded around the queen's face. A tiny, knowing smile pulled at her mouth.

"No, My Lady, no one has seen me," the knight answered. "It is shift change."

The queen locked me in her gaze like a fox staring down a hare. "Then make haste, for these corridors are not safe."

I woke with a start. Sweat pooled between my breasts. The sheets clung to me. The air was hot and clammy. I ran a hand through my hair, pulling it away from my face and kicked off the sticky sheets. It had been years since I'd dreamed of the queen in the castle. When I used to dream of her, Dr. Parket called it something like "projecting my past experiences"—subconsciously making up stories to fill the emotional gap. Yes, I missed my mother. I still did, but I was sure my dreams had more to them. I didn't feel like it was my mind making up stories; it felt like my mind trying to remember something I'd tucked so far in that it was almost irretrievable. I was glad Dad had agreed to no more psych visits after the move. Fifteen years of someone else digging into my head were enough. He was keeping his word so far—I'd just have to deal with these moments of weakness by myself.

I rolled out of bed and stepped onto the wood planks. I'd need to get an actual carpet before winter hit or the floor would be freezing. Something glinted by my heel. I bent to pick it up thinking it was probably a wayward piece of glass from the window breaking yesterday. I was relieved that I hadn't stepped on it. As my fingers touched it, I realized it wasn't glass.

It was a green flake of mica. Where were these flakes coming from? Was someone playing a trick on me? Would Lawrence do that? He was the only one who'd been in my room besides Dad. I'd probably just stepped on it outside and it stuck to the bottom of my shoe. I laid it on my bedside table and crossed to the window seat.

The sky was bright and clear. No sign of a storm. Dad was already outside snipping away at the tangled vines around the fence line with a pair of shears. What was it with guys and cutting things down?

I dressed in a pair of denim cut-offs and a black tank top, grabbed my brush from the top of my dresser and pulled it through my hair. Sweeping the long strands off my face, I pulled it into a ponytail. Even high up on my head, the fringed ends tickled the small of my back. Maybe I should've taken Dad up on his offer to get my hair cut in one of the best salons in the city before we moved, but I'd been growing my hair out for two years. What if the hairdresser took off too much and people could see my scars? What if the haircut made me look like a dork? It was more comfortable to just leave it alone.

The mirror above my dresser reflected the trees. Their bright green leaves beckoned me into the sunshine. I returned to my own reflection, pulling my ponytail over my shoulder. It hid most of the scarring anyway.

Mother stared back at me from the picture stuck to the edge of the mirror, but so did the leering grin of the king. Anger toward him bubbled to the surface. I grabbed the picture and tore it in half, tossing the king and his leer toward the garbage can. The torn piece fluttered to the floor. I propped the other half back up, satisfied.

Finding the shorts I wore yesterday in the pile of dirty laundry on the floor I rummaged through the pocket and pulled out the key I'd found in the tapestry. I rolled it in my hand. Perhaps today was the day I'd give the lock a try. I closed my fingers around it and stepped into the hall.

The floor creaked under my feet and I paused in front of the locked door. I bit my lip as nerves took flight in my stomach. My hand shook, but I slipped the key into the keyhole. It fit. I turned it. With a pop, the door squeaked open.

I stood in the doorway. Perspiration beaded on my forehead. Finally I got the nerve to step into the room. Shelves full of books lined the wall to my right. I ran my finger over the spine of a small red book with gold lettering. *Weird.* There wasn't a speck of dust on it. I pulled it off the shelf and flipped open its pages. A line drawing of a unicorn stared out at me. It was different than the unicorns I was used to seeing—it looked more like a goat and less like a horse. Flipping through the pages I decided it was a bestiary of sorts. I replaced it on the shelf and pulled the sheet off a chaise upholstered in green velvet in the middle of the room and another off a small writing desk under the windows. Again, there was no dust. An eerie sensation grew around me. I'd had to clean the whole house from top to bottom. I had the dry, chapped hands to prove it, but this room was perfect. Nothing was out of place. There was nothing that could've caused the key plate to become hot the other day. Nothing looked out of the ordinary, except another sheet hanging on the wall. It must be covering a piece of artwork. I yanked it down and caught my breath at the tapestry that was revealed.

The dragon seemed to blink in the bright morning light as if I'd woken him from a deep sleep by yanking the curtains open. The wool threads he was worked from shimmered in a deep emerald hue. He looked like my dragon. Like Bailean.

I ran my shaking hands over the hanging—the details were so finely worked. There was not a single strand of color out of place. He was so beautiful. I wondered if Dad had ever seen it. Such a beautiful piece.

I nearly called out to him, but a sudden protectiveness came over me. I wanted to keep it for myself just a little while longer. A secret. Something no one could spoil. A warm wind wound around my ankles.

I'd just have to keep the door locked. I wouldn't tell Dad I'd found the key. If he asked, I'd tell him it was no big deal. "I don't need the space yet, and when I do, I'll find a locksmith to change the lock." Yes, that sounded reasonable. I walked out of the room, but I could've sworn that the dragon in the tapestry winked at me as I shut the door.

chapter eight

I dropped the key back into my pocket and rushed to the window seat and looked out. Dad was still battling the tall vines clinging to the fence line. I cranked the handle to open the middle window. It was still jammed up and took all of my strength to get it to crack just an inch. Exasperated, I yelled down to Dad. "Hey! Do you think you could help me with these windows? They're stuck and I could really use some air flow up here."

My dad waved and nodded. "I know I promised to work on them the other day. Sorry! I'll look at them when I'm done with this!"

"Great," I mumbled. "That'll be like, next week." I walked toward the long window at the end of the peak. At least there was no crank on this one. The lock turned smoothly and I raised the sash, expecting a cool breeze to waft in. There was nothing but more oppressive heat.

Which is why I was surprised when I heard a *creak*, like someone stepping on a floorboard behind me. Wilhelm's face loomed in my imagination. He'd given me the creeps and I hoped I'd never see him again—but he did know where I lived and where my bedroom was...

I was overreacting, but I peered over my shoulder anyway. No one was in the room, but the door on the wardrobe was ajar. That must have been what I'd heard. My hand shook as I pushed it shut, making sure the catch caught this time. My fingers lingered on the smooth wood. I remembered the *screech* of wire hangers on the bar, and my chest tightened. I yanked my hand away from the wardrobe and shook my head. "It's just your imagination. Nothing is there."

Still, I fled down the stairs and shoved my bare feet into my gray low-top Converse. I pushed through the screen door and let it slam behind me. I needed to get outside, take a breath of fresh air. Rounding the corner of the house, I walked toward Dad and his snip-happy shears, leaving behind the wardrobe, and the terrifying memories of the last day I'd seen my mom.

"Dad? Lawrence is coming by later."

My dad looked at me and pushed his glasses back up his sweaty nose. "Oh, yeah?"

"Yeah…" I bit my lip. It'd been so long since I'd gone out, but I didn't need to ask permission. "I mean, I'm going into town with Lawrence today, so he's picking me up."

Dad quit chopping, pulled off his glasses, and wiped the sweat from his face with his T-shirt. "What are you doing in town?"

I shoved my hands in my pockets and leaned casually against the fence. "You know that cool tapestry I found under the window seat?"

Dad nodded and made an affirmative noise.

"Well, Lawrence is gonna help me hang it on the wall, but we need some hardware."

Dad nodded. "That reminds me. We really need to find you a car before school starts…and a part-time job." He wiped his sweaty forehead on his T-shirt sleeve. "Have you eaten breakfast?"

I shook my head. "Not yet. I woke up really hot, which is why I was trying to open the windows." My hand went to the locket nestled under my tank top. "I was having this weird dream."

Dad nodded and pointed to my chest. "Still wearing that every day, huh?"

I pulled out the locket and studied the design. It was the exact design of the queen's locket in the dream. "Anna said it belonged to her…to Mom."

Dad peered at the etched design as if he couldn't quite remember what it looked like, but I knew better. He probably had every etched line, every scratch, memorized. He chewed on the inside of his cheek. "Well, she would probably know. Anna knew your mom when she was a little girl."

I know her. Anna's statement replayed in my mind. Had she just misspoke? Anna didn't seem the type of person to do that. Still, I kept a tight rein on the hope blossoming in my chest. I opened the locket, turning it so he could see the flake of mica. "Why do you think Mom kept this flake of mica in it?"

Dad shrugged. "Don't know. It must have meant something to her."

I held up the locket so the flake caught the light. It glittered in the sunshine. How would Dad react if I mentioned what Lawrence and his aunt said about the mica? "If dragons were real, I would think that their scales might look like this."

My dad groaned. "Oh, Sophie. We aren't going there again, are we? He was an imaginary friend when you were six."

The fire in the pit of my stomach flared. I wanted to scream. To tell him that my dragon had been there as long as I could remember, not just when I was six. I wanted to say that I didn't make him up to protect myself from the bad memories of my mother being beaten in front of me. My six-year-old self wanted to say that he was *real*. That *Bailean* was real. But I didn't know quite what to believe. My gut told me to believe; everyone else told me I was crazy—except Lawrence and Anna. They believed me. They didn't think I was nuts.

I lassoed my anger and plastered on a fake smile. "Relax, Dad. I said *if*. You don't really think I still believe in dragons, do you?"

Dad sighed. "Don't make me have second thoughts about the psych visits."

"Can't you just have a little fun? I remember a time when imagination was encouraged in this family." I waved as I headed for the gate. Hopefully my smile would make him think I was just fooling around with him.

"Where are you going?"

"For a quick walk," I called over my shoulder.

"Could you fold the laundry before you leave with Lawrence?"

"Sure!" I waded through the tall grass in the backyard. Dad had mowed the front yard, but he'd wanted to finish trimming away the vines on the fence before he tackled the back. The shade of the trees near the stream was a welcome relief from the heat. I followed the trail to the house Lawrence shared with his aunt. Perhaps Anna could explain why no one believed in dragons except for us. She seemed to know everything else.

I splashed over the creek and trotted deeper into the woods, taking the steep stairs two at a time. As I entered the garden, I heard Anna humming. It was a lullaby…then it hit me. It was the song Bailean used to sing to me—the one I'd been humming yesterday! "Hi, Anna. Where did you learn that song?"

Anna turned from the plant she was trimming. A wide-brimmed straw hat shaded her deeply tanned face. Her long white hair was braided and hung over her shoulder. She wore a deep blue apron over a plain dress. She looked like a villager in some medieval realm. The lullaby continued softly in my head even as the woman answered my question. "Oh, it's a very old tune handed down from my ancestors."

Anna curled her arm around mine and led me to the bench by the pool. The rough stone was still cool under the shade of the trees edging the yard. The morning sun had not yet warmed it. "Every child of Bristol knows the melody, but the words are only known to a special few."

My palms grew clammy. The words to the tune she hummed danced along my tongue. "Do you know the words?"

Anna shook her head. "Just the tune, though I think someone made some words up a few hundred years back, called it teh Skyeboat Song. But those aren't the real lyrics."

I stared at her. "So the words to the Skyeboat song—the song about Bonnie Prince Charlie escaping to France—those aren't the real words?"

"Oh, they're the real words to some." Anna laughed gaily, but I was totally confused. She patted the back of my hand. "You've heard the saying about words having great power?"

I nodded.

"Songs have even more power. Music and words combined are the most powerful thing in the universe."

My heart skipped a beat. What was Anna on about this morning?

"You are a child born with a special gift." She scooped up a handful of cool water from the pond and ran her hands over my forehead and down the sides of my neck. The cool water slowed my racing pulse. My mind whirled back to the story Mom used to tell me when she tucked me into bed, about the dragon that had brought me into this world. I'd always thought it was just a story, but could it be true? How much of it was true?

Desperate, I grasped Anna's hands. I needed someone to tell me the truth. I needed to hear something that would validate all my memories of Bailean. "The story my mom used to tell me, about a dragon bringing me into this world—it's true then?"

Anna squeezed my hands, her eyes lighting up. "It's true."

All the hair on my body stood on end. Shocks of electricity swept through me. I shook my head, wanting so much to believe, knowing deep down it was right. Could I just let go of all the heartache? Let it shed like a snakeskin and emerge? "It can't be. It has to be a story—a fairy tale she made up."

"It's not. I was there. You were born right in this house. Brought into this world in the presence of a golden dragon."

Anna pointed with her pruning shears to the small room on the backside of the cottage. She chuckled. "There was barely enough room for all of us."

The old woman dropped the shears into her apron pocket and patted my hand. "Come inside; we'll get a glass of water."

I rose and followed Anna into the cottage. I'd been right to follow my gut on this one. There was more to Anna than she let the world see. Anna knew things—things I needed to know. She might sound like a lunatic to the rest of the world, but my body felt the truth of her words. It resonated in my bones with the frequency of certainty.

Inside the cottage, dried flowers and plants hung from the rafters. The place was clean and comfortable, with pale-colored walls and rustic wooden trim. It all looked so ordinary—how could something so amazing have happened here in such a normal place? Anna gestured for me to sit at the small round table while she pumped a handle over the sink and filled a glass.

I took it gratefully and sipped, hoping the cool water would help clear my mind. I took in more details: built-in cabinets loaded with glass canning jars, baskets filled with a variety of colorful vegetables, a few plants that I couldn't identify, and a fish bowl swarming with tadpoles. Involuntarily I made a face of disgust. Why would someone want a bowl of slimy fish-frogs in their kitchen? I blanched as I remembered Lawrence joking about eating frog legs.

Anna interrupted my gruesome thoughts. "Would you like to see the room you were born in?"

I bit my lower lip but nodded. It was all a little too weird. Why didn't Dad tell me I was born in this cottage? Again I felt the niggling suspicion that secrets were being kept from me.

Anna led me down a narrow hallway and opened the first door on the right. Sunlight filtered in through a rectangular window. A light summer breeze pushed through the room. It was a little bigger than my room, maybe fourteen foot long and twelve foot wide. Parallel to the doorway was a narrow, dark wooden bed made up with crisp white sheets. Above the bed hung a painting of a stick fighting the pull of the river current. Built into the wall near the foot of the bed was an old-fashioned stone hearth. Hanging on the wall next to the door was a tapestry even larger than the one I'd found in my room.

The tapestry, like mine, was a pastoral scene. Sheep grazed in the hills and a turreted tower of a castle peeked over the foliage in the distance. Interlaced ribbons made a golden border around it, and in the forefront, a shepherd dallied with a maiden under the shade of an oak tree. He paid no attention to his grazing charges. The ribbons tying the girl's corseted bodice flowed out with the wind. I stepped closer to inspect a dark shadow in the background—it was a creature, with horns, but it wasn't a ram. It was a reindeer just like in the tapestry I'd found. I could tell by its shaggy white chest. Why was a deer grazing with the sheep? *Weird.*

Anna interrupted my perusal of the tapestry and gestured to the tightly dressed bed and washstand. "It's all prepared for Samantha when her time comes."

A pile of white blankets and extra sheets were folded on the end of the bed. An old-fashioned washstand was placed in the corner with a spray of lavender stuck in a pitcher that sat in a large bowl. The room looked like a still life painting.

"The baby will be born here? Not in a hospital?" I asked.

"I can handle almost any complication that rears its ugly head."

"And if you can't?"

Anna propped her hands on her hips and sniffed. "If I can't handle something, the hospital is just a few miles away."

I took in the stark furnishings again and ran a hand along the pristine sheets. I liked the way the sun cascaded through the window above the bed. "This room reminds me of that painting of the dog curled up in the sun."

"That's because it is the room in the painting." Anna smiled.

I was taken aback. "It is?"

"Mr. Wyeth, the artist, used to come and paint every summer. He was a good lad." Anna ran her hand over the simple wooden frame of the painting above the headboard. "And quite good, as I remember. He gave me this one. Called it *Wishbone*—that was his nickname for me because he thought I gave him luck. He stayed in this room when he came calling, as long as there were no babies to be born."

I gestured at the room. "You'd think Dad would've told me about all this."

Anna shook her head. "The night you were born was a cold winter's eve. The wind was howling like a pack of wolves, and the snow was falling thick as carpet. The largest flakes I've ever seen. It was beautiful and the dragon arrived just in time."

"So, my dad wasn't here because there was a storm?" I guess that made sense, but why would Mom have come up here alone so close to having me? If he would've come and seen the dragon for himself, then he'd have to believe. I wouldn't have had to go through all the self-doubts. I wouldn't have loathed myself all those years for being different.

"You'll have to ask him, dear. I can only tell you about the dragon."

"You've seen a lot of dragons?" I whispered.

"A few," Anna answered.

My heart missed a beat. Anna believed dragons were real. Like, really believed. I licked my lips, afraid of where my mind was going. Before the years of therapy had convinced me I just had a strong and wild imagination, I'd believed dragons were real too. Did I dare to truly believe again? Did Bailean come back to me because I was finally accepting my own truth?

"Shall we return to the garden?" Anna suggested. "I need to finish watering the flowers before the sun gets too high."

My stomach growled. I put a hand over it as if that might quiet its protests for food. I needed time to think about all this: the mica flakes, the lullaby, Bailean. "I should probably get going. I haven't eaten breakfast yet, and I have to do chores before I go into town with Lawrence."

I gazed down the hallway, hoping to see Lawrence poke his head out of one of the other doors. "Where is he?"

Anna turned toward the kitchen. "He's working this morning with Henry. What are you going to town for?"

I followed Anna down the hall. "I found a tapestry in the window seat in my room."

Anna gathered a basket from a table by the entryway and opened the back door. "A tapestry? Under the window seat? Well, now, that's interesting."

I narrowed my eyes at her back. "Why's that interesting?"

"Well, most people hang tapestries on a wall."

She had a point. "Do you know why Gran would've hid it?"

Anna shrugged. "Describe it to me."

We pushed through the back door and strolled across the lush lawn while I shared my recollection of the tapestry: the faded colors, frayed corners, and shimmering threads. But also how at night, when the moon shone through the window, I would stare at it and wonder what was in the glade besides the stag.

"What do you think is in the glade?" Anna asked.

I shrugged, feeling a little silly. "Besides what I can see?"

Anna nodded. What was she playing at?

"Okay." I laughed nervously and tried to conjure up an image of what was beyond the glade. "I guess there could be a castle in the distance that you can't see because of the trees… and maybe a small pond where frogs laze around in the shade. Only they aren't frogs, but princes who've been transformed by a witch."

"That sounds…almost pleasant," Anna laughed. "A window into another world—one where magic exists for everyone."

A world where magic existed! Where doctors didn't try to convince people that they were crazy? Where fathers pretended to be trolls because trolls really existed? I drew a breath. "It's real then?"

Anna's smile was thin. She put her hand on my shoulder and guided me toward the forest path. "That's something you have to find out for yourself. Thank you for paying an old woman a visit."

"But is that where my mother—" I turned to badger the old woman for more information, but she was deep into the garden already, humming as she deadheaded the lilies. The shadows of trees billowed around her like a cape in a breeze. Why did no one ever want to give me a straight answer? Did they think I couldn't handle it? Was I going to be treated this way my whole life?

chapter nine

I burst through the kitchen door, panting from the jog uphill from the creek. Dad was at the sink guzzling a glass of water. Bits of green leaf stuck to his T-shirt and sweaty forehead. I took a deep breath to calm the swirling emotions in my head, and crossed the room.

"Where've you been?"

I jerked a mug from the cupboard and joined Dad at the sink, turning on the cold water and letting it run for a minute. "Talking to Anna."

"Everything okay?" Dad peered at me over his half-full glass, eyes narrowed.

I filled the mug and then gulped it down, not trusting myself to speak yet. I hoped the cold water would numb my irritation. I wiped my mouth with the back of my hand. "Why?"

He shrugged his shoulders. "You look a little green around the gills."

I averted my eyes. I couldn't tell him what had happened with Anna or it'd be back to the psychologist and meds for sure. He'd never believed I was telling the truth anyway; his version of the truth was so far from mine. To get off the meds last year, I had to tell the doctors that I'd lied. It made me nauseous to think about it. I'd said I made up the stories because I needed to protect myself from the feelings of being abandoned by my mom. I'd said Bailean was imaginary. That Mom had walked out the door, leaving me behind like one would leave a dog at home while shopping. I carefully composed my next words.

"It's probably the heat…and I haven't eaten anything yet. Two things that make me crabby."

I set down the mug gently, slid a bowl out of the cupboard, and rummaged in the dish drainer for a clean spoon. Every movement was at a carefully controlled pace. If I could control my external world, I could control my reactions. My fingers were still a little shaky—leftover nerves. I hid it by not keeping still. I desperately wanted to find out how Dad knew Anna, about why he wasn't there when I was born.

He raised an inquisitive eyebrow.

"How do you know Anna?" I blurted.

Dad rubbed his face with the inside of his shirt and took off his glasses. "Like she said, she was Gran's best friend. I'd see her when your mom and I came up to visit."

I nodded. Of course, but it felt like he was leaving something out. I bit the inside of my cheek, framing my next question. There was more he wasn't telling me, but how could I pry without him getting suspicious? "Is that all you know about her?"

"Why? Is there something else I should know?" He cleared his throat. Clouds darkened his expression. The wrinkles in his forehead said *I'm worried about you.*

I shook my head and elbowed him gently out of the way, opened another cupboard door, and reached in for the cereal. "Stop worrying. I'm okay!"

He sighed and held up his hands in a surrendering gesture. "Okay, fine." But the worry lines didn't go away.

Under his watchful eye, I poured cereal into a bowl. It was like he was measuring my mental wellness according to how much cereal I planned on eating. "Are you going to eat it for me, too?"

"Now that you mention it, I will join you. Second breakfast and all that." He grinned.

I removed the milk from the fridge, poured it in my cereal, and then left the carton on the counter. He was trying to smooth things over. I sat at the kitchen table. "Better watch those second breakfasts or you'll start looking like a hobbit."

My dad patted his flat stomach. "Girl! This physique is supa-fly." He grinned as he sat across from me.

"Really, Dad?"

He shrugged. "Isn't that what you kids say nowadays?"

A snort of laughter found its way up, and I rolled my eyes. "Maybe when I was fourteen."

We sat in silence for a minute or two, crunching away, before Dad looked at me. His face was awash with worry again.

I groaned through a mouthful of mushy corn flakes. "Ugh. What now?"

"Look, Soph. We've had our troubles, but those are in the past. We came here for a fresh start. I really want the slate wiped clean—for both of us."

"Yes, I know." I kept the eye roll in check. Did we really have to go over this again?

"I'm glad you've found a friend." He pushed the last bite of his cereal around with his spoon.

The rest of his unspoken thought hung in the air between us. It wasn't the direction I thought he was going, and I was relieved he didn't bring up the psychologist again, but if that wasn't where he was going with this conversation, then where *was* he headed? I swallowed my mouthful. "But?"

Dad leaned back in his chair. "Be careful. I know how a young man's mind works, even if he does seem innocent enough."

I banged my spoon on the edge of my bowl. "Oh, come on!" A groan rumbled in my throat.

"I just don't want you to put yourself in a situation you can't handle. It's not like you've dated a lot." He shoved the last mushy spoonful of cereal in his mouth.

I glared at him. "In six months, I'll be able to drink myself into a stupor if I want to. And, I *did* grow up in New York. I can handle myself. Why are you still so worried about me?"

He shrugged. "That's what dads are supposed to do. Worry about their kids."

"So you worry about me because you're *supposed* to?" I was baiting him, and I knew it. My chest tightened as I anticipated the coming verbal conflict.

Exasperated, Dad put down his spoon. A dot of milk spread out on the table and traveled in the cracks of the rough wooden surface. "No, Sophie. I worry about you because I love you and I want your life to be full of happy stuff."

"Then why did you make me stop believing in happily ever after?" I shouldn't have said it, but I couldn't help myself. Conflicting emotions simmered just under the surface like a lake of lava. Sadness filled a part of my heart that understood I'd missed out on a normal childhood. Anger because no one believed my mom was taken away. Irritation that I couldn't seem to control the beast inside me and, at some point, when it had been bottled up long enough, it always lashed out.

Dad's jaw tightened. He swallowed his answer, pushed his chair away from the table, and stood up. Gathering his dishes, he walked away from me. He rinsed his bowl and put it on the counter. Every movement he made was deliberate. When he spoke, his words were clipped. "I'm going into the office to see what I can do to prepare for classes."

"You've still got six weeks before classes start," I said. A little bit of whine wrapped around my words. I cleared my throat.

"Yes, but I haven't taught intro courses for a long time. It's going to take some preparation." He started to walk out of the kitchen. Shoulders square, jaw set in a firm line.

"So, does that mean I'm eating dinner by myself tonight?" I wasn't sure if I was ready to be alone. My heart fluttered.

Dad paused and looked at me over his shoulder. "Well, you *are* an adult."

He threw my words back in my face. I swallowed and crossed my arms. "Fine."

Dad turned on his heel and ran his fingers through his hair. He adjusted his glasses. "I was thinking I'd give you money to get something already made at the farmer's market. I'll be home by six."

My body tingled with the sudden rush of relief. "Promise?"

"Promise."

I bit my lip and tucked the unease into my back pocket. It would be okay. Most of the afternoon I'd be with Lawrence. Maybe I could talk him into staying for dinner.

Dad's gaze bore into me. "You made me a promise, Sophie."

I picked at a hangnail so I wouldn't have to meet his eyes. "What promise was that?"

Dad cleared his throat. "You know the answer to that. What I want to know is, do you intend to keep it?"

My insides swirled with a burning shame. I saw myself in the psychiatrist's office, propped in the middle of her purple couch, my legs dangling off the edge. Dad sat in the chair across from me, leaning forward, bloodshot eyes boring through me. In my mind's eye, I looked small, like the couch could swallow me whole, and everything else in the room loomed larger than life. I was only eight, but I still remember the moment my life changed forever. "Bailean isn't real. He's just my imaginary friend and I make people uncomfortable when I talk about him."

"And you promise that you won't talk about him anymore," Dad had said.

That day I'd made a promise I could no longer keep.

How could I when everyone I'd met told me dragons were real? That magic existed. I looked at the floor. My voice squeaked awkwardly as I tried to answer. I cleared my throat and tried again. "Yes."

Dad fished his wallet out of his pocket and dropped three twenties on the table. "Buy what you need at the hardware store. The farmer's market is open on the town green this afternoon. Get us something we don't have to cook in this horrible humidity." He bent and kissed my forehead.

I patted the bills. "Thanks."

"I'm gonna hit the shower before I head out." He rubbed his shoulder. "I feel like I've been battling a hydra."

"There are no mythical creatures in Vermont, Dad," I said, and stood. "Except Champy. They've got photo evidence of him." With my bowl in hand, I made my way to the sink. I half-filled it with hot soapy water and started washing the breakfast dishes.

"I was speaking metaphorically," my dad muttered. He struggled to keep his tone even. "Have fun this afternoon."

"You, too." He left the kitchen and I rinsed the bowls.

The melody of the lullaby was on a loop in my mind, repeating as I folded the laundry, straightened my dad's tie before he left, and hit the shower myself.

The water running over my back eased some of the discomfort I'd been feeling all morning. I hadn't realized just how much I was looking forward to going out with Lawrence until I started daydreaming about him in the shower. It was a good thing he wasn't around to see me blush.

As I stepped into my bedroom wrapped in a towel, a breeze moved over my skin. *Finally.* Dad must have gotten the other windows open while I was folding the laundry. The pile of photographs I'd shoved under the bed beckoned. I pulled it out and dumped the pictures on my bedspread thinking that I should find a box to put them in before they got ruined.

I grabbed a handful. The one on top was the ice cream picture that had made Lawrence laugh. Thinking about his laugh made me smile, so I set it aside. The next picture was of me and Mom on the swings at the playground. Another at kindergarten graduation. A picture of me with both front teeth missing. I dug deeper into the pile, butterflies flitting around in my gut, but there were no photos of my dad until I was around two. Not only that, there weren't any photos of him with Mom before I was born, or with me as a baby either. The photo at the bottom of the box was of Dad and me at eighth grade celebration. I was wearing a black dress and combat boots and my eyes glared accusingly at the camera, red holes ringed in charcoal-black makeup. Neither of us was smiling. That was the year things had really gone downhill. I'd totally given up.

I stretched out on the bed and rubbed at my wrist. Too young to really understand the consequences of my actions, I'd been determined to leave this world. I was certain I didn't belong here. Like Bailean, I was just someone's imaginary friend. I'd felt caught between reality and the lies adults tell their children. Those scars had faded, but the feelings still lurked under the surface, undermining every good intention I'd had since.

I found an empty box and flung the photo into the bottom, covering it with the others, but one I hung on to for a moment. My mother was smiling as she posed with me on a swing, but she didn't look happy. It was the kind of smile you plaster on when you want people to think you are happy. I knew that smile all too well. I pulled the photo to my chest and flopped back on the bed. Why? Why was Mom so unhappy?

~She knew they'd eventually find you.

I sat up so fast I almost threw myself to the floor. My heart pounded like the time I'd let my so-called friends in eighth grade talk me into snorting speed and then riding a roller coaster at Luna Park. The cereal in my stomach threatened to revolt.

~ Calm down. Take a deep breath.

I looked wildly around the room and held the towel tighter to my body. The wind gusted through the windows raising goosebumps up my arms. The small voice in my head felt different this morning—more present. More persistent. It *wanted*—no, *insisted* it be heard.

~ Relax.

A tingling sensation started at the nape of my neck and traveled down my arms. "Bailean, is that you?" I lay back on my bed and stared at the green canopy, forcing myself to take deep even breaths. Nerves made my thigh muscles quiver. "Why won't you show yourself to me?" I whispered.

~I'm here, right in front of you. You just have to believe.

I closed my eyes, desperately wanting to believe again. To know the voice in my head was real—that it belonged to someone other than myself. That I wasn't…crazy.

"You are Bailean. You are real. And you are a dragon." Warm breath skimmed my shins, but I didn't dare open my eyes yet. "You protected me."

My face grew hot with the heat in the room. My skin searched for the cooling breeze that was traveling through the windows just a moment ago.

~It is my job to protect you.

Tears sprang to my eyes. "Then why did you leave me?"

~I didn't leave you… It was you who shut me out.

He thought I had abandoned him. All those years, I'd tried to talk myself into believing that he was just a figment of my imagination, a childhood friend. The doctors had said he was a way to cope with everything life had thrown at me—that he wasn't real. Not a warm flesh and blood creature like the one standing before me now. Why did I believe them? Why didn't I trust myself? Why didn't I trust what I knew to be true?

His heat radiated on my shins. His voice, deeper now that he was grown, but still familiar in my head—talking the way we'd always talked. It had been years since I'd allowed myself to lower my walls, to open myself up enough to let his voice in, past the pain, the worry, and the self-loathing. But it felt good. It felt right.

~Yes. It is right. And right now, we need your help. We need you to save the other dragons...and Brindle.

"What's Brindle?" The name seemed familiar on my tongue... Anna. She'd said something about Brindle the other day. What was it?

~Your mother told us stories about Brindle.

A picture in my imagination bloomed to life: a white castle on a hill, a bustling seaport below, dragons perched in trees dripping with jeweled fruit. Had Anna told those stories to my mom when she was a little girl? "But Brindle was just a town in the stories. Mom made it up."

~Not all of the stories your mother told us were fairy tales. Come, let me show you.

The room spun and the day's heat fell away. Relieved, I opened my eyes. I was standing in the middle of a large gathering. Surprised, I groped for my towel, but was pleasantly surprised to find I wore a long cream dress, and over it a blue apron-like thing. It was different from the apron I saw Anna wearing earlier though. This one tied up the front like a corset.

~It's called a kirtle.

I heard a chuckle in my head and it reminded me so much of Lawrence that I turned to look for him. But it was Bailean who appeared out of a shimmery fog. He was much bigger than I remembered. When I was young, we both fit in the wardrobe. Now I wondered how he even fit into my bedroom. He was the size of the Mammoth skeleton at the American Museum of Natural History. His emerald scales shimmered like polished armor in the sun. Heat radiated from his massively muscled body. Whisker-like fur floated around his nostrils and wisped back along his smooth neck. His shining amber eyes, the same color as Lawrence's eyes, shone from their deep sockets. I had a brief moment to wonder if that's why I found Lawrence so attractive, because his teasing manner and eyes reminded me so much of my dragon.

Bailean was beautiful, but I didn't think I was here to admire him, as much as he might like that. I turned my attention to the people in the crowd.

"Where are we?"

~*This is Brindle.*

The people were all dressed like medieval villagers—but not like in movies where they look a little too clean, or at the faires where they only half-assed dressed or wore sneakers under their period gowns. These people looked real.

~*That's because they are real. But they can't see you. You are in a memory.*

"Then why am I dressed this way?"

~*I thought you'd feel more comfortable. I can remove it if you like.*

I held up my hand. He might be a dragon, but that didn't mean I would be comfortable wearing only my birthday suit in front of him. "No thanks! I'm good."

Looming over the crowd was a large white building with heavy wooden doors and wide stone steps. Nailed to one of the doors was a proclamation bearing a seal: a blue shield with a crouching panther under a gold crown. Feeling like I was in slow-motion I climbed the granite steps, my hand sliding along the iron banister. The fancy script on the parchment declared that all the young women in the village eligible for marriage must assemble before noon. The faces of the women in the crowd were tight with anxiety. Some were flushed with suppressed emotion; others were openly wailing. Mothers patted daughters consolingly. Fathers stood cross-armed and red-faced. The crowd split as a carriage thundered into the square, pulled by two strong-legged horses. The door to the conveyance flew open before the driver had a chance to halt. A young man, perhaps a few years older than me, peered out.

"Who is that?"

~*That is King Stuart, the fifth.*

King Stuart, *the fifth,* had light brown hair, a strong jawline, and eyes the color of a summer sky.

"Why are all the girls upset? He's cute!"

~*His beauty is shallow.*

The handsome young king jumped from the carriage. A sickness spread in my gut as I saw the intertwined dragons on his belt buckle. He wormed his way through the crowd. He paced around the women on the church steps, pausing here and there, twirling a lock of hair and raising it to smell its fragrance. When he approached the youngest in the crowd, he cupped her breasts as if they were his own to fondle, then slid his hands down her body to measure the width of her waist. He frowned and moved on. The young girl turned into her mother's arms and shook. I was pretty sure it was sobs of relief.

The king then noticed the tallest maiden in the crowd. She had long, graceful limbs and a softness to her that spoke of a gentle nature. The king's tongue darted out to trace the track her tears had taken. She shut her eyes. He pinched her chin between his fingers and forced her to face him. "Tell me why you cry. Does not every girl wish to be a queen?" His other hand grabbed hers and forced her to cup his groin. "Am I not enough to please you?" The hand that had held her chin released and twisted in her hair. He forced a brutal kiss upon her lips as he moved her other hand in a stroking motion along the front of his pants.

Sick to my stomach, I strode forward to help her, even if I did have to knock him on his royal ass.

~It's just a memory, remember? You can do nothing to help.

I stopped midstride as the girl whimpered and tried to pull away. The king scowled and shoved her to the ground.

Stuart gestured to the cowering women in the crowd. "This is all you have to offer your king?"

The women scattered, fading into the congregation. King Stuart turned on his heel and glared at the crowd. "I demanded you find me the fairest maiden in the land, be she poor or be she wealthy. My only demand was that she be beautiful."

The cruel man paused in the middle of his tirade. I followed his gaze to a black-haired beauty in the crowd. She was petite, beautiful, with full pink lips, and hair that shone like a raven's wing.

"This one," the king announced. He pointed his scepter at her, and bit his lower lip. Then he strode forward, the crowd parting before him.

"No," I whispered, but his eyes gleamed with lust.

"She will be my queen." He stopped close enough to her to run his finger over her exposed collarbone. His voice turned to liquid sweetness. He nearly purred like a tomcat getting a scratch between the ears. "Please tell me your name, fair damsel."

"My name is Gwendolyn, My Lord," she replied, her voice clear and strong. "But I am not eligible for marriage. I am already married. And with child." She placed her hand on her slightly protruding belly, punctuating her statement. She smiled at the kingdom's ruler, though to me, it looked like more of a self-satisfied smirk. I smiled with her, glad the king was thwarted.

The king's smile faltered, but he caught himself and bowed with a shallow dip of his head. "I beg your pardon. Who is the lucky gentleman? I must congratulate him."

Gwendolyn turned slightly to her right, accepting the arm of a dark haired gentleman who stepped forward. "May I introduce my husband—" Gwendolyn looked into the pleasing face of her husband and smiled.

"Ah, yes, the Duke of Wirth," the king sneered. "You didn't tell me you had such a fetching wife."

"One always protects their most valuable assets, My King." The Duke smiled and bowed, dropping his head low.

A snarl of madness replaced the sovereign's sneer. Sound disappeared, seconds turned into minutes as I ran forward. Gwendolyn pushed at her husband, her mouth open to shout a warning, but it came too late. A sickening crack shattered the silence as the heavy, jewel encrusted end of the king's scepter smashed the back of the duke's skull. The gray contents spilled out for all to view as he crumbled to the street.

Bile rose in my throat. I put the back of my hand to my mouth to keep from retching. I tried to remind myself that this wasn't happening right now—that I was seeing something akin to watching a movie. It was hard to remember when the iron stench of blood filled my nostrils.

Gwendolyn dropped to her knees and turned over her husband's body, rolling him onto her lap. Blood soaked her gown and streamed over the cobblestones. She cradled him like a child, his eyes staring up at her, but unseeing. My heart squeezed into a tight, angry ball.

The king grasped Gwendolyn's hand, pulled her to her feet, and raised her arm as in victory. "Hail, Queen Gwendolyn!"

There were a few murmurs through the crowd, but most voices were stunned and mute. The villagers could not look away from the crumpled body on the cobblestones. King Stuart glowered at the crowd and led a sobbing Gwendolyn in a circular path around her dead husband as he caught every eye.

Gwendolyn's free hand crumpled the side of her skirt. Her brows scrunched together and the corners of her eyes turned down. Her chest rose and fell in quick motions. "Hail me as your queen!" she whispered.

I was stunned. I couldn't have heard what I thought I heard. Then, she repeated it. "Hail me as your queen!" she screamed.

"Hail, Queen Gwendolyn!" the crowd responded. "Long live the queen!"

chapter ten

he memory Bailean had pulled me into faded to a deep nothingness. No light seeped from the corners, but my eyes were full of the terrible images I had just witnessed. My stomach churned as I relived the sickening crack of the man's skull, the crowd hailing their new queen at her command. Had she been in on it? The expression on her face when her husband was killed had been so heart breaking. My mind swirled. Why would Gwendolyn have demanded to be hailed queen so quickly? Unless she had planned it with the king…? I wracked my brain for any other sensible answer, but nothing came to me.

I swallowed the disgust and found my voice. "Why? Why did you show me that?"

~*You need to understand.*

"Understand *what?*"

~*Where you come from. What we are fighting for. What he is capable of.*

The blackness softened and the hushed crackle of a fire filled my ears before its light spread out and warmed the darkness. A groan split the stuffy air as a white walled chamber came into focus. Gwendolyn was propped in a narrow bed.

"Push, My Queen, I can see her raven hair." The midwife was crouched between the queen's legs.

I suddenly felt awkward and out of place. I was a stranger intruding on an intimate moment.

"How do you know it's a girl?" the queen puffed.

A tall woman held Gwendolyn's hand. She perched on the edge of the bed offering unintelligible murmurs of encouragement. She smiled and patted the queen's hand. "It won't be long now."

I gasped when the woman looked over her shoulder at the midwife. My heart stuck in my throat. It couldn't be!

But it was. I moved closer.

Warm brown eyes filled with sympathy each time the queen rose with a labor pain. Her long, sandy-brown hair draped over her shoulder. Her speech was calm, her tone soothing, like the voice I remembered from my childhood.

The midwife's assistant was my mother.

Any thoughts about that fled as the queen yelled and the babe's head emerged. The midwife's hands were eager and at the ready. She cleared the tiny nose and mouth with a swipe of her deft fingers and helped the newborn rotate its shoulders. My heart sped and my palms grew clammy. I licked my lips, intent on the scene.

Gwendolyn groaned again, and a final push had the infant lying in the midwife's arms. A cry passed over the queen's lips as she slowed her breathing from the shallow labor pants. My mother wiped the queen's brow with a wet cloth.

"It's a girl. Just as the dragons prophesied." The midwife's brows knit together.

I grimaced as she cut the umbilical cord, severing child from mother. The room buzzed like a hive of bees, a thousand wings vibrating in sync. I didn't realize that I hadn't heard the baby cry yet until it suddenly wailed. It had a strong voice. The midwife quickly silenced the baby with a light touch to her lips and a whisper of, "Quiet, little one."

With the babe swaddled in the crook of her arm, the midwife turned to the wall. I turned as well. A large tapestry hung behind us. It showed embroidered willow trees shading a flowering glade where a dark stag stood. My mouth dropped open. It was the same tapestry I had found in my room.

I scowled at Bailean and pointed to the hanging. "How the hell did that get there?"

Bailean shifted next to me. *~I think the better question is how did it get into the window box in your house?*

Before I had a chance to wrap my mind around that puzzle, the wool loops of the tapestry rose and shimmered like waves on the ocean. A sparkling green mist filtered into the chamber. The mist reminded me of the day at the creek when I saw all those little green orbs floating about Lawrence. I would have to ask him about that. I made a mental note as a dragon pushed out of the wall hanging, noticeably warming the space. It was almost as if a space heater had been placed in the room.

Wonder made my fingers tingle and my eyes grow wide. This dragon was even larger than Bailean. Gold scales glowed a rosy hue from the firelight. Thin membranes stretched between the row of spikes that crowned her head like an Elizabethan collar. The dragon reached for the baby.

"You were right, it is a girl," the midwife said. She swaddled a sapphire blanket around the infant and placed the small bundle into the dragon's golden claw.

The dragon gently unswaddled Gwendolyn's daughter, inspecting her. She surprised me with her gentleness and dexterity. Were all dragons that gentle? Or just the female dragons? Did they all revere newborn life no matter where it came from? I knew the lore about dragons being the protectors of the universe, but I'd heard the opposite as well. The story of St. George came to mind.

"Wait! Is that you?" I half-asked, half-accused Bailean, but I answered my own question. It couldn't be him. Bailean was green. Did dragons ever change color?

~She is sweet perfection, my Lady. Bless you, Anna, for delivering her safely.

For the third time in a short span, my heart pranced in my chest. Anna? As in Lawrence's great aunt? I shook my head. This couldn't be a real memory. It had to be a dream. Still, I stared hard at the midwife. She was less wrinkly and dressed differently than when I'd seen her this morning, but there was a definite resemblance. Was Bailean showing me *my* birth? How could that be? I peered harder at my surroundings.

It was very much like the room I'd seen this morning, but with subtle differences. For one, it was bigger, and the walls weren't as white. And the tapestry on the wall—it was different. We weren't in the cozy cottage I'd visited this morning, even though at first glance, it looked like it. A million questions surfaced on my tongue.

~Hold your questions. You may find the answers yet.

The dragon lowered the child, but the queen turned away. The dragon's voice whispered in my head. *~Don't you wish to hold her?*

"No. Just take her away!"

~I will name her Sophinestra, after Ronan's mother.

I flinched at the name. So close to mine.

A knock thundered upon the door of the chamber.

The dragon slid toward the tapestry. *~Come now, Maria. We must go.*

Maria. I stared hard at the midwife's assistant. There was no doubt it was my mom—or who I'd *thought* was my mom. I suddenly felt off balance. I reached for Bailean, and he steadied me with his strong grasp.

"I command you to unlock this door!" Another round of incessant banging echoed into the chamber. The dragon placed the small blue bundle into the arms of the small woman. *Maria.* The woman I had thought was my mother. The woman who had raised me. The woman I'd seen beaten and dragged from our New York apartment when I was six. It was all coming back to me. Everything I'd tried to forget—to block out of my memory. My heart beat in my ears, as loud as the banging on the chamber door. My chest tightened and cramped. I covered my mouth to soften the sob that wanted to rupture. Tears streamed down my face.

The dragon approached the tapestry; Maria followed with the babe—me—cradled close to her chest. As they melted into the scene, Anna bundled the afterbirth, then took a deep breath and murmured something I couldn't quite hear over the racing beat of my heart. The sparkling mist vanished. The tapestry rolled itself up and disappeared. A whitewashed wall appeared in its place. The chamber door burst open with an earth shattering crash, the wood splintering as it met the wall. A cold wind howled through and snaked around my ankles.

"Where is the child?" the king snarled, his shadow looming in the doorway. He seemed scared to step over the threshold. Snowflakes clung to his cloak like delicate embroidery.

"Majesty…" Anna curtsied, lowering her eyes. "The child…I'm sorry, sire. She was born still and…deformed." The lie tumbled from Anna's mouth like a rehearsed line in a play. She held the bundle out to him. "Do you wish to hold her before I—"

"No," King Stuart said, lips curling. He stepped away from the door, wiping his hands down the front of his jacket as if they'd been soiled. "No. Toss it to the dogs."

chapter eleven

I woke with a sobbing scream. My heart pounded in my ears. My jaw hurt from clenching. It'd been a terrible dream. I looked down, pulling up the towel that was no longer wrapped tightly around my body.

Not a dream, then. I tried to shake it off and I blinked at the brightness of the mid-morning sun. My head was fuzzy, my mind unfocused. The sound of hammering downstairs made me think Dad must be fixing something. Then I remembered that he had already left the house. The hairs on my neck stood up. Adrenaline quickened my breath. The sound came again, more persistent, and my ears perked. Knocking. The king! My fists clenched around the towel. Not that a towel would be able to protect me. Sirens blared in my head. My gaze darted to the door. It was open. I saw the blue numbers of the clock sitting on my bedside table. I was in my bedroom, in Vermont. I wasn't in Brindle. I looked at the clock again. 12:34.

Lawrence. *Lawrence* was knocking on the door.

"Crap!" I scrambled out of bed, wrapping the towel tight before peering over the railing. "Come in, Lawrence!"

As his onyx-colored head appeared in the entryway I darted back into my room. Rummaging through my drawers, I pulled out my favorite pair of blue underwear and a matching bra. I tossed the towel on the floor and stepped into my underwear. I'd just finished latching my bra when the bedroom door opened.

Surprised, I turned my back and crossed my arms over my chest. "Lawrence!"

"Oh my God, I'm so sorry," he stammered. I glared at him over my shoulder. His blush was crimson.

"I'll…I'll just wait for you out here…in the…um…in the hallway." He started to close the door.

I shoved my legs though my cut off jean shorts. "Don't worry about it now." I pulled up the zipper and buttoned the waist. I pawed through my closet for a suitable shirt, pulling out a gauzy, off-the-shoulder top. I held it up and looked at him through my eyelashes. "This one you think?"

"I like blue." Lawrence eased into the room, arms crossed over his chest. He shifted from foot to foot, uncomfortable. "Where'd your dad go today?"

"He went into his office for a little while." I took in his shifty eyes and spotted cheeks. "Look—it wasn't any worse than seeing me in a bathing suit, right? In fact, a lot of bathing suits are much skimpier. So, get a hold of yourself." I pulled the shirt off the hanger and shoved in my head and arms. I walked toward Lawrence who was lingering in the doorway and grabbed my hairbrush off the top of the dresser.

"It's just—" He ran his hand through his hair with a shaky hand. "I expected you to be dressed."

I pulled the brush through my long hair. It was all knotted up from falling asleep on it while it was still wet. "I'm sorry. I fell back to sleep after showering…and had a *really* terrible…" It wasn't a dream, but would he think I was crazy if I told him it was a memory seen through the eyes of a dragon? "A really weird dream."

"Oh, yeah?" Lawrence's eyes lit up. He stepped close to me and twisted a curl of my hair around his finger. "You know, I'm kind of a dream guru. Tell me about your dream and I can tell you your innermost thoughts."

I leaned toward him, settling my arms atop his, my hands curled around the muscles just under his elbows. His lips were so close I could feel the heat radiating off of him. Would he totally freak if I just kissed him? "I think I'll skip the dream interpretation on this one. Maybe next time?"

Lawrence nodded, his eyes never leaving my mouth. "Anything you say."

I pulled away, letting my hands slide over his arms until our fingertips snagged. I smiled and grabbed a hair elastic from my bedside table, shoving it in my pocket. My fingers ran into something hard—the key! I'd almost forgotten about it. I pulled it out of my pocket and set it on the dresser.

Lawrence tossed his head toward it. "That the key to your gran's locked room?"

I nodded.

"Have you opened it yet?"

"Not yet." The lie tumbled out without warning.

"Do you want to open it together?" Lawrence rubbed his hands together in anticipation.

I smirked. "Why? You think we're going to find pirate gold?"

Lawrence shrugged. "I don't know. It's a mystery though—so it's exciting." He grinned.

I laughed. "I think it can wait. The market is only open so long, right?"

He shrugged. "Yeah, just for the afternoon."

I pushed past him and knocked on the door as I passed. "It will be even more fun to open it if we wait." It would be fun torturing him all afternoon.

I trotted down the squeaky stairs and wiggled my feet into my sneakers. I stood and tucked my hair behind my ear. A strange look crossed Lawrence's face as he studied me.

"What?" I asked. "Are you dreaming of what's behind the mystery door?"

He smiled. "No. I haven't seen your hair down before. It's always been in braids, or a ponytail. You look like one of the heroines in my aunt's books with your 'shining, raven-colored hair'."

I swatted him. I was no one's heroine. "Shut up!"

Lawrence opened the door and bowed low. "Ladies first, of course."

"If you insist." I stepped outside and down the front stairs holding my hands as if I was wearing a long skirt, my nose perched in the air.

Lawrence chuckled behind me.

The humidity was building again. It was going to be another hot one. I was glad that the floor-length skirt and corset days were long over.

An old Ford truck sat in the driveway. It was a muted turquoise color and had a little rust around the wheel well—not so much that it looked like it was falling apart, but just enough that it had a vintage flavor. The truck bed was made of wood and shone with varnish. The door didn't squeak as I opened it, either. I hopped into the passenger seat. "Cool ride."

Lawrence grinned and turned the key. "Thanks. I've worked on it every summer since I was thirteen. Anna thought I was crazy for wanting an old truck. But she doesn't mind now that she doesn't have to bum rides off of Henry or Samantha."

The truck roared to life and Lawrence shifted into Drive. The road was a little bumpy, but with the windows rolled down and the air sweeping through the cabin, it was less of a struggle to let go of the tight, anxious feelings I'd woken up with this morning. I grabbed the top of the door panel as the truck hit a big bump in the road. "Are all the roads around here like this?"

Lawrence laughed. "Nothing runs straight in Vermont, but you'll get used to it."

The lonely wooded road eventually gave in to civilization. Houses appeared, with kids playing in the yards. Lawrence pointed out the library, the elementary school, and the lone doctor's office.

When we finally reached the downtown area, striped awnings shaded store display windows. Tall black lampposts stood sentinel on the tree-lined sidewalks. Large containers of flowers were interspersed every twelve feet or so near the freshly painted wooden benches. The sidewalks were clean—not like the sidewalks in the city where trash and debris were common. It was almost as if I'd traveled back in time.

Lawrence pulled into a space in front of a tall brick building and put the truck in Park.

"This is the hardware store?" The shiny wooden door had a charming oval window in it and dark green striped awning above. *Sam's Olde Towne Hardware* was painted in script-style letters in the large display window to the right of the door.

"Sure is. Let's go." Lawrence pulled the key from the ignition and tossed the key ring on the floor before opening the door and sliding out of the truck.

"Don't you lock the doors?" I asked.

Lawrence laughed. "For what?"

I shrugged and hopped out of the cab. "I don't know. Aren't you worried someone will steal your truck?"

Lawrence shook his head and patted the hood. "Nope. Everyone knows she's mine."

I raised my eyebrows and smirked. "She?"

Lawrence grinned but didn't offer an explanation.

We met on the sidewalk in front of the store. "So you know what kind of hardware to get, right?"

Lawrence shrugged. As he opened the door to the store, a bell jingled above, announcing their entrance. "I'm sure we can figure it out."

A guy about our age with short, slicked-back hair popped out from one of the aisles. His pants were belted around his butt and pooled around his ankles. Under his red store apron he was wearing a black T-shirt. A diamond earring shone in his left earlobe. "Well, hello, Lawry. Long time no see. Who's this fine young thing you've brought in to meet me?"

Lawrence and I exchanged a glance. Really? Who'd this guy think he was—Eminem?

Lawrence put his arm around my shoulders. I didn't argue. "Don't call me that. And I didn't bring her in to meet you, Roger."

"What up, my lady?" Roger said, completely ignoring Lawrence. His eyes took in my measurements. I closed my hand into a fist. It would be pretty hard to ogle me with a black eye.

"Not much," I said. Then, just to get his goat, I snuggled under Lawrence's protective arm. "We came in to get some hardware. Lawrence is helping me hang something in my bedroom."

"Ooh, I can help you out in your bedroom…if you know what I mean." He leaned into my ear and spoke low, but just loud enough for Lawrence to hear, too. "Obviously, I know more than he does about *hardware*."

Lawrence's face flushed. He took his arm away from my shoulders.

"Uh, thanks Roger." I pushed him away, and flashed Lawrence a smile. I grabbed his hand. "But Lawrence and his *hardware* is my business, not yours. And he is exceptional in that department."

Lawrence rocked on his heels. His complexion had settled. He hefted the weight of my hand in his, and then with a half-smile, he snapped his fingers on his free hand and pointed to Roger. "You heard the lady. *Exceptional.*"

I squeezed his hand and let go. I strolled down the aisle, pretending I knew what I was looking for to give Lawrence a moment to gloat. Roger whispered loudly. "Dude, you're blockin'!"

"I am not 'blocking'," Lawrence whispered back. "She's my girl, and obviously not interested in what you have to offer."

His girl? Blood rose to my cheeks. I liked the sound of that.

"She just needs to get to know me. You'll put in a good word, right?"

Lawrence scoffed. "We haven't hung out since we were ten. No way I'm vouching for you."

Roger's voice caught in his throat. "Whatever." He stomped away, hitching up his pants.

Lawrence approached with his hands in his pockets.

"Your friend seems nice," I teased as I fingered a package of thin vintage-looking nails.

"He's not my friend. Hasn't been since we were kids."

"So you aren't blocking him, huh?" I tried not to smile.

Lawrence ran his hand through his hair. A lopsided grin spread across his mouth. "Um…no. I wasn't *blocking* him. You wanna bite at ole' saggy-bottom boy? Be my guest." He gestured down the aisle as if opening a door.

"Yeah, no thanks." I laughed.

Lawrence pointed at me. "Whoa! You're doing it again!"

I wandered down the aisle, but I couldn't get rid of the smile no matter how much he teased me, so I changed the subject. "What are we looking for?"

"I think the easiest way to hang the tapestry would be a rod. Come this way." He laid his hand on the small of my back and steered me toward the back corner of the store. A little thrill rose at the sensation of the heat of his hand through my thin shirt. I hadn't felt this way when I'd grabbed his hand, but maybe that was because I was just pretending in front of Roger. But this—this touch was genuine.

"So we're looking for a curtain rod?" I asked.

"A little heavier than a normal curtain rod, but yes…like this one." He pulled a long black rod encased in plastic from a hook, but I was drawn to the aged-looking bronze-colored rod next to it. It had leaf-shaped finials.

I pointed to it. "What about this one? It kinda matches my bed frame."

Lawrence placed the black rod back on its hook. "Whatever you like."

I turned the package over to see the price tag. "Twenty-four dollars and ninety-five cents."

Lawrence looked at the package in my hand. "More importantly, it stretches from forty-eight to seventy-two inches. So, it's long enough."

"How do you know? We didn't measure the tapestry."

Lawrence smiled and tapped his temple. "It's my super power."

"Measuring by sight is your super power?" I asked.

"No! Knowing things I shouldn't know. That's my super power."

I cocked my hip and raised an eyebrow. "Oh, yeah? And what else do you know that you shouldn't?"

Lawrence smirked as he walked away. "Wouldn't you like to know?"

I chased after him, the rod in my hand. "You're such a punk!"

After paying for the rod, we climbed back into the cab of Lawrence's truck.

I settled into the seat and pulled the belt over my lap. "Ready to check out the farmer's market?"

"Yep." Lawrence swung his arm behind me as he let off the brake. His thumb brushed against my shoulder, sending a warm rush up my neck. The truck rolled out of the parking spot and onto the road. He smiled at me as he shifted from Reverse into Drive. We coasted down the road and pulled into another parking space in front of a huge lawn with a gazebo in the middle.

There was a band playing in the gazebo, and the bass flowing out from the speakers vibrated against my skin like a mosquito buzzing near my ear. At least a hundred people milled about, shopping in the merchant tents, standing under the shade of the trees that lined the green, or clapping to the music. Families had little wagons filled with produce and picnic baskets. Kids had swirly line designs painted on their faces that sparkled in the sun.

"Wow," I said. "It's like the quintessential small town where children grow up wanting nothing more than to leave it and then come back to raise their kids." It was almost too perfect of a scene.

Lawrence pointed to the brick buildings across from the town green. "That's the college your dad is teaching at. Let's go say hi."

I narrowed my eyes at him. "Why?"

Lawrence shrugged. "I just thought it might be nice to stop in since we're here. You're planning on going to school there in the fall right? I mean, I assumed you were going to since your dad is teaching there and free tuition and whatnot…"

I grinned. He was nervous. That was a good sign. "You're babbling." I opened the truck door and stepped into the oppressive heat. Going to see where my dad worked wasn't a terrible idea. It was a little weird, but my Dad would probably appreciate it. "We'll still have time to hit the market, right?"

I glanced over the truck at the sandwich board on the green proclaiming the hours and days of operation: Tuesday and Saturday, noon to four.

He shut the door and met me in front of the truck. He reached for my hand. "We'll have plenty of time for both, and we'll put your dad's mind at ease."

"At ease with what?"

"With you being out with me. A *boy*."

A smile pulled at the corners of my mouth. How did he know exactly what I'd been thinking? His long fingers wrapped around mine. His hands were darkly tanned from the summer sun; his nails were even and smooth. I pulled him forward. "C'mon. Show me the art building."

We crossed the road, hopped over the curb, and walked between two red brick buildings. On the far side of campus gleamed a three-story white stone building. Across the front, engraved in the arch over the door, were the words *Stein Hall Visual and Performing Arts Center.*

Lawrence pointed. "The auditorium is on the first floor as well as the professor's offices. Classrooms and studio spaces are on the second and third. Student artwork is displayed in the hallways, and there is a small gallery in the back of the building."

"How do you know all that?" I asked as we climbed the stairs.

Lawrence released my hand and held open the door. "I've had a piece or two hanging here."

"I didn't know you were an artist."

Lawrence shrugged and smiled. "There's a lot you haven't learned about me yet."

He turned to the left and strode past both sets of double doors that led into the auditorium while I wondered what kind of art he did. Was he a painter? No, there wasn't a speck of paint on his clothes or under his nails. Maybe he was a sculptor. I pictured the muscles in his arm tight as he gripped the handle of a hammer and chisel. A light sheen lit his body as the sun bore down on him from windows high above his cathedral-like workspace. Wait—was I picturing Lawrence or DaVinci? I shook the daydream from my head and trotted along beside him. He turned down a well-lit hallway and stopped at an open door. I squeezed in front of him and peeked inside.

Dad was scribbling furiously on a yellow pad of legal paper. Deep lines etched across his forehead and his hair was crazy, like he'd been running his hands through it in frustration. I leaned on the doorjamb with Lawrence peering over my shoulder, so close his radiating warmth made me tingle and the smell his aftershave lingered in my nostrils.

"Still refusing to use a computer?" I asked.

Dad looked up, startled at the intrusion. Then he smiled and the worry lines smoothed out. "Sophie! Lawrence! How nice of you to visit."

"Hello, Mr. Lincoln," Lawrence said.

"How did you know where to find me?" My dad came around his desk and leaned against the front edge.

I gestured to Lawrence as I stepped into the office. "Lawrence knew where you were."

"Really?" Dad asked.

Lawrence stuck his hands deep in his pockets. He was still leaning nonchalantly in the doorway. A small, nervous smile lit up his face. "I've taken a few art classes."

My dad grinned from ear to ear. "That's fabulous. I didn't know you had an interest in art. Will you be taking any classes here this coming school year?"

Lawrence grinned back at him. "It depends on how this summer goes... I live with my other aunt most of the time—in a different town."

"Well, it would be very nice to have a familiar face in class," Dad said. "What are you interested in studying?"

An art history book stood open on my dad's desk. A full color photograph of a tapestry was on the right hand page. It reminded me of the one I'd found in my room, which reminded me of the tapestry at the Cloisters. It was closer to one of those. This tapestry was of a medieval lady sitting on the ground, holding a mirror in her right hand. The front legs of a kneeling unicorn were in her lap, his face reflected in the mirror. A lion stood on her left holding a waving pennant. I ran a finger over the lady's rich brocade dress. The lion and the unicorn were smiling, but the lady wasn't. The caption under the photo caught my interest. "A panel from the six tapestry series titled, The Lady and the Unicorn. This panel is historically thought to represent sight."

I recognized Dad's scribbled notes in the margin.

Sight. But what kind of sight? Regular, five senses sight? Second sight? Magical sight? What is the significance of the unicorn's reflection in the mirror? Why does the lady look so sad and the animals so happy? Why the combination of the real and the imaginary?

That was a good question—why the combination of the real and imaginary? But Bailean, he was real, even though people had tried to convince me that he was imaginary. Did that mean the unicorn could be real, too? Could the mirror be reflecting a world where unicorns and dragons actually existed? Not just for me, but for everyone, like Anna had said? Was that the world I'd seen this morning? Could it be Brindle?

I saw another light scribble in the book's margin and peered closer. *Are unicorns imaginary or just extinct? Is the mirror a portal to another world?* I ran my fingers over my Dad's notes. I bit my lip, fighting the anger rising inside. He'd never believed me, but his notes were the same questions I'd asked myself. The same questions I'd been chastised for. What was he hiding? Why wasn't he being truthful with me? I curled my fingers around the locket hiding under my shirt.

"You're looking thoughtful over there, honey." My dad interrupted my study of the book. He closed the cover and turned over his paper pad.

I stared at him. He didn't want me to see what he had written. He was hiding something from me. "I…I was just looking at the picture. It reminded me of the tapestry I found in my room."

My dad laughed, but it sounded forced. "The tapestry you found isn't from the Middle Ages. Although, it is very old." Dad tapped the book and looked like he was making connections in his head. "I should spend some time studying it. Try to discover its origins."

Lawrence glanced at the clock on the wall above my dad's desk. "Are you ready to go to the market?"

I nodded and came out from behind the desk.

Dad threw his arm around me. He squeezed me in a half-hug. "It's so nice to see you smiling again, Sophie. You guys have fun."

Lawrence waved. "See you around, Mr. Lincoln."

"Drive safe with my girl," Dad called after us.

"Bye, Dad." I sauntered down the hallway, in no particular rush. My mind was still on Dad's notes. He didn't want me to know he was questioning things, too. He was hiding it from me on purpose. Did that mean that he might believe me if I tried to convince him Bailean was real? I sighed. It wasn't worth the chance of being hospitalized again.

We strolled out of the building and back into the heat. The bright sunshine was gone, filtered through puffy white clouds edged in gray. Soft rolls of thunder lingered distantly in the air.

Lawrence reached for my hand. "You're awfully quiet."

"Sorry. Just thinking."

"And?" Lawrence drew the word out, exaggerating it.

"So much for your super power." I smirked.

Lawrence chuckled. "Well, I don't know *everything*."

I held my breath. How should I put it so Lawrence wouldn't think I was missing half of my marbles? "Do you believe things exist without being able to see them?"

"Of course," Lawrence said. "Wait. What kind of things did you mean?" He stopped on the curb and looked both ways before settling his hand on my lower back and ushering me across the street.

I smiled. That was the second time he'd touched me like that. "Never mind, it's silly."

"Oh, come on! If you believe in it, it's not silly."

"No." I shook my head again. "It doesn't matter."

Lawrence slowed to a snail's pace. "I'm going to walk this slow until you start talking."

I shrugged and walked away. "Fine, I'll just grab dinner and walk home."

Lawrence jumped into action and clamped his hands on my arms. His grasp was surprisingly strong. He forced me under the protection of a large oak tree as the first few drops of rain pattered upon the merchant tents. "Oh, no you won't! Talk!"

I avoided his gaze and twisted the ends of my hair. There was no way he'd believe me, even if he did believe in dragons.

Lawrence lifted my chin with his finger. "Wasn't I the one who told you to talk to my aunt about the dragon scales?"

I looked into his eyes. "You don't think dragons just exist in stories?"

"The important thing here is what you think."

I picked at the skin on the side of my thumbnail. I couldn't muster the courage to look at him again. "I don't know what to think. My mom…" Not my mom, but the woman who'd raised me. Tears pricked my eyes.

"What about her?"

"She told me I was born in the grasp of a dragon."

"And you don't believe her?"

"I thought it was just a story…until I met Anna and…the dreams."

"The dream you had this morning?"

"Yeah…but it wasn't a dream. Not really. It was more of a memory—but it wasn't *my* memory. I just called it a dream because…" Because it was too hard to believe that something that awful really happened. That it was the truth.

Lawrence rubbed his thumb across the top of my shoulder. "Hmmm. Not a dream, more like a memory—but not *your* memory."

"I know; it sounds stupid. If I told my dad any of this, he'd probably have me hospitalized again."

"Again?"

I swiped at the tears clinging to my lashes and sniffed. "Yeah. In eighth grade I tried to off myself. I couldn't take the pressure anymore."

Lawrence sucked in an audible breath. "Well…I'm glad you didn't succeed." His whisper was warm and moist against my shoulder. His lips were so close to mine. So soft. So gentle. I wanted his lips on my skin.

"So, this memory. What was it?"

I took a deep breath to help clear my head. "You promise not to laugh at me?"

He made a cross over his heart. "Promise."

When I didn't speak, Lawrence reached for my hand. His fingers curled around mine and he led me around to the backside of the oak tree, away from any peering eyes in the market crowd. "I've had my share of bad memories. You can trust me with yours."

A glowing warmth filled my belly. My heart melted a little when he smiled at me, encouraging my confession. I bit my lip, hesitant to let it out, but the tightness in my shoulders was unbearable. I couldn't keep all these secrets to myself anymore. "I had a friend when I was little. His name was Bailean, but he wasn't human."

I tried to read his face. His expression remained interested but not surprised by what I said.

"After my mom, uh…went away, my dad and the psychologists told me Bailean wasn't real, and soon he no longer came around. In eighth grade, I saw him in the alley by our apartment, but by then I had convinced myself he was imaginary, like my dad and the doctors told me. I thought I was losing my mind and so…"

"You tried to off yourself…" Lawrence breathed.

Tears slid from my eyes and over my cheeks. I swiped at them and nodded. Seeing Bailean had been the icing on the cake. My throat burned as I pushed the memories of that dark time back into the recesses of my mind. It was a minute before

I could continue. I swallowed. "When we moved here, I started seeing things again, and finding scales of mica, and everyone I've met says something about dragons."

"So...your imaginary friend was a dragon...like Barney?"

Without second-guessing, I punched Lawrence in the ribs and laughed despite the tears still sticky on my cheeks. "You butthead. Barney is a dinosaur."

Lawrence grinned and rubbed his ribs. "Go on."

I drew in a long breath. "This morning he came to me again." A shiver of dread ran through me. Telling Lawrence about the memory was almost as bad as seeing it the first time.

"What happened?" Lawrence asked.

"He showed me something—a scene. Like a movie. In it, the king killed my mother's husband, but it was almost like she was in on it. She commanded the crowd to hail her as their new queen. She was pregnant, Lawrence. The baby was *me*. The husband was my *father—my real father*. So who is Jack? And why did I think Maria was my real mom all these years? What if it was all *real*?"

Lawrence coaxed me close. I laid my head on his chest as the pent up hurt flowed out with my tears. "So neither of your parents is your birth parent?"

I shrugged. "I don't know. It's so confusing. When I went to see Anna this morning, she told me I was born in the room at her house, but the memory the dragon showed me was in someplace called Brindle. So, are the memories Bailean showed me true, or is your aunt's story the truth?"

"Perhaps they are both true."

I pulled away to look into his face. My hand fell to his chest. The beating of his heart was strong and steady under my palm. Why wasn't his heart racing like hers? "How can that be?"

"There are a lot of people who believe in parallel universes."

"So you think that there are two worlds, and somehow I'm connected to both of them?"

Lawrence ran his other hand through my hair. "Yes."

"And I thought you would think *I* was crazy," I murmured and snuggled back into his shoulder. I wound my arms around him. "A world where dragons actually exist?"

His heart quickened under my touch. He cleared his throat. "Why not?"

"If I was born there though—why I am here? In this world?"

Lawrence dipped his head. His murmur was warm against the top of my head. "That's the mystery isn't it?"

I sniffled. For all his lankiness, smooth hard muscles rolled under his damp T-shirt. I patted the spot that was wet with my tears. "Thanks."

"For what?"

"When I was little, my dad didn't believe me when I told him that Mom was taken away by men dressed like the king at the faire. The police said I was confusing recent events, and the psychologist said I was using an imaginary friend as a comfort tool. It's just nice to have someone believe in me."

Lawrence tucked his hands under my ears, cupping my chin in his palms. He gave me no choice but to look at him. "We all need someone to believe in us." He kissed the tip of my nose and that made me giggle. "What do you say we pick up some dinner and go hang that tapestry?"

"Okay." I stared into his eyes, not wanting him to let go. It'd been so long since I'd allowed anyone besides my dad this close. I wanted to stay here longer, to feel Lawrence's warm skin on mine, to taste his sweet lips. I closed my eyes and inhaled the spicy sweet aroma of his aftershave. His hands lingered for a moment, then slid down my neck and over my shoulders.

He encapsulated my hand in his. "C'mon," he whispered. "Let's finish up before it starts to pour."

chapter twelve

Lawrence set his toolbox and the hanging rod by the staircase and followed me into the kitchen. I pulled open the refrigerator door, put the enchiladas we'd bought at the market on the shelf, the lettuce in the vegetable drawer, and lingered for a minute while the cool air rushed out at me like a sea monster exhaling. The air was thick, humid. The little bit of rain that had fallen while we were at the market hadn't been enough to wash it away.

I grabbed the pitcher of lemonade and held it up for Lawrence's inspection. "Want a glass before we get started?"

He nodded. "I'd love one."

I poured two glasses, and Lawrence gulped his down before I'd even had a chance to sip mine. I poured another half glass for him to take upstairs, but he downed that, too. He set the empty glass on the counter. "Ready?

"I'm following you," I said.

Lawrence walked from the kitchen, pausing to grab his toolbox and the hanging rod by the staircase before heading upstairs. I lingered behind him, watched his arm muscles contract with the weight of the toolbox. My heart fluttered a little. I was glad I'd gotten a chance for a prolonged view— even if it was from behind.

I set my glass of lemonade on the dresser as Lawrence propped the hanging rod beside my bed. "Penny for your thoughts?"

I blushed at the corny saying and busied myself by fishing the ponytail holder out of my pocket and pulling my hair back to keep it out of the way. There was no way I was telling him what I was thinking. "It'll cost you more than that."

Lawrence smiled and surveyed the walls. He pointed to the empty wall by the pale green wardrobe. "Well, we'll have to move that cupboard, but that wall is probably the best. It will keep the sun off the tapestry. Keep it from fading more."

I shivered. No way in hell I was touching that wardrobe. Sure, I'd gotten to where I could be in the same room with it. But that was as far as I was going. I gestured to the wall by the door. "Couldn't we put the tapestry on that wall instead?"

Lawrence sized up the tapestry. "I think that could work. Let's see if this will be high enough." He grasped a corner of the tapestry and pulled it up. I dragged the other corner to the wall. Lawrence could easily reach the top of the wall, but no matter how hard I stretched, I just wasn't tall enough.

Lawrence laughed. "Don't worry, I can tell by my side that it'll work."

"We can't all be giants," I retorted, then I startled as a piercing crack of thunder filled the room. "Holy shit! That sounded like it was right over the house."

My bedroom lights blinked and then went off, leaving the room in a weird grayness. Lightning zigzagged outside. Wind rushed through the open windows carrying the scent of the rain and the forest.

"I knew that little bit of rain was just a warning." Lawrence frowned and let the tapestry slide to the floor.

I held onto my corner as he opened his toolbox, pulled out a yellow drill, and shoved a battery into the bottom. He set it on the floor and opened the packaging for the rod, fishing out the screws.

"How did you learn to do all this stuff?" I'd never even hung a picture on a wall.

Lawrence handed me the screws. "Henry taught me. He's been like a big brother." With one hand, he lined the bracket up on the wall. With the other hand, he grabbed a screw from my palm. "Can you hand me the drill?" he asked.

I dropped the corner of the tapestry and passed the drill to Lawrence.

A shrill whine filled the room as the drill forced a screw into the wall. Lawrence moved down the wall and lined the other bracket up.

Another clap of thunder exploded overhead. We both jerked. And then laughed.

"Storms make you nervous?" Lawrence screwed the other bracket into the wall.

I shook my head. "Not normally." But there was something about the intensity of this storm. It was almost preternatural.

Picking up a corner of the tapestry, Lawrence showed me the back. "See this long pocket? We have to slide the rod through it."

I was surprised that a rod pocket was already sewn onto the back. Gran must have had this tapestry hanging once before. I grabbed the rod, removed the decorative end, and handed it to Lawrence. Then I twisted the pole to its longest length and guided it through the pocket.

The end of the pole emerged on his side of the tapestry. "Ready?" Lawrence asked.

I nodded and held up my end as Lawrence set the rod in the cradle of the bracket and twisted the finial back on with a twist of his wrist. He then walked over and grabbed the other end from me. His hand lingered in my palm before he raised the rod and settled it in the bracket. I stepped back to admire our handy work. Lightning flashed, filling the room with a quick brightness, and thunder shook the windowpanes. The trees in the tapestry sparkled; a green line of energy ran through their leaves like an electric arc.

"Did you see that?" I pointed to the tapestry.

"See what?" He was turning the finial into place.

"The way the lightning lit up the trees in the tapestry?"

"Missed it. I bet it will look even more beautiful when the sun comes through those windows though." Lawrence bent to put his drill back in his toolbox. I stared at the hanging, willing the lightning to come again. All I got was a long, loud rumble that sounded like Mother Nature snoring.

The door to the wardrobe creaked open. I recognized the sound instantly. My chest tightened, anxiety tingled at the edge of my consciousness, but I turned casually and walked toward it, fighting the storm of emotions: a tight space, a shallow breath, a shadow. I shoved the door shut; my eyes filled with tears.

"You can't see me…you can't see me…"

chapter thirteen

"Sophie!" Lawrence pulled me into his chest with one arm while the other wrapped around my back. He held me tight, as if trying to keep me from falling. He breathed into my hair. "It's okay…shhh. It's okay. You're safe. You're safe with me. We'll protect you now."

He was warm. The vice-like grip he had on me was comforting. A shuddering breath struggled to inflate my lungs as I broke into an uncontrollable sob. I clenched Lawrence's shirt in my hands and buried my head in the crook of his shoulder.

He sat on the edge of the bed and gathered me onto his lap. His hand stroked my hair, soothing away the fright, and then he began to hum. The notes of Bailean's song vibrated from his vocal chords against the top of my head. I pulled away and looked into his face. His eyes were wrinkled with concern, his brow crinkled between his eyes. "Are you all right?"

I swallowed. "How do you know that song?"

"What song?"

"The one you were just humming. How do you know it?"

"Do you recognize it?"

I chewed on my lower lip as Lawrence searched my face with his golden eyes. "Yeah," I finally answered. "It's my dragon's song. He sang it to me when I was upset or scared."

"What were you scared of?" Lawrence whispered.

"The man. The man that took my mother." I wound a strand of hair around my finger.

"What is it about the cupboard that scares you so much?"

I shrugged, feeling like that six-year-old child long ago that no one believed. I looked away. Wrapped my arms around myself.

Lawrence pulled my chin with his finger until I looked at him again. "You can tell me. I'll protect you."

"You'll protect me?" I asked.

Lawrence nodded. "Of course."

"Protect me from what?"

"Whatever you need protecting from…although, I'm not sure I can protect you from a dragon."

I gave him a small smile. "Why would you need to protect me from Bailean? He's my friend."

A grin lit up Lawrence's face. "Oh, you know. Dragons and virgins and all that."

I punched him in the shoulder and rolled off his lap. "You're such a dork."

Lawrence chuckled as he rubbed his shoulder.

Without thinking, I launched myself at him, forcing him to sit back on my bed. I leaned into his face so we were nose to nose. So close I could feel his breath tickle my lip. His skin smelled like cloves and oranges. I pressed my breasts against his chest. "How do you know I'm a virgin anyway?"

His tongue darted along his lips, moistening them. "I have super powers, remember?"

I laughed.

Lawrence eased back on the bed, pulling me with him. His body was taut under mine and so warm. He drew me down, his hands firm on my back, guiding me toward him. My breath hitched as my heart raced. His muscles moved under me as he lifted his head to press his lips into mine. Deft fingers pulled out my hairband. My hair fell, curtaining us off from the world. Slowly, I let my tongue explore his mouth and he pulled me closer, rolling over so that I was now under him. I loved the gentle pressure of his weight on my body. His hand traced the curve of my neck. I tried to shy away, but he nuzzled into the crack, his warm breath tickling my ear.

"Don't hide from me."

Soft lips caressed the scars that disfigured my skin. I shivered as he moved down my shoulder and over my collarbone. Then he returned to my lips. My hips strained against him. His kisses were making me senseless.

Breathless, Lawrence shifted and lay next to me, stroking the curve of my hip with a light, teasing touch.

The room had grown dark as the storm moved in but his eyes were still bright. I combed a hand through his bangs, pushing them off his forehead. "I don't want you to stop."

He smiled. "That's why I did."

"You are a punk." I punched him in the shoulder.

Lawrence laughed. "When I make you mine, I want to take my time." He kissed me again and I melted into his arms.

When I came up for air, I was lightheaded and giddy. There was an intense buildup of pressure in my body that had found no release. I curled into him and his hand continued to caress my hair, trail down my arm.

We lay together until the storm died down. A gentle breeze swept through the room and ruffled the tapestry. My eyelids were growing heavy when Lawrence spoke again. "If the cabinet freaks you out, we could move it out of here."

I rolled on my back and looked at the bed canopy. "Then my dad would ask why I moved it, and I'd have to tell him and he'd get worried about me again. I'll just deal with it. Face my fear."

"Hey, you two!" Dad poked his head in through the door. "What's going on in here?"

We exchanged a glance as if we were two naughty children caught doing something we weren't supposed to be doing.

"Oh, hello, Mr. Lincoln." Lawrence rolled to a sitting position and gestured to the tapestry. "We were just admiring our handiwork."

Dad leaned against the doorframe. He looked tired, but his smile was genuine as he took in the tapestry hanging on the wall. "Looks good. Are you staying for dinner, Lawrence?"

Lawrence stood and stuffed his hands in his pockets. He shrugged and looked at me. "To tell you the truth, I hadn't really thought about it, Mr. Lincoln."

Dad waved a dismissive hand. "Please, call me Jack. C'mon you two, let's make some dinner. It's the least we can do to repay Lawrence for his help."

I grabbed Lawrence's hand for a lift up. "You heard the man. Let's go eat!"

We followed my dad down the stairs and into the kitchen as the whir of the refrigerator motor kicked in. The digital clock on the stove blinked.

"Electricity is back on!" I celebrated with a little jig.

"Don't count on it for long," Dad said. "We're supposed to get another bad storm tonight. There are even tornado warnings out."

"Oh, that's just great," I mumbled as my happy jig faded. I pulled open the fridge and grabbed the bag of enchiladas. I had a vision of a tornado picking up the house and carrying it to a different world, like in the Wizard of Oz. I hoped when it landed, it didn't kill one of the resident witches. I handed the package to my dad and grabbed the lettuce, tomatoes, and a red pepper to make a salad.

"Can I help with something?" Lawrence asked.

My dad gestured to the cupboard to his right. "Open that cupboard there and grab the plates. Silverware is in the drawer next to the stove."

Lawrence grinned at me, slid the plates out of the cupboard, and gathered the forks and knives. I tore the lettuce leaves and tossed them in the salad bowl. Then I cut the tomatoes and the pepper into bite size pieces and tossed them in, too.

Lawrence opened the refrigerator and peered into its brightness. "Italian dressing good?"

"Yep," I answered.

Lawrence had placed two plates right next to each other and one across from those. He'd also folded the napkins into little origami birds. They made me laugh.

"Cute birds." Dad put the now-steaming enchiladas on the table.

"If you're going do it, you might as well do it with style," Lawrence said.

Dad let out a short burst of laughter and pulled his chair up to the table. "I like this guy."

I smiled. I did, too.

The storm Dad mentioned at dinner rolled in on moans of soft thunder. Streaks of light crackled in the starless sky. A cool breeze flowed through the window. I lay on my bed staring at the tapestry. Every time the sky lit up it sparkled, as if it was being energized by the discharge of electricity. My mind wandered around Lawrence's parallel universe theory. It wasn't any stranger than thinking that Bailean was real.

The wind shifted and blustered around the room carrying a strand of warm air. My ears perked up at the sound of a snort, like a horse blowing. Hair rose on the back of my neck. I clenched the edge of my pillow and bit my lip.

~He is real.

The leaves in the trees of the tapestry bubbled and shifted. A green, sparkling mist swirled about the room. The reindeer from the tapestry tossed his head and then he stepped out of the hanging, his antlers shining with an inner light. My heart raced as he approached. Was he real or was I dreaming? I didn't remember falling asleep. I pinched my arm. The sting told me everything I needed to know.

The bull's hazel eyes pierced clean through to my soul. I saw sadness in them, but also hope. Deep in my gut, I knew that being able to see Bailean wasn't just because I'd started to believe again. I propped myself up on an elbow. "Are you from Brindle?"

~Yes.

A shudder ran over me, leaving goose bumps in its wake. It was different saying it aloud. Almost like it was more real. "Does that awful man still rule there?"

The deer shifted his weight. His tail switched. *~Yes.*

"He took my mother…but you already knew that, didn't you?"

The reindeer winced and closed his eyes. *~ The king has destroyed many things—relationships between kingdoms, bonds between families, and nearly all of the enchanted tapestries.*

"What do the tapestries have to do with any of this?"

~They act as a portal between our worlds. If someone looked at your tapestry in Brindle, they would see the same scene you see. Your tapestry has a twin.

I wondered who owned the mirror of my tapestry. My skin crawled at the thought of some stranger literally just walking into my room. "So the tapestry is kind of like a wormhole?" The scribble in my dad's book flashed in my mind…*a portal between worlds.* He knew. Dad knew and yet he'd convinced me that I'd made all of this up. Drove me to the edge of insanity. I clenched my fists, anger boiling inside. I had to do something with the energy that was building inside me or I'd blow. I stood and paced the floor.

~To limit the travel between worlds to only his chosen few, the king destroyed almost every tapestry in the kingdom. But some were smuggled out before he could get to them.

I turned to the deer. "Bailean has come back because he needs me to do something. Something no one else can do." I looked him in the eye, daring him to tell me a lie.

~The king is obsessed with finding you because of your special abilities, but don't worry, we'll protect you.

The back of my neck prickled. *We'll protect you.* That's exactly what Lawrence had said earlier.

The reindeer nudged my hand with his large head, like a dog. I smoothed my fingers over the soft fur on the side of his face. Short, stiff velvet still covered the base of his antlers, but the tops were smooth bone. His muscles shuddered under his shaggy coat.

~They tortured Maria when she wouldn't tell them how to find you.

My stomach turned sour. My disbelief came out in a whisper. "What? Tortured her because of one little girl?"

His eyes filled with tears. *~All for one little girl.*

I flung up my arms in exasperation and then locked my hands behind my head, trying to keep control of myself. What was I expected to do? I didn't even know where Brindle was or how to get there. How was I supposed to help? "I don't get it! What does the king want from me?"

~ A dragon chooses a child before it is born, and imbues the child with special powers at its birth. Some children are given the power to see what others cannot. Some are memory keepers—historians—and others can take on the form of another. You are the Duke of Wirth's daughter, and you were born in the grasp of the Golden Dragon. The rarest of all dragons. The only one who can give the gift of Dragonsong.

I didn't believe what I was hearing. It was "the Chosen One" speech I'd read in every fantasy book of my youth. There *had* to be more children born with "Dragonsong." It just didn't make sense to put all that power into one person. I shook my head but the words to Bailean's lullaby came unbidden anyway. "I don't want it."

~You don't have a choice. It is yours already. He caught and held my gaze. There was something about this creature that struck

a chord. The smell of roses hung in the air between us. The fragrance carried on the rain and wind from the open window.

Rain crashed into the windowpanes and drummed on the roof. His ears flicked toward the door, and he dissipated in a fog of green sparkle. I threw out my hand. "Wait! I have more questions!"

But it was too late; his figure had already reappeared in the tapestry. My bedroom door opened and Dad stuck in his head.

"Everything okay, Soph? I thought I heard you talking."

"Sorry." I balled my fists, trying to counter the lingering sensation of the smooth antlers, the smell of the roses. I tried to shrug away the uneasiness, the unanswered questions. The knowledge that there was something expected of me because of a gift given but never wanted. A gift I didn't even understand. I had an overwhelming urge to talk to someone who could help me put all the pieces together, someone who would understand but not judge my sanity—okay not just someone, but Lawrence. I sighed and plopped on the bed. It would have to wait until tomorrow. I looked into Dad's worried face. "Just muttering to myself about all these damn thunderstorms. We are definitely going to lose power again."

My dad ran his hand through his disheveled hair and yawned. "Yeah, well it's late. You should get some sleep."

I nodded. "I will."

Dad nodded and with another loud yawn started to pull the door closed.

"Dad?"

The door popped back open. "Yeah?"

"Can you tell me why you've tried to convince me that magic isn't real, but make notes about portals to different worlds in your textbook?"

Dad's shoulders tightened. He scratched his neck absentmindedly. "Can we have this conversation in the morning?"

I shook my head as tears gathered on my eyelashes. I clasped my hands together to keep them from shaking. I had to know. I couldn't go on trying to believe I was someone I wasn't. It wasn't fair to anyone, most of all myself. The words stuck in my throat. I swallowed hard. "You—you aren't my real dad, are you? I mean, you raised me, but you didn't donate the sperm, right?" His face paled and I searched for words that would soften the implications, but I couldn't find any.

Dad walked across the room, sat next to me, and sighed. "What makes you ask me that now?"

I shrugged. The tears plopped into my lap. After his reaction this afternoon about Champy, I didn't dare tell him the memory Bailean showed me. "I was looking through the pictures the other day—you know, the box I dumped when the window in your room broke? Mom's hair is so much lighter than mine, and her eyes are brown, and your hair isn't dark either—I don't look like either one of you. Plus, there are no photographs of me when I was a baby—nothing before I was like, two."

My dad ran his hand over the back of his neck. I could see him struggling to find the right words. "I met your mom at the museum when you were about eighteen months old. I instantly fell in love with you both. When we got married, you got my last name in the bargain. I know we've been through some really tough times, but I wouldn't change the fact that you are my daughter for the world."

"Thanks." I put my arms around his chest and buried my head in his shoulder. It was weird at first, like maybe I was too old to want to be held.

I started to pull away, but he wound me back in. The awkwardness melted away as if it had never been there. "You're still going to call me Dad, right?"

I laughed. "You got it, Jack."

Dad ruffled my hair and settled his chin on top of my head. "I'm glad. I didn't know what to do when your mother—"

I stiffened, but held my tongue. He didn't know Maria wasn't my real mother.

He sighed deeply. "We'd never discussed if we would tell you, or at what age we would tell you if we did. But, I don't consider you my adopted daughter—just my daughter."

"Even when I do something stupid?" I picked at a loose button on his shirt.

"Like try to set the high school on fire by blowing up the chemistry lab? Yeah, even then."

I smiled. He really did love me. Who would've kept a kid around this long if he didn't? "Did Mom ever tell you anything about my real dad?"

"Just that he died before you were born."

"Did she tell you how?"

My dad went rigid. His thumb rubbed my arm nervously. "She said he was…murdered."

A burning sensation flared in my chest. Silent tears ran down my face until I could hardly breathe. I shook in Jack's arms as I cried. I was so hoping that he'd tell me a story. One that contradicted the memory Bailean had shown me. How could someone be so cruel? The king had murdered my father for one reason and one reason only. He'd wanted my mother.

~*And the child she carried.* Bailean's voice whispered in my mind.

"Why?" I sobbed. It was a question meant for Bailean but my dad answered it.

"Sometimes people do terrible things."

To his credit, Dad didn't tell me that everything would be all right, or that I shouldn't be upset about a man I never knew, and he didn't shush me. He just let me cry, the tears falling like the rain outside. When I'd cried myself out, I sniffed and ran a hand under my nose. He smoothed my hair away from my face. "It's late. Are you ready to go to sleep now?"

I untwined from his embrace, nodded, and pulled my legs onto the bed, folding them under my body.

"Goodnight, bug."

I smiled at my childhood nickname. Dad stood and walked out of the room. He pulled the door halfway closed.

"You can leave it open," I said with a yawn and snuggled into my pillow.

He smiled and nodded. "See you in the morning, then?"

"We'll talk about the notes in your book then, right?" I asked.

"Yes." Dad sighed. "I'll tell you everything I've discovered about your mom's disappearance. All right?"

I nodded. *Finally*. Finally, I'd be able to share things with my dad without him threatening to send me away again. I buried my head in the pillow and cried tears of relief.

As he shuffled across the hall, I saw lights travel across my wall. I sat back up and looked out my window. Two headlights beamed up the driveway.

"What the hell?" Dad mumbled, speaking my exact thought aloud.

I climbed out of bed and waited at the top of the stairs as he opened the front door.

A familiar lanky form in a bright yellow raincoat stepped into the hallway. My heart raced and then dropped into the pit of my stomach. If Lawrence was here this late, something must be wrong.

"Lawrence! What the hell are you doing here? It's like one o'clock in the morning," my dad said.

I ran halfway down the stairs, heart thumping in my throat. "What's wrong?"

"I'm sorry to bother you, Mr. Lincoln, but it's Samantha. The baby is coming, but something isn't right. Anna needs another woman's help. She asked me to come get Sophie."

I swallowed down the dread fear and ran back up the stairs. "Give me a minute to get dressed!"

"Why aren't they going to the hospital?" My dad's voice traveled up the staircase behind me.

"The storm is too bad. The stream has flooded over the road and Anna's afraid it would be more dangerous for Samantha to travel."

"Crap," Dad muttered. "Well, I suppose I'll just be in the way if I come with you."

I paused in the middle of pulling my shirt over my head.

"Actually, sir, I could use some help keeping Henry calm," Lawrence said. "If you don't mind."

I smiled as Dad dashed back up the stairs. His door slammed against the wall. He must have flung it open. I finished pulling my shirt down, pulled my hair back into a ponytail, and then jammed my legs into a pair of jeans. I pounded back down the stairs before slipping on my sneakers. "What does your grandmother think is wrong?"

"The baby is breech," Lawrence said as my dad came back down.

My dad's hands trembled above his chest for a moment, and then he took an audible breath and adjusted his glasses. "Breech. That's not good, but manageable for a midwife as experienced as Anna. Is there anything I should bring?"

"Not that I can think of, sir." Lawrence opened the door and the three of us dashed to the truck. Lawrence wasted no time putting it in gear. The wipers slashed back and forth, not able to keep up with the torrential rain. The motor whined with each swipe.

My dad flung an arm around my shoulder, his hand gripping me protectively, the other hand braced against the dashboard. He squinted and peered at the road through the windshield. "It's a good thing you're driving, Lawrence. I'm not familiar with the road in this direction."

Lawrence white-knuckled the steering wheel. His brow creased in concentration. He swerved suddenly as a limb fell into the road. I gasped and my hand grasped his leg, squeezing the muscles of his thigh. His skin blazed through his jeans. I loosened my grip, but kept the physical contact between us.

Energy flowed like the lightning zigzagging across the night sky. Leaves and tree limbs were scattered everywhere. No lights could be seen from any of the houses.

"Damn electricity is out again," Dad mumbled.

The truck bumped over the washed out gravel road and I recognized the storybook house at the edge of the woods. The windows were brightly lit. I slid my hand off of Lawrence's leg as he pulled in the circular driveway at the side of the house. He put the truck in Park and turned off the ignition. "Are you ready?"

I bit my lip and took a calming breath. My heart was threatening to shoot out of my chest. "As ready as I'll ever be."

chapter fourteen

We piled into the cottage kitchen. A low fire burned in the hearth and a small black cauldron steamed over it. The smell of lavender infused the room. Thirty or so candles burned on the table, bathing the entryway in a warm glow. Henry came around the corner. His hair was sticking up; his clothes were rumpled. He looked like he was having one heck of a night.

"Thank the gods," he said, grabbing my hand and pulling me down the hall toward the birthing room Anna had shown me the other day.

"I don't know how Anna thinks I can help." I stumbled, caught myself, and then quickened my pace to keep up with Henry's long strides. Nervous butterflies swarmed in my gut.

As Henry pushed open the door to the birthing room, Anna brushed Samantha's hair away from her forehead. A slight blue glow emanated from under her fingertips. My jaw dropped in awe.

"I know it's hard," Anna said. "But resist the urge to push. We don't want this little darling any further in the birth canal than he already is."

Samantha nodded, eyes bright and feverish looking.

My heart tugged. Samantha was in pain. My fingers tingled, wanting to help, but not knowing where to even start. My thoughts slid back to the memory Bailean had shown me of my own birth. I could get a cool washcloth. Or hold Samantha's hand. I stood frozen with indecision. I felt as much a stranger here as I had standing in the birthing chamber with Bailean.

Henry dropped my hand and strode to his wife. He bent to kiss her forehead. "Sophie's here. She's going to help; everything will be okay."

How did he know everything would be all right? How was my presence a comfort? Everything in me said to flee.

Anna walked around the bed and encircled my shoulders with her arm. It was almost as if she'd read my mind and was keeping me from running away. She led me toward the washbasin. "Sophie, you're just in time. I need you to wash your hands."

I nodded and swallowed hard. Finally. Some instructions. This all seemed a little too real now that I was here. My breath caught as I looked into the bowl. Bile burned the back of my throat. The water was pink, tinged with blood. My heart pounded in my ears. I looked at Anna for guidance, but she was bent over the small hearth where steam swirled over a pot of simmering liquid. I reached for the water, pulled my hands back. Drew a deep breath. Do it for the baby. Without further thought, I dipped my hands in the tepid water, picked up the bar of soap, and lathered my skin in lavender scented bubbles. Anna brought the pitcher and poured hot water over my hands. I flinched at the nearly scalding temperature, but suffered through it. The high temperature was necessary to kill any germs lingering on my skin.

Lawrence poked his head into the room. He gave me a nod as I dried my hands on a clean linen towel, and then he addressed Henry. "You should come with me for a bit, Henry. Let Anna and Sophie do what they need to do."

Henry looked at Samantha, shaking his head, but Samantha put her hand on his arm. "Go, Henry. You can't order your son out of me. Anna will call you back in when it's time."

Henry's troubled gaze lifted to Anna. She nodded at him. With a big sigh, he curled his shoulders and shuffled out of the room.

As soon as the door was shut behind him, Anna clapped her hands together. "Let's get this baby turned, shall we?"

"I don't know how you expect me to help." I lifted my thumb to my mouth but caught myself. I chewed on the inside of my cheek instead.

Anna beckoned me to the foot of the bed. "Come. I want you to put your hands on Samantha's belly."

I met Samantha's gaze as I placed my hands on her round stomach. She was breathing hard and grimacing again. A strong bump from the baby made me gasp and pull away. But then I let out a nervous giggle. "I've never felt a baby move before."

I put my hands back on Samantha's belly and the baby wiggled again.

"Right now, he has his head up by Samantha's ribs. But we need him to turn the right way. Have you seen pictures of babies in the womb?"

Nodding, I visualized the drawing from my freshmen health science book. The baby should be engaged head down in the birth canal, the head almost twice the size of the body. Instantly, I was sorry for my neighbor. A clap of thunder made us all flinch.

Samantha moaned, her free hand curling around her belly. "I need to push," she said, through gritted teeth.

"Not yet, dear." Anna patted her arm consolingly. "We're almost there."

Closing my eyes, I pictured the baby from the book again, but this time I pictured him with a head full of strawberry-blond hair like Henry.

"Can you see him?" Anna asked.

I nodded, assuming Anna meant being able to see the baby in my mind. I imagined a bright light at the end of a tunnel and smiled as the baby turned his head toward it. He stirred under my hands.

~*Sing.* Bailean's voice commanded in my head.

What? I thought, taken by surprise. The vision of the baby turning in the womb nearly startled out of me. I squeezed my eyes tighter, doubling my efforts. Sing what? How was singing going to bring a baby into the world?

Before I could blink my eyes though, a song formed in my mind. I started to sing the song about Bonnie Prince Charles, but different words kept wanting to replace the lyrics I knew. It took a lot of concentration to sing the right words. Was I confusing two different songs?

~*Don't think, just sing!*

I took a breath and sang.

"Speed bonnie boat, like a bird on the wing,
Onward, the dragons cry

I shook my head. That wasn't right.
~*Keep singing!*
I took a shaky breath and continued.

Carry the lad that's born to be king
Over the sea to Skye
Come to me lad, come to me now
Thunder clouds rent the air;
Baffled, our foe's stand on the shore
Follow they will not dare."

The words leapt from my tongue like they were on fire. Samatha's groans grew louder with each line. Under my hands, the baby turned away from his mother's heartbeat and searched for the source of the song. I sang the verse again, even though I knew they weren't quite right, and imagined the baby's head making its way toward me. Samantha cried out, lurched forward, and grabbed Anna's arm.

"It's working!" Anna said. "Keep singing!"

I took a breath, the tension in my shoulders giving a little until Samantha screamed. "Henry!"

The door burst open and Henry rushed into the room. He'd probably had his ear to the door the whole time. A prolonged roll of thunder shook the floor. Startled, I quit singing, my eyes flying open at the intense brightness of the lightning. A strong gust of wind rushed through the room. The candles flickered and went out. The glowing embers in the hearth were the only illumination. A warm body pressed into me. A draw of breath tickled my neck. *Bailean.* The dragon grasped my hands in his claws and positioned them between Samantha's legs. Before I could protest, a warm, heavy wetness pressed into my palms.

A wisp of green sparkle—like someone had sprinkled glitter—swirled about the newborn.

~Clear his nose and mouth.

"Shouldn't Anna be doing this?" I heard the panic in my voice.

~Grab the corner of the linen. It's just to the right on the edge of the bed.

I fumbled for the bed sheet. My fingers clasped around it as Samantha's voice rose again. The baby emerged further.

Wait! My mind shrieked against the panic building in my chest. I wasn't prepared for this.

~You must do it anyway.

I swiped the linen across the baby's face. Henry was bustling about behind me relighting some of the candles, but my eyes were adjusting. I saw a hint of light colored hair in the firelight.

"Okay, Sophie's got everything in hand. Push again when you are ready," Anna said to Samantha.

"I do?" My voice was three octaves higher than normal. My knees shook.

Anna patted my shoulder. "You're a natural. Rotate his shoulders a bit, that's it. Now pull on him gently…gently. You've got him."

I gazed in wonder as the little one drew breath for the first time, his lungs expanding and filling with air. He cried and everyone in the room let out a collective breath. The tenseness in my muscles released and I laughed. My whole body shook with nerves as I wiped the baby off with a dry towel. I couldn't imagine doing this every day—I mean, I could do it every day. I just don't think I would ever get used to it. No wonder it was called a miracle. It was amazing. I held the baby as Anna cut and tied his umbilical cord.

~Well done.

The dragon's memory of my own birth played in my head. The little one in my arms had been born in the grasp of a dragon, too. I offered the baby to Bailean as I had been offered twenty years ago, but he was nowhere to be seen. Only a quickly dissipating mist told me he'd actually been in the room.

"Give him a blessing, Sophie," Samantha said.

I lifted my gaze to Samantha. Henry was standing next to her holding her hand, a look of wonder and awe on his face. I smiled at the newborn in my arms. "Welcome to the world, little one. It's one crazy place. But you've got parents who love you very much and some pretty cool neighbors, if I do say so myself. My one wish for you would be that you are always able to see the world from someone else's eyes." I swept his fuzzy hair off his forehead and whispered in his ear. "In this way, you will always know the truth behind the lies." I kissed his forehead and then smiled as I gave him over to Anna. She swaddled the infant in a clean linen, then snuggled him into the crook of Samantha's arm.

A light knock came at the door. My heart immediately set to racing. I remembered the king coming into my mother's birthing room. I reached out for the wall, steadying myself against the spinning room. I closed my eyes, took a deep breath.

Lawrence's voice carried through the sliver of space between the door and jamb. "Is it safe for us to come in?"

Anna pulled a clean sheet over Samantha. "I think it's safe for a few moments," she said.

He pushed open the door and they entered slowly, unsure of themselves. Henry smiled and whooped out a glad cry, grabbing Jack's hand and pumping it up and down. "Come! Meet my son!"

"It's a boy?" Dad's eyes lit up as he walked into the room.

"It's a boy." Henry took the bundle from Samantha and cradled him. "William Henry Stuart."

My insides churned. ~*Stuart? As in the king of Brindle, Stuart? It's just a coincidence. Right, Bailean?*

~*Bailean?*

My dad let the baby grab his finger. He waggled it to and fro.

"So nice to meet you William Henry," Lawrence cooed.

"Oh!" Samantha gasped. "I feel like I need to push again."

Henry's eyes widened. "Two babies?" he asked Anna.

"No, no." Anna shook her head. "The afterbirth. Why don't you take the baby out and let me help Samantha get cleaned up?"

Henry pecked Samantha on the forehead. "I love you."

"I love you, too."

"You too, Sophie," Anna said and waved me out. "Wash up. You've done enough for tonight. Thank you, my dear."

"I couldn't have done it without you," Samantha said to me.

I nodded and walked over to the washbasin. I scrubbed my hands and forearms in the lavender scented water. My mind was still reeling, body amped up by adrenaline. I could barely find my tongue. "You would've done fine without me. I had no idea what I was doing."

Samantha grinned. "Neither did I."

I smiled back.

As I entered the kitchen, Lawrence was busy relighting the candles. The lightning and thunder had calmed, but the rain was still coming down in torrents. I sidled up next to Lawrence and grabbed an already-lit candle, tipping it toward the blackened wick of another.

"You don't need the candle to do that, you know," Lawrence whispered in my ear. His breath was moist on my cheek.

"I would need matches then." I bumped him with my hip. "And I'm currently out of those. So…"

Lawrence looked over his shoulder and I followed his gaze. My dad and Henry were occupied with the new baby and chatting away. His gaze returned to me, settling on my face. "You still haven't figured it out, have you?"

I raised my eyebrows and sighed. I was too tired to play games tonight. Couldn't he just tell me what was on his mind? "Haven't figured what out?"

"Your gift. Your…*abilities*. You don't need matches to light a candle."

"Oh? So now I can light candles with the power of my mind? Is that kind of like your super power?" I scoffed.

Lawrence held up an unlit candle. He tipped it toward me like it was a glass of champagne. His golden eyes sparkled with mischief as he wet his lips with his tongue. My stomach clenched and flip-flopped. Butterflies rose from my guts and took flight in my chest. Was he going to kiss me right here? In front of my dad?

Lawrence smiled and puckered his lips.

Then he blew as if he was blowing out a birthday candle, and a bright flame danced to life at the end of the wick.

chapter fifteen

"H-how did you do that?" I whispered. I frantically looked over my shoulder, praying that my dad hadn't seen what I'd just witnessed. He would totally freak out and I would never get to see Lawrence again.

"You can do it, too." He seized another candle and held it out to me.

"No, I can't." I pushed the candle away but he held it up to me again.

"Yes, you can." His eyes darted over my shoulder. "Don't worry, he's not looking."

I puckered my lips and blew gently, but I didn't think anything would happen. I was right. The wick stood tall in the wax, unlit. I raised my eyebrows as if to say I told you so. He nodded at me, encouraging me to try again. I took a deep breath and blew harder this time.

Still nothing.

I pushed the candle away with a sidelong glance at my dad. Thankfully he wasn't paying any attention to me. "I can't do it. I feel stupid trying again."

Lawrence stared at me—hard. His intense gaze made me shiver. I'd never seen him looking so fierce. Where was the good-natured boy I'd met a few days ago?

"You have to believe you can do it. You have to expect the flame to rise."

I shook my head, still not convinced.

Lawrence picked up another candle, twirled it in his fingers. "Tell me what you remember about the birth."

I shoved my hands in my jeans pockets. "I put my hands on Samantha's stomach. I felt the baby kick. I pictured what he looked like and then I imagined him coming toward my voice, toward the firelight."

"Why did you start singing?"

I blushed. I wasn't going to tell him the reason I sang was because Bailean commanded me. What if Dad overheard? "It was just…to calm my nerves. So my mind didn't go to that crazy place my body was trying to take it."

Lawrence smirked, candlelight dancing in his eyes.

He knew. Somehow he knew I'd just lied to him. My palms grew sweaty.

He pressed the candle he'd been twirling into my palm and curled his fingers around mine. His voice was husky, but insistent, when he spoke. "Imagine. See it in your mind. Draw the flame up. That's all you need to do."

It was almost like he was a completely different person than the Lawrence I'd met a few days ago. I liked this new confidence. I studied his long, thin fingers wrapped around mine. I roved over the lines etched into his knuckles, got lost in the curves, in the way his fingers curled together. Lawrence cleared his throat and broke the spell, encouraging—no—demanding I try again. I drew a breath, closed my eyes, and pictured the fire blazing in my core. As if the world had frozen in this one moment, everything faded: the soft chatter of my dad and Henry, the rain pounding the roof, the howling winds driving across the landscape. It was only Lawrence, me, and the candle grasped in our hands. I coaxed out my inner fire, controlling it like I had never done before. Usually it controlled me. A bead of light traveled up my throat and filled my mouth. My mind drew a small yellow flame at the top of the wick; made it dance until it glowed bright, and then I blew.

Time seemed to slow around me.

"Open your eyes," Lawrence whispered.

I peeked through my eyelashes, almost afraid to look. A warm yellow flame glowed before me. I let out a surprised little laugh, pressed the candle into Lawrence's grasp, then picked up another. I drew out my flame again. A white spark of light spiraled around the wick.

Lawrence chuckled. "Hey, slow down!" He gestured with his head toward my dad and Henry.

"Who cares?" I was floating. The butterflies in my stomach might carry me away. I lit another candle and placed it on the table with the others. The room was as luminous as a church service on Christmas Eve. I reached for Lawrence's hand and twined my fingers around his. We stared at the glow, basking in the warm light. Outside, the storm raged on, but inside I was cozy and safe.

Safe.

Something I hadn't felt in fifteen years. Lawrence's amber eyes were even more striking in the candlelight. Energy buzzed in the small space between us. He stepped closer, his thighs making contact with mine. His heat radiated like a blast furnace. His shoulders rounded as he bent toward me. He was so close I could smell the fragrance of his soap—cinnamon and citrus and cloves. I closed my eyes.

A cool hand on my shoulder drew me back to earth. Lawrence dropped my hand and stepped away.

"Are you ready to go home?" my dad asked. He gave my shoulder a gentle squeeze.

The lightness fluttered away, replaced by the blackness of disappointment. "Oh. Can't we stay for a little while longer?"

My dad turned his wrist and wrinkled his brow. "My watch says 2:48 A.M. I think that's late enough."

I opened my mouth to protest again but snapped it shut. He was right. It was late. Plus, he'd promised we'd talk about Mom in the morning. "Okay, let's go."

"Thank you, Sophie." Henry looked down at the swaddled bundle in his arms.

"Tell Samantha and Anna that I'll visit tomorrow." I smoothed little William's strawberry-blond hair and smiled.

Lawrence pulled open the door. A great breath of rain-laden wind greeted us. The candles on the table flickered but burned on. We stepped outside. I ran to the truck and clambered into the cab. Lawrence and my dad climbed in on each side, sandwiching me in the middle. The rain ripped through the leaves of the trees bordering the driveway with a fierceness I'd never seen in the city.

"We are going to have quite the clean-up in the morning," Dad said.

"Let's hope the bridge doesn't get washed out." Lawrence started the engine. He shifted into Drive and turned the wipers on high. He pressed on the gas to pull out of the driveway, but a loud crack made him slam on the brake. My dad threw a protective arm across me as I flew forward, hands outstretched. A large tree crashed down, missing the windshield by mere inches. Branches scraped against steel. Leaves fluttered all around them.

"Damn it," Lawrence slammed the gearshift into Reverse and pulled away from the downed tree.

"What'll we do now?" I breathed.

"We could take the path through the forest," my dad said.

Lawrence shook his head. "It isn't safe to cross the creek right now." He put the truck in Park and turned off the engine. "You'll just have to stay with us."

My dad leaned forward, looking past me. "Are you sure there's room?"

"We'll make do." Lawrence nodded and pounded his hand on the steering wheel. His eyes flashed like lightning.

I would've sworn on the closest Bible that a wisp of smoke floated about him, like the old saying about steam coming out of your ears. Was he mad that we'd have to stay? "Are you sure it's all right? You seem pretty upset."

Lawrence sighed. "I wouldn't hear of anything else. I'm not mad at you. I'm mad that you were almost killed by a tree. In a storm we have no business being out in."

Wow. I rubbed my hand over the smooth denim of my jeans, not knowing what to say. He pushed the door open and held it for me. I slid out and ran back into the house.

Anna came around the corner wiping her hands on a white linen towel. "What's the matter? Is everyone all right? I heard an awful noise."

"A tree fell across the driveway," I explained.

"Jack and Sophie need to stay until the storm clears." Lawrence shut the door behind him.

"That's fine. Put Sophie in your room. I made up a cot in the birthing room for Henry and we can put Jack up on the sofa." Anna gestured for my dad to follow her. "Come. It's been a long night and we could all use some rest."

"I really appreciate this, Anna." Dad trailed her through the kitchen and into a small sitting area on the other side.

Lawrence grabbed a candle and gestured for me to follow him down the hallway past the birthing room. I admired his wide shoulders and narrow waist. Why hadn't I noticed how nicely he was built when I first met him at the river? I liked that Lawrence, but this one... This take-charge version of him was…dare I think it? Sexy.

He pushed open the door at the end of the hall, a Cheshire grin on his face.

"What are you grinning so big for?" I stepped through the door as Lawrence shook his head and looked at the floor.

"Nothing. Just thinking about…stuff."

His face wasn't giving anything away, so I turned to studying his room. A trunk sat at the end of a double bed. A small dresser with an oval mirror above it was pushed along the wall, and a desk with books stacked in the corner was just to the left of the window. In the corner sat a strange looking guitar. The room was tidy. Nothing was out of place. It was almost like he never stayed in it. There wasn't even a stray sock to be found. "Are you sure this is your bedroom?"

Lawrence's grin returned. "Why would you ask me that?"

"I've never seen a boy's room so clean."

He rubbed the back of his neck and placed the candle on the top of his dresser. The mirror magnified its glow, sending a warm orange hue throughout the room. "Anna makes me keep it clean—otherwise, it would probably be a disaster." He pulled open a drawer and rummaged through it, handing me a pair of boxers and a T-shirt. "Here, you can sleep in this. And there is a towel hanging on the back of the door."

I took the bundle of clothes. I was exhausted from the day, but how was I ever going to fall asleep in his bed? Wearing his *underwear* no less. My mind was already spinning around his change in manner. His sudden take-charge attitude. "Thanks. Uh…where's the bathroom?"

Lawrence pointed across the hallway. "Just across there. I'll make sure I put a candle in there too. Good night, Sophie."

"But, where are you going to sleep?"

He shrugged, but a half smile lit up his face. "Don't worry. I'll find somewhere to crash." He pulled the door shut behind him and I pressed my head to it for a moment, thinking about how he had lit those candles with just his sweet breath, how I could feel his warmth when I stood close to him, how his amber eyes seemed to see right through me, how I was so close to feeling his lips upon mine again. I shivered, but I wasn't cold.

"You know," Lawrence's husky voice murmured through the door. "It's going to drive me crazy all night that you're sleeping in my bed…in my boxer shorts."

I smiled and bit my lip. My heart tap-danced on my ribs. "Goodnight, Lawrence." I tossed the boxers and T-shirt he gave me onto the bed and stripped off my cold, wet clothes. I pulled the towel off the hook, dried myself, and then soaked up the excess rain from my hair. I draped the wet towel over the bedpost and hung my shirt and camisole, followed by my jeans and underwear on the hook on the door. Then I slipped on the soft cotton boxers and the T-shirt, which hung to my mid-thigh. I pulled the shirt up to my face and breathed his scent. It was a good smell, a comforting smell—like the smell of someone you'd known and loved your whole life.

Reluctantly, I dropped the shirt and pulled the elastic holder out of my hair. I brushed my fingers through the tangled, damp strands. Bailean's song buzzed in my mind and I hummed as I pulled down the covers and climbed into the bed. The sheets were cool and I found myself wishing Lawrence and his internal furnace were next to me. Despite how exhausted my body was, my mind spun with everything that had happened: the trip into town, the storm, the baby, the candles…the magic. Magic was real. Dragons were real.

Did that mean Lawrence's theory of parallel worlds was real, too? Did I live here but really belong in some other place? Was my real mother still alive in that other place? I clasped my locket in my hand, wishing more than anything that it were true.

The storm raging mirrored the storm of questions in my head, but the rhythmic pounding of the rain lulled me to sleep. My eyelids fluttered closed as I grew warm under the blankets.

I didn't know how long I'd been sleeping when a sharp crack of thunder made me bolt upright in bed. It shook the house and when my eyes adjusted, I swore I saw a face at the window lit up by the blanket of lightning above. I drew the covers up under my chin, like the homemade quilt could protect me. The room grew unusually warm and sweat beaded on my forehead. I tried not to breathe and I waited for another patch of lightning to light up the window. My eye was drawn to a sparkling green mist twinkling in the corner of the room. Bailean's song softly filled the recesses of my mind and eased my fright. I relaxed back into the pillows, closing my eyes once again.

~I told you I'd protect you.

My hair was gently brushed away from my face. A soft kiss pressed upon my lips. I smiled, imagining that Lawrence had snuck into the room.

~Would you like it if he did?

"Yes," I whispered. Deep down, I longed for his touch. Ached for it. So much so, that I dreamed of his fingers lightly tracing the curve of my hip, the dip and swell of the muscles in my arms. A warmth spread down my chest and between my legs. I kicked off the covers, the cool air on my damp skin a relief.

Lawrence's voice infiltrated my dream. *We can be two halves made whole, Sophie.*

It sounded so delicious—like a poem from long ago. A gentle but firm pressure made me arch my back and reach out, grabbing for something that wasn't there. It was a dream after all and one couldn't hold onto a dream.

chapter sixteen

I woke to the good-natured yelling of men. Rays of warm sun streamed through the window. I stretched and tossed off the covers, taking a good look at Lawrence's room in the daylight.

Tiny bright lights sparkled on the windowsill. A shiver ran up my spine as I remembered the arousing dream I'd had last night. I ran my hands through the tangles of my hair, mulling over the feelings and sensations. They were so strong, like the dream had been real.

Flinging my legs off the edge of the bed, I stared at the sparkling at the window. I eased myself toward it as if it was a huge hairy spider that needed to be dispatched. The hair on my body rose. The shiny flakes of mica and bits of something softer, like moss, came into focus on the sill. I pressed my finger into the bits and held it up to study in the sunlight. The tiny flakes were green, like the flakes I'd found in my room. The other stuff was like flocking, or the shed velvet from an antler. I thought of the reindeer from the tapestry and tried to dust off my finger, the fuzzy bits tumbled to the floor, but like glitter, the mica flakes wouldn't budge. A warm breeze filtered through the open window. Had the window been open last night? No. It had been closed against the storm. Outside, Henry, Lawrence, and my dad were already cutting up the tree that fell across the driveway.

I turned from the window, intent on asking Lawrence about the glittery bits. I reached for my clothes, but they weren't on the back of the door. Perhaps Anna had grabbed them to hang on the line while I was still sleeping. She'd probably opened the window as well.

There was a pile of papers on Lawrence's desk. I sifted through the drawings. One was of a castle at the top of a steep hill. There were smaller drawings, which looked like parts of the castle, others looked like interior views. The drawings were highly detailed, with notes like *tower room, always guarded* and *dungeon entrance—spiral stairs—not good for combat* written here and there in tiny, but meticulous letters. I shuffled through the other drawings: more details of the castle walls, decorative gates, a portrait of an elderly man. Lawrence had captured the kind eyes and smiling mouth beautifully. The word *Gafford* was scrawled under the drawing. Where had I heard that word before?

The memory swirled in on me. The man in the castle hallway—the one in the green surcoat. He'd told the queen that Gafford had been taken to the dungeon. I traced the tiny letters, my mind working on a solution. I put the drawing down.

The last one in the pile was a drawing of me. He'd drawn me in a thoughtful moment, head raised. Lawrence was very good, and I found myself flattered that he'd chosen me as a subject. I set the drawing gently on the pile on the desk. I was good at drawing animals, and portraits of people when I took my time, but Lawrence's skill was instantly recognizable. He'd drawn me from memory.

I pulled open the bedroom door and wandered into the hallway. Samantha was cooing at the baby so I popped my head into the birthing room. "How's little William?"

Samantha looked up with bright eyes and a smile on her face. "Here, because of you." She gestured for me to come into the room. I obliged and sat on the edge of the bed, tucking my hair behind my ears.

Samantha held out the baby to me. "Here, take him for a minute while I fix my pillows."

The baby lay in the crook of my arm before I could reply. The little bundle of warmth was soothing. The small noises he made endearing. I held a finger next to his hand and William's long thin fingers wrapped around it. I cooed at him and hummed a bar of the song I'd sung to him last night. I smiled as he blinked his blue-gray eyes up at me and wondered what thoughts were forming in his mind. Was he even capable of such things? "He's just as I pictured him last night."

Samantha clasped my arm and gave it a squeeze. "You were wonderful. I've never heard anyone sing like you. If you knew how to play a lute you'd make a killing at the Renaissance festivals. Henry can introduce you to some people. Everyone always listens to what he says, I'm sure he'd have no problem convincing them to give you a job."

My face filled with heat. I stared at the baby so Samantha wouldn't see the blush creeping into my cheeks. "What's a lute?"

"It's kind of like a guitar, but its predecessor. Come to think of it…I think Lawrence plays."

I remembered the funny looking guitar in Lawrence's room. That must be what she was talking about.

"The two of you would make a great team."

Lawrence and I a team? The blush on my cheeks deepened as I recalled the dream. I shook my head. "I don't know about singing in front of people… I'll think about it." I handed the baby back to his mom.

"You're a natural with him, you know." Samantha swaddled William tighter and put him in the bassinet by the side of the bed.

"I've always liked babies." I tossed my hair over my shoulder. "How long will you stay here with Anna and Lawrence?"

Samantha leaned back into the pillows and sighed. "Oh, a couple of days. But we'll head home soon."

I nodded and stood. "I'm going to see if I can find Anna. I think she took my wet clothes to dry them or something because they're missing this morning."

"Oh, that's Anna, always one step ahead of everyone else."

"Can I get you anything before I leave?"

"Thank you, Sophie, but I'm fine." She gestured with her head to the content little bundle. "I'm just going to nap a little while the baby isn't hungry."

"Okay. I'll see you later." I turned to leave the room, eyes grazing the tapestry on the wall. The sudden shock of the scene made me stop in my tracks. I stepped closer. The stag wasn't with the sheep in the hills this morning—the tapestry had changed.

"It's beautiful, isn't it?" Samantha said.

I nodded, giving her a small smile before waving and stepping into the hallway. No one was in the kitchen, which meant that Anna was more than likely in the garden. I shoved my feet into my sneakers and grimaced. They were wet and cold. I'd have to set them in the sun to dry once I was home. I walked out the door and into the summer sunshine.

My clothes swayed on the laundry line attached to the house. The men hauled brush and limbs from the fallen tree out of the driveway. Shirtless, Lawrence's olive skin glistened in the sun. He had rolled up the cuffs of his khaki pants. The top of a pair of blue plaid boxers peeked out of his waistband. I was suddenly very aware that I was still wearing his boxers, too. His muscles bunched under his skin as he pulled a branch away from the pile and dragged it toward the forest. Almost unconsciously, I ran my fingers down my throat, lost in lusty thoughts, as he strode back to grab another limb. I'd never before thought of a man as being beautiful, but Lawrence was a fine example. I could stand here all day and watch him work.

"You're awake."

I had to shield my eyes from the brightness to see Anna strolling toward me. She wore her old-fashioned, wide-brimmed straw hat and carried a pair of shears. A woven basket with a long handle hung over her arm. Flowers and plant cuttings were piled high in the basket.

"Good morning." I smiled and pulled my jeans off the laundry line. They were a little stiff, but at least they were dry, unlike my sneakers. "Thanks for hanging my clothes."

Anna dismissed me with a wave. "Wasn't me, dear. You'll have to thank Lawrence for that."

He'd been in the room! My eyes shifted to Lawrence dragging another limb. He glanced at me over his shoulder and I waved. He winked and smiled back. My heart lifted with sudden joy.

"Men!" Anna said. "They're all little boys when it comes right down to it. Still love to play with sticks and rocks no matter how old they are. Will you join me for breakfast?"

Reluctantly, I pulled my gaze away from Lawrence. "I'm going home, but thank you. And thank you for letting us stay last night. It would've been a really miserable walk home in the storm."

"That's what neighbors are for, dear." Anna stuffed the gardening shears into the basket on top of the cuttings. "I hope you understand why I asked Lawrence to bring you over last night."

I cocked my head. "He said you needed me to help with the baby..."

Anna smiled and patted my arm. "I didn't need your help, child; you needed mine."

"What?" I blurted. What did she mean by that? Anna was the midwife, not me.

The old woman sauntered away and into the house. My gaze followed her. She had a habit of leaving me with unanswered questions. Was last night just some ploy to get me to finally believe in magic? To put away the years of self-doubt and mistrust? In the hazy glow of the candlelight, I had to admit, I'd believed. But in the light of day, was the conviction still there?

I looked at Lawrence again. His gaze held mine. The locket grew hot on my breast, the skin on my arms tingled, and the hair on the back of my neck rose.

Yes. I believed. I smiled at Lawrence and he smiled back.

Drawing a cleansing breath, I walked over to my dad. "I'm going to walk home. Hopefully take a shower."

Dad wiped his brow with his shirt and then readjusted his glasses. "We're almost done here. I'll be along shortly."

"Okay." I turned to Lawrence. "I'll see you around?"

He pointed to his T-shirt and shorts and grinned. "I'll have to get those back at some point."

I blushed. "Oh, yeah. I'll put them in the laundry and give them back this afternoon. See you later." I headed toward the forest path that led across the creek.

"Be careful, honey!" my dad yelled after me. "The stream is probably pretty full after so much rain."

I waved away his concerns and turned on my heel to yell back. "I will. And congratulations, Henry!"

"Thanks!" Henry waved goodbye.

As I turned and jogged down the stairs and into the shade of the forest, footsteps pounded behind me. Lawrence called my name. As he drew close, I smiled. I wanted to touch him so bad. I reached for his arm. Let my finger trail down his browned skin. "So, you came into my room this morning?"

Lawrence dipped his head and grinned. "I had to see how cute you looked in my under clothes."

I took a step closer to him. "And?"

"And what?"

I punched him in the arm. "What do you mean, 'and what'?"

Lawrence laughed and put his hands on my waist, tugging me forward. My heart jumped into my throat as he leaned down. His lips were soft. He smelled so good, but a wave of self-consciousness hit me. I hadn't brushed my teeth or even drank a glass of water yet this morning. I probably had the worst morning breath. As if he'd read my thoughts, Lawrence pulled away. "I'd better get back."

I bit my lip and reached for his hand. I didn't want him to stop, but I didn't want him to kiss me with dragon breath either. "Wait." My mind raced with all the things I wanted to ask him—the glitter, the face in the window, the fact that he always seemed to know what was on my mind. "Why…why does it seem like you always know what I'm thinking? It's a little unnerving. Am I just that easy to read?"

He grinned and looked at me through his lashes. "Well, you are kind of easy to read. You wear your emotions on your face and in the curve of your shoulders." He hesitated, massaging his thumb along the fleshy part between my fingers and thumb.

"But?" I prodded.

"We…you and me, we have special powers."

I raised my eyebrows. "I know that… well, I'm learning."

"Lighting candles is just the lowliest form of our gift." Lawrence straightened and squared his shoulders.

I shrugged. "What do you mean?"

Lawrence's eyes flashed. His pupils shrank to slits. *~Well, we can do this, for one.*

"You just talked in my head like…" *Bailean.* He even sounded like the dragon. I wondered if my mind made everyone sound the same. But the deer the other night, he didn't sound like Bailean.

~You heard me?

"Of course I heard you! I just said I did!"

~See how your mind is open to me? Lawrence smiled and licked his lips. *~That's why I can read you so well.*

"So how do I do it?" He definitely had the advantage and I didn't like that.

~You already do it—you just weren't doing it consciously. Remember the first time we were in your room together? When you thought I was a prude?

My cheek grew red hot. I didn't mean it.

~You meant it then…you just don't think that anymore. He grinned. *~Picture a thread that connects us. Then just send the thoughts you want me to know down the wire.*

I screwed my face up in concentration. I pictured a silver thread connecting us, like the telephone wire stretched between poles. A hot spot grew on my forehead as the thread snaked between us. I felt a jolt of energy as it connected to Lawrence. I sent him a thought and imagined it pulsing over the thread. *~Like this?*

Lawrence's laugh reverberated in my mind. *~You shouldn't have to try that hard, but yes.*

I narrowed my eyes at him. *~So you have been reading my mind this whole time? Even the first day I met you?*

"More like your emotions. I tried not to pry too much, since you hadn't given me permission. But some things came through the static loud and clear."

My stomach sank. I'd had some mighty unnerving thoughts about him…especially last night. He was going to think I was some kind of slut.

Lawrence laughed and pulled me close, his chin rested on my head. I heard his heart beat—steady, strong. "It's okay. I had those thoughts, too. I don't think you're anything but a normal young woman."

I pulled back to look in his face. "How do you have magic?"

"I am a child of Brindle, like you."

Both of us from a different world? It couldn't be a coincidence that my grandmother's house and Anna's house were so close. I had this sudden feeling that Lawrence and I were meant to find each other. That maybe we'd known each other in some other life.

I stood on my tiptoes, wrapped my arms around his neck. "Kiss me."

Lawrence licked his lips. His heart pounded against my shoulder. He dipped his head and suddenly his lips were on mine, soft at first, and then more demanding. My blood surged through my veins. I met his demand with my own, breathing in the scent of him. He pulled away, panting, unable to speak for the want of air.

~Last night when you helped bring William into the world, did you feel a difference in your power?

"Y-yes." I stammered, thinking about the birth. "When I held him in my hands, I had this impression that anything in the world was possible." *Like I could sing anything into existence.*

Lawrence raised his eyebrows. Shit! I'd have to learn how to keep thoughts to myself as well as broadcasting them. Surely there was a way to keep my mind from leaking all over the place.

~It takes practice…speaking with your mind and only letting out what you intend to be known.

Lawrence tightened his grip on me. The little string in my core coiled and burned. His mouth moved over mine and I followed his lead. He was definitely not the strange, inexperienced frog-boy I'd thought him to be when we first met. He deepened our kiss to prove me right. Then he picked me up and crushed me against a smooth birch trunk. I didn't protest. The hard surface pressed into my back. Lawrence's mouth moved from my lips and down my neck. I didn't even protest as he caressed my scars, explored them with his fingers and then his mouth. The world around me disappeared—just as it had last night when we'd stood in the kitchen. It was just me and Lawrence and nothing between us but the need to belong to each other. I clung to him. His lips moved over my bared skin searing his touch in my mind. He let out a moan and pulled away.

"Don't stop," I whispered. I would burst into flames if he continued, but I didn't care. My body craved to be a phoenix. To be reborn in his embrace.

"I must." Lawrence's breathing was ragged. He ran a hand through his hair. "You make me feel all these things…stir up passions I've long ignored."

I grabbed his hands and pulled him back into me. "You don't have to ignore them. I don't want you to."

Lawrence buried his head in my shoulder. His breath pooled in the hollow of my neck. "This connection between us…it makes our desire…our longing to be together…stronger. Who knew it would blossom so quickly?" He chuckled.

"You mean back when I thought you were a frog-loving weirdo at the creek?" I giggled.

"Yeah." Lawrence straightened up and grinned back.

"I don't think that anymore."

"Yes, you do, but now you like it." His lips pressed into mine again, but he pulled away before it could get steamy. "Jack is probably getting suspicious. I've been gone too long."

I sighed. "I guess you're right. What are you going to tell him?"

"I'll tell him that I escorted you home, just in case the creek was still raging."

"You can meet me here later though, right? When you're finished clearing the tree?"

Lawrence took a step back, his hands dropped from my waist. "I'll be here. Four o'clock, sharp."

"It's a date."

He climbed the stairs. At the top he turned and waved before disappearing. I turned and started down the path. The mid-morning air was still cool in the forest, the humidity carried away by last night's storm. The creek had swollen and no longer meandered through the woods but crashed like a bear in the underbrush.

"Hello, beauties," I purred to the ferns growing along the pathway. I stroked a finger down one of the fronds, and the fern stretched toward me, blushing red. "I'm glad you weathered the storm all right."

Bluish-purple irises stood tall at the water's edge. I cupped a bloom in my hand and wondered if it had been me or Anna that had made the coneflower turn colors last week. I closed my eyes and pictured the iris in my hand—the beautiful golden yellow beard, the delicate white stripes that flowed into a blue petal fall. Then I pictured each petal turning a bright red, like the blush on Lawrence's cheeks when he'd walked in on me dressing. I giggled, opened my eyes, and let go of the flower. The stem huddled with its sisters, a bright red bloom in a sea of blue.

If I could make flowers change colors, light candles—and dare I believe it—sing babies out of wombs, what else was I capable of? I was suddenly drunk with my own power. I wanted to turn toadstools into faeries, make the trees sing. I wanted to ride on the wing of a dove—no. I wanted to be the dove. To float on the swirling currents up into the clouds.

The stones I'd used to step across the creek before were hidden in its watery depths. I wrapped my clothes in a tight bundle and held them to my chest as I stepped into the stream. The cold water rushed halfway up my legs, surprising me with its strength and fiercely cold temperature. I closed my eyes and imagined the water running warm. The current flowing past me warmed like bath water. Then a strange sound, like the pop of an air bubble surfacing, made me look down at the stream. I gasped at the white belly of a dead fish floating off. Then another rolled to the surface by my knees. Was I doing that? Was the water too warm for the fish? I immediately pushed the thought of warm water out of my head and struggled to cross the fast moving current, each step carefully placed. I'd have to put more thought into using the magic inside me. Shivering, I pulled myself out of the creek and raced up the path toward home.

Home. Is that how I thought of it now?

I chastised myself all the way up the path, until the iron fence came into view. How could I have been so thoughtless? I'd read enough faerie tales to know that there was always a price for using magic. So what price was I going to pay?

I pushed those thoughts from my mind and walked quickly through the field toward the house. The sun was warm on my shoulders, and Lawrence's kisses still lingered on my skin. I thought back to how the feel of his lips on mine made me feel breathless, the soft caress of his fingers along my collarbone. If I were a star, I'd be the one glowing the brightest in the sky. At this moment, my world was perfect. The boy next door was beautiful and sweet. I'd discovered within myself amazing abilities. And my anxiety had kept its ugly head buried in the sand for a whole twenty-four hours—the longest I'd gone without a flare up in the last seven years. I almost congratulated myself. The gate creaked as I opened it and jogged across the back yard.

I turned the handle to the back door and walked in, a smile still plastered on my face. The warmth of Lawrence's hands lingered on my body. A shuffle in the kitchen drew my attention out of my head.

Two men stood before me.

My stomach clenched. Dread iced my limbs.

One of the men stood cross-armed by the refrigerator. He was massive; hulk-like muscles bunched under the sleeves of his shirt. The creepy delivery guy, Wilhelm, smirked, an emerald ring gleaming from his finger. I turned to flee, but a third man stood between me and the door.

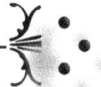

chapter seventeen

My guts twisted with the sickening click of the latch. I took in the light brown hair, the blue eyes. I didn't want to look, but my eyes traveled down to the intertwined dragons on his belt buckle. He was older, but unmistakable. King Stuart.

He reached out, long fingers tracing the side of my face, his thumb skimming over my bottom lip. Hot bile crawled up my throat, leaving a burning track.

~Lawrence! He's here! I need you. I hoped he would hear me, but my mind was so scattered that I couldn't picture the thread that connected us.

Wilhelm peered over the king's shoulder and smirked at me. "I told you I found her, sire," he said. His slit of a mouth curled at the edges in a grin. He stood so close to the king that if he were to turn around abruptly he'd probably break the guy's nose. "Looks just like the queen, doesn't she?"

The king narrowed his eyes. "The resemblance is uncanny. I didn't expect her to be this old though. That plays into my favor."

"What do you want from me?" I whispered.

The front door opened and my heart fell into my toes. I turned toward Dad as he walked in, his nose in the mail he was flipping through. King Stuart pressed his body against my back, his hand snaking over my mouth. He made a shushing sound in my ear.

"I hope you're almost done in the shower, bug!" Jack sauntered into the kitchen, oblivious of the danger lurking just before him. I tried to scream, but the giant leapt into action, pinning Dad's arms behind his back.

"What the hell?" my dad yelled. The mail fluttered to the floor.

Wilhelm rounded on my dad, punching him in the gut. He doubled over, trying to catch his breath.

I wrenched my head out of the king's clasp. "I'll do anything." I panted. Tried to catch my breath. "Just don't hurt my dad." ~*Lawrence! Please hear me!* I sent him an image of the men in our house.

"Oh, you're very accommodating now, aren't you?" Stuart chuckled. "Much more accommodating than Maria ever was."

Inside, I flinched at her name. "Please!" I pleaded to both the king and Lawrence—willing him with all my might to hear me. My eyes met Dad's. "Do you believe me now?"

"I'm sorry," he said, his voice cracking. He struggled in the giant's hold.

The heavy drape of guilt and anxiety that had stunted me for fifteen years flew away. I ran toward Dad, but the king reeled me back in with a vice-like grip.

Wilhelm whacked my dad in the back of the head with the pommel of a knife. His head drooped to his chest. The image of my real father being murdered flashed before my eyes. I screamed. Tears stung the backs of my eyes. The giant proceeded to bind his ankles and wrists.

"No!" I screamed again.

"Relax. He'll just have a little bit of a headache, dearie. No permanent damage done," the king purred. He shoved me toward Wilhelm. "Tie her up."

I glared at Wilhelm as he strode toward me. His snicker seemed to echo off the kitchen's shiny surfaces.

"It will be my pleasure." He shoved me, turning my body around so that my face flattened on the windowpane of the kitchen door. I grasped for the knob, struggling to unlock it. I needed to get away, but Wilhelm pressed into me. "I don't know where you think you're going."

My breath fogged up the glass. A thin, prickly rope was wrapped around my wrists. My neck grew warm as Wilhelm shoved his face into the crook between neck and shoulder. His damp breath chilled me to the core. What had been arousing just minutes before with Lawrence turned perverse. "Share some sweet kisses and I might go easy on you."

Tears burned down my cheeks. "Not on your life."

"Wilhelm," the giant chided in a deep voice. "Now is not the time."

Wilhelm twirled me around and pushed me forward, his grip like an iron brand around my arm. "Shut up, Dougal."

The men marched me upstairs. My thoughts whirled. Of course—the tapestry. It was a window into another world, just as Anna had said. Why hadn't I thought of it earlier? All the clues had been there. And Wilhelm was here when I'd found the tapestry under the window seat. I should have tried harder to put the pieces together. My heart fell into my stomach.

When we entered the room, I nearly gasped. It had been turned upside down. All of my belongings were scattered, my bed curtains torn from the rails. What had they been looking for? The wardrobe stood ajar. I gasped as I became aware of the change in my tapestry. The stag was gone. Just as it had been this morning in Anna's house. Wilhelm steered me forward. I braced myself for the smack into the wall.

I was suddenly weightless, and yet I felt myself moving forward through a deep blackness, by gravity or some other force I couldn't name. My inner fire flared, making my throat burn. Were the king and his men behind me? Or had they thrown me into a part of their world where I would never be found? Would I ever find my way back home? My mind reeled as my body shuttled toward some unknown ending.

Abruptly I stopped and pitched forward. By the time the world stopped spinning, I was retching over a wooden floor. I'd just portaled through a piece of art they way I'd always dreamed, but I felt like I was in a nightmare.

Wilhelm, Dougal, and Stuart loomed over me. A pile of clothes landed at my feet. "Put these on. Lawrence, give her a hand, would you?"

A pair of strong hands slipped under my arms and lifted me from the floor as the other men strode off. I looked up into amber eyes. These eyes were not soft, but sharp as flint. I recoiled, managed to swallow the burning in my throat. "L-Lawrence?"

He tugged the blouse over the T-shirt I was wearing— his T-shirt. "It will go better for you if you don't fight," he whispered.

~Lawrence! I need you.

Lawrence's eyes flashed brightly. *~Don't speak to me as if you know me.*

My eyes grew wide and I drew in a long breath. *~What do you mean? How did you get here so fast? How did you know?*

Lawrence shook his head, eyes narrowing. *~I can't answer your questions right now.*

What the hell? My mind scrambled for a reply. I sized him up like a prize fighter. Tall. Thin. Muscular. Olive skin, dark, handsome features, golden eyes. Was he still my Lawrence?

A grim line scored his face.

~How can you work for King Stuart? He took Maria! He killed my real father! I bit my lip, holding back furious tears. What about the stolen moments we'd shared this morning? Had it meant nothing to him? Had his words been nothing more than empty promises?

~Being one of the king's guards was the easiest way to get close to him. Step into the dress and stop asking questions.

A hard wall pushed against my mind. He'd blocked me out. Hurt draped over my shoulders like a cloak. I lifted one foot, and then the other as Lawrence pulled the kirtle over my shorts. How did he get here so fast? Did he know those men were in our kitchen? What if he was only kissing me to stall in order to give the king's men more time to get to me? My stomach suddenly felt like I'd swallowed a pound of lead.

Lawrence loosened the rope binding my wrists.

Pins and needles traveled up my arms. I sucked air through my teeth at the unpleasant sensation. When the worst of it passed, I wiggled my hands through the sleeves of the dress and pulled up the kirtle. Lawrence pulled the laces tight and fastened them, his fingers brushing my breast. I blushed at the hot awareness that traveled down my torso. He was tying me up for God's sake. Taking me prisoner!

Lawrence seized my locket. It had fallen out of my shirt, probably when I fell through the portal. He rubbed his thumb along the etching on the face, and then pulled it with a swift jerk. The chain broke away and I started to protest. His hand covered my mouth and he leaned into me, his eyes just inches from mine. The scowl on his face squelched my outcry. He dropped the locket into the front of his shirt with a furtive glance over his shoulder.

Why was Lawrence acting this way? What did he want with my locket?

He pointed to the woolen slippers on the floor. "Change your shoes."

Using my big toes I pried off my sneakers and stepped into the woolen shoes. The other men loitered in the kitchen, drinking. Where had the giant gone?

"Why you being so nice to the girl? Ya think she's your sister?" Wilhelm mocked and threw his head back, laughing.

~*I'm sorry.*

~*For wh—*

The impact of Lawrence's hand on my cheek made me sees stars. He tossed a cloak around my shoulders and pulled my hands roughly to him. Why was he doing this? Minutes ago he was crushing kisses on me in the forest. Now it seemed he was a completely different person.

He looped the rope around my wrists again, but it wasn't as tight as when Wilhelm had done it.

"We're ready to travel." Lawrence pulled the hood of the cloak over my head. I was glad as tears were trembling on my lashes, but I didn't want him to see me cry.

With a smirk, Wilhelm gestured toward the door. "By all means then, *Casanova*. Our king is anxious to get to know her better."

Lawrence didn't rise to his own defense, but his shoulders stiffened before he yanked me toward the door.

The cabin door was pushed open without him even touching the doorknob. The rattle of bridles and the stomp of hooves echoed in the night. I was escorted outside. I could see little but the stars shining above, a distant flicker of a candle in a window. It seemed the world had turned its back on me. Closed its eyes so that it could plead innocent of any wrongdoing. A strong grip encircled my upper arms. The giant lifted me onto a large, black horse. He had the strength of Atlas. He met my eyes briefly. I expected to see an intimidating expression, but instead I saw empathy, maybe even a little guilt.

"Why?" I whispered.

In an instant, the look was wiped from his face. The hard stare returned to his hazel eyes before he turned away.

Lawrence climbed up behind me. His arms wrapped around me as the giant handed him the reins.

King Stuart called to Wilhelm and gestured to the cottage with his head. "Burn it."

"No!" I cried. "You can't!" It was the only way I knew to get back home.

"What's the matter, sweetheart?" Wilhelm sneered. "Afraid you'll never see dear old Jack again?"

I looked away. I had to be smart about this. I couldn't give him any more ammunition against me. Tears burned twin paths down my cheeks.

Dougal cleared his throat. "The tapestry has done its job. We've no more use of the old midwife's cottage."

His comment made me pay attention to the cottage before me for the first time. Thatched roof, flowery vines creeping up the chimney. It was a near perfect twin of Anna's cottage in Castleton. The room she'd shown me wasn't the room I'd been born in. The room where I'd been born was in this little cottage in Brindle. So close, yet so far away.

The giant's horse pranced in a circle. "Light it up, Wilhelm, as Stuart commanded."

Wilhelm saluted with a gleam in his eye. "Yes, sir, with pleasure."

I choked back a sob as flames licked the thatched roof of the cabin housing the mirror of my tapestry. What would happen to the tapestry in my room? How would I get home now?

Flames quickly consumed the thatched roof and worked their way down the sidewalls. I turned away from the searing heat.

Wilhelm laughed harshly and urged his mount forward until I could see the fire reflected in his eyes. "This is just the beginning, bitch."

I chafed in opposition to the term; my heart grew steely in its armored cage. I was no one's dog.

Dougal and his horse trotted off behind the king, and Lawrence gave our mount a squeeze.

"Where are you taking me?"

"The castle, and it would be best if you kept your mouth shut," Lawrence replied.

I tested the fat lip his backhand had given me with my tongue. It was tender. Probably would be for a few days. I tested my link with him now that no one was watching us. *~How many like us were born in Brindle?*

    ~A few.

    ~Do you know them all?

    ~No.

I shifted in the saddle, all too aware of the proximity of his body. Lawrence's strong arms encapsulated mine, our thighs rubbed together with each step of the horse. I tried to clear my thoughts. Why was Lawrence giving me such short answers? Was he really on the king's side? Had it all been a ruse to get me to Brindle and give me to the king? Was Anna in on it?

    ~No.

Damn it. I really needed to learn to keep my thoughts to myself. I scooted forward, away from the warmth radiating off his body. I couldn't think clearly with him so close. *~What's your plan?*

    ~To get you through the night.

    ~That's it?

    ~That's enough.

chapter eighteen

The dungeon floor was cold. The only respite from its icy touch was a small pile of damp straw. I curled up in the corner and wept. The tapestry, my only portal home, was gone. The scent of the consuming flames still lingered in my hair and clothes.

The small flap at the bottom of my cell door creaked as a plate of mush was shoved through. An old woman's creaky voice carried through the passageway. "That's all you'll be getting today, so eat up."

I made no effort to rise. The pains of hunger had left yesterday. I wasn't even sure how many days had passed. I tested my bruised lip. It wasn't tender anymore. That was good, I guess. Though it didn't seem to matter much anymore. I closed my eyes as more tears flooded my cheeks.

I ran my tongue along the cracks and craters that had formed in my lips. I needed water. I bit the inside of my cheek, an old trick to get my mouth to produce saliva. It wouldn't come, but a hot spot formed deep in my core. My body convulsed as my hand flew to my stomach.

~*Lawrence?*

I waited for his answer. My blood pounded in my ears. My lungs burned from holding my breath. But no answer came. I rolled to my back. A single star shone through the small window at the top of the high-ceilinged cell. Briefly I considered wishing upon it, but it had never worked before. No tears tonight, though the loss of home cut me deeply. I was too dehydrated. The gray mantel of unconsciousness seduced me back into its arms.

rust your gut.
        I awoke with a start.
~ *Trust your gut.*

I scanned the bleak cell. *Bailean? No, Lawrence.* The sharp-edge in his voice made all the difference. But I couldn't trust him. I couldn't trust anyone—not until I knew what I was doing in Brindle. And how Lawrence got here before me. I rolled over and tried to stand, but dizziness brought me back down. I stayed still until the world stopped spinning.

How many days had I lain here? How many nights had passed? The small window high above was bright with the sun but still I shivered. How I wished those rays could warm me with their gentle touch.

I extended my arm, pretending I could twine my fingers around the rays of light. To my surprise, the pale yellow light grew fingers. It stretched toward me like an alien thing, pulsing with energy. It stroked my cheek and made my face glow warm and rosy. In a few moments, my whole body tingled with warmth. The stiffness in my muscles eased.

"Thank you," I whispered as the ray receded. With everything that had happened, I'd almost forgotten that I had the power to change things. Here I could try that power without being careful. Who would see me testing my magic in a dungeon cell? I wiped my eyes on the fabric of the cloak and ran my sleeve under my nose. It was time to buck up. I was in Brindle after all…this was where I came from, where I supposedly belonged… I just needed to think.

Through the bars of the small window in the door I could make out a large open space. Cobwebs streamed out from the iron braces that held small torches in the passageway. Well, what did I expect, enchanted dust busters to keep the dungeon clean? A cold wind howled and seeped through the barred door. It carried the bitter smell of trash, damp earth, and decaying flesh. My eyes watered from the stench.

The clamoring echoed through the dungeon. It was unlike any sound I'd ever heard. Then I realized it was the sound of footsteps on the stairs. The cavernous dungeon made it sound as if a whole army was approaching. Slowly, I crawled forward to peek out of the flap where slop was shoved in twice a day, if I was lucky.

"Grab that torch there," a guard ordered. "Let's play some cards."

"Damn," a red-haired man said. "I always forget how the devil breathes down my neck in this hell hole!"

The men broke into raucous banter. The torch taken from the wall now lit a low table. Bales of straw were arranged for the men to sit upon. They gathered their cards as they were dealt.

"Huzzah to the queen, fair faced is she…" The melody floated through the dungeon like a moth soaring out of the darkness and into the soft light of the moon. *Maria*. It was a voice I instantly recognized. Emotion welled up within me.

Clang! One of the guards kicked a cell door. The reverberation of the metal made my ears ring. "Shut it or there'll be no supper for you, devil squatter!" He turned back to his cronies at the table with a yellow-toothed smirk. "Not that she'll be getting much anyways. King Stuart said to halve her rations daily now that we've got the girl."

The girl? Were they talking about me?

"I don't believe that dragons exist." One of the guards tossed a pair of cards on the table.

"Shush!" Another guard made a pinched face. "It's treason to speak in opposition to the king."

"Play your cards! Don't matter what we think no way…" The man's voice trailed off as he stood abruptly, dropping his cards on the table.

"Stand up," he ordered.

I strained to see around the door as the other guards rose and bowed.

"Your Majesty," the head guard said.

My stomach dropped into my shoes. Not the king.

"The queen wishes to see the girl."

Not the king, but the queen. *The queen?* My lips pressed together. I scratched my ear and then patted down my hair. I must look terrible. I released the flap and stood. My head grew light and I had to lean against the door for a minute. As the dizziness from being weak and dehydrated eased, the contradicting feeling of relief that the visitor was not the king flooded my limbs. I tried to wet my lips, but my mouth was too dry. I strained, trying to see past the guards through the barred window in the door.

The head guard stammered. "I was told no one was allowed to see her but the king. Not even the queen, Sir Edward."

An elderly gentleman stepped into the light. Bears embroidered in silver flashed in contrast to his faded green coat. It was the man I had seen in the dream (or was it a memory?), though he was older now. "Surely our queen can see the prisoner and no one will be the wiser."

"I'll just be a minute." The queen's voice was soft in the cavernous space.

"But, My Lady…" The head guard removed his hat and twisted it in his hands like a dishtowel.

"Would you dare deny your queen a few minutes with a daughter she hasn't seen since her birth?"

My kneecaps shook. My fingers tightened around the bars. My mother, my *real* mother, moved into the circle of torchlight. Her dark hair glowed alongside her porcelain skin. She was beautiful in a way I would never be. Her aura spoke of elegance and patience. Yet I had seen her, in the memory Bailean had shown me, command the crowd to hail her as their new queen. Just moments after the murder of my father.

I stared, trying to hold my heart in such a way that it was indifferent to her, but a mixture of awe and resentment needled its way in.

With quick steps, the great lady approached the cell. Her eyes shone with unshed tears. "Sophinestra," she whispered. "Is it really you?"

I shrugged. The cage around my heart tightened.

"I was so hoping that braggart, Wilhelm, was mistaken, but there's no mistaking you. I feel like I'm looking into a mirror… except—" Her eyes traveled to the scars on my neck.

"Except she has her father's eyes." Edward finished the sentence for the queen and smiled gently as he approached.

Queen Gwendolyn turned to him. "Edward, please see to it that Sophinestra is given plenty of dry straw, clean water, and a blanket."

I jutted out my chin but could do nothing about the rasp of my voice. "My name is Sophie, *not* Sophinestra."

Edward nodded and turned away. Gwendolyn turned back. Her voice shook and came out in little breathy gasps. "I see. If I know Stuart, he'll only keep you down here until he's sure that you will be grateful enough to be taken away from this place to do whatever he asks. All you need to do is play your part. Can you do that?"

I blinked. I tried to keep my face still as stone, but my heart pumped overtime. What part was I expected to play?

Gwendolyn narrowed her eyes. "I know you are powerful, the Golden Dragon made sure of that, but you must also be smart. Stuart is cruel and will think nothing of using the ones you love to get to you. I am proof of that."

The head guard stepped toward them. His right eye ticked nervously. "I must insist that you take your leave now, My Lady."

The queen waved a dismissive hand. "Yes, yes. I'm coming." To me she said, "I'll be back as soon as I can manage it." With a sniffle, Gwendolyn strode across the dungeon, disappearing from sight, but I could hear the tap of her shoes on the stones as she climbed the stairs. Her footsteps faded quickly. I felt more alone than I had since I'd been unceremoniously dumped into this cell. I shook off the feeling. My mother didn't care about me anyway—she hadn't even held me when I was born. Refused to even look at me.

The cell door opened and I stepped back. Edward brought in a pail of water and a mug. He smiled apologetically. "I don't know how clean it is, but at least you won't get wet from trying to drink from the bucket. Being wet is a death sentence down here."

I nodded and cleared my throat. "I appreciate it, sir."

"Please, call me Edward." He handed me the mug and poured water in it. I gulped it down. Panting, I held it out for a refill. "Thank you."

This time I drank it more slowly, not wanting to get a stomachache, though it tasted like Heaven.

"I will push for your quick release." Edward took a bundle from the guard and handed it to me. It was a thick wool blanket. He waved a hand at the guard still standing in the cell doorway. "You heard the queen. Fetch some dry straw for the prisoner."

He waited until the guard had trudged down the corridor before speaking again. "I will come every day to make sure you have clean water and that you are kept warm." He kicked the plate of mush on the floor. "This won't do either. I'll send a servant boy down with some real food."

I wrapped the blanket around my shoulders. I'd warmed myself up, but I didn't know how long it would last, and I wasn't sure how often I could use my magick without suffering some kind of consequence. "Would it be too much to ask for some socks?"

"Socks?" Edward asked, a puzzled expression crossing his face.

Crap. What did they call socks a long time ago? "Um… stockings. My legs are cold."

"Of course." Edward nodded.

The guard who said he didn't believe in dragons entered the cell loaded down with straw. He tossed it in the corner mumbling under his breath about prisoners and special treatment.

"Watch your mouth." Edward slogged back out. "You're speaking to my granddaughter."

*Grand…*what? My heart leapt into my throat.

"She's been looked after, Sir Edward," the head guard said. "Now I must insist that you leave."

Edward clasped my hands and met my eyes. His pupils narrowed into slits so quickly that had I blinked I would've missed it. A pinching deep in the skin between my eyebrows made me open my mind to him.

~Yes, you are my granddaughter. I'm your father's father.

I nodded in understanding and watched Edward walk away, the touch of his warm hands lingering on my own.

As the days wore on, the guards grew less vigilant. The servant boy Edward had promised had brought me some long socks, thankfully made of wool and thick enough to help keep out the damp, seeping cold. I'd long ago devoured the roast beef, cooked carrots, potatoes, and bread he'd sent. Furry little visitors popped their heads out of the straw, looking for crumbs.

There were so many mice down here, none of the guards paid much attention to them…the gears in my mind whirled and clicked into place. No one paid attention to the mice! Could I? Was it possible? Would it work? At this point, almost anything was worth a try.

Pushing up a lump of straw in the corner, I draped the blanket around it. I hoped it would pass muster—hopefully, if the guards poked their head in, they would think I was sleeping. Lawrence's directions echoed in my head. *You have to believe that you can do it. You have to expect the flame to rise.* It had worked with the candles. Surely the magic would work here in Brindle—it was a place full of magic—wasn't it? Granted, I hadn't seen any since my tumble through the tapestry, but after the way Anna talked about it…

The little voice I liked to ignore scratched at my thoughts though. Could I trust what Lawrence said? I had no idea what he was up to or why he'd given me to the king so easily. For some reason, even though I questioned his motives, something made me think I could trust him about the magic part at least. He was the one who showed me how to use it back in Vermont. There was only one way to find out for sure though.

I squatted, wrapped my arms around my knees and tucked my head. Curled into a tight ball, as small as I could get, I imagined myself shrinking. Smaller than the rocks the walls of my cell were made from, smaller even than my shoe. I pictured whiskers sprouting from my cheeks and downy fur along my neck. My muscles tensed as my face twitched. Something akin to needles tried to push themselves out of my skin. My nose stung, like it was raw from a cold, and my ears were hot, sensitive. Pressure crushed my lungs until I could hardly gasp.

My tailbone burned as I imagined it growing into a long pink tail that curled out from under my skirt. I gasped for a full breath and a moan escaped from the pain drawing a breath caused. A red haze filled the room and a wave of agony rolled over me. Then, as suddenly as it had engulfed me, the pain was gone. My heart pattered like a rolling drum and my lungs expanded with cool air. The sounds of the dungeon were all around me, funneling into my alert ears. I heard water trickling over the stone floor, the shuffle of the guards snoring in the corner, someone mumbling about fleas. I held out my hands—they were curled into tiny pink paws.

I whimpered even as I celebrated. I was a mouse. I. Was. A. Mouse! A sudden sinking settled in my stomach. Would I be able to turn back?

My nose twitched with scents—the sickly-sweet smell of decaying straw, the earthen smell of stone, and the wet-dog smell of damp wool. I made my way out of the maze of fabric that were my clothes, scurried past the water pail, and gazed at my reflection in a small puddle. Amazing. I actually looked like a mouse—well, almost. My eyes were still green, and there was a patch of black on the top of my head where the hair was longer, and I was more the size of a rat—okay, so it wasn't perfect, but it would do. I grinned as I shimmied under the cell door and peeked left and right. Which way to go? A familiar tug at my core bid me to go right—deeper into the dungeon. My whiskers shivered, but I followed my gut.

Running was the only thing that kept my anxiety at bay. It lurked just under my skin. It quivered there, ready to make its entrance. The howling wind I'd heard before grew into an insistent cry. I kept tight to the wall, pausing in the dark corners every once in a while to look at my surroundings, to make sure no one was coming, but this part of the dungeon was abandoned, the doors hanging ajar. An urgent need to run as fast as my stumpy legs could carry me propelled me forward. I found it strange that the abandoned part of the dungeon was more frightening than the occupied cells. I skidded around a corner and stopped dead in my tracks. This was the end of the tunnel. There were no more twists or turns. No dark corners. But in the last cell a momentary golden light shone through a small hole in the wall.

chapter nineteen

I crept forward, tail stiff, ears alert, sticking close to the wall. The cold from the rough stones seeped through my fur. The end of the dungeon tunnel felt a million miles away. A chilling wind swirled in little eddies, ruffling my whiskers. Shivering, I squeezed my eyes into slits to protect them from the breeze. My paws were sensitive to every bump and sharp edge of the paving stones beneath them. Rising on my hind legs my body automatically used my tail for balance. I didn't even have to think about it. I patted the wall, looking for the small hole I'd seen from the entrance of the tunnel. Through the gap I popped in my head and sniffed. Musty. Dusty. Old. A streak of golden light jumped and shimmered in the dark chamber beyond.

I pulled myself up, my back feet scrabbling to catch hold of something. A bit too pudgy, I had to wiggle but finally my claws caught a ragged bit of mortar and I was able to launch myself through the gap and tumble into the darkness. Another golden spark floated into the air, briefly lighting up the room— hundreds of rolled up tapestries and gilt framed paintings littered the floor—as far as I could see. The glow faded and I held my breath, praying for another spark of—was it magic? Another spark did rise—like fireworks without the mosquitos.

King Stuart hadn't *destroyed* the tapestries like the reindeer had said. He'd hidden them.

The only way I might figure out why he'd hidden them instead of having them destroyed was to unroll the tapestries and see what doorways I could find. But I couldn't do that as a mouse. They were just too heavy. My anxiety spiked as I remembered the pain of transforming. Would it hurt just as much to return to my true form? I chewed the inside of my lip—I couldn't think of any other options. With the tapestries rolled up, even if I did crawl into them, I wouldn't be able to see much, and I couldn't do what I needed to do as a small bit of fur.

Face your fears. You learned to sleep in a room with that damned wardrobe in it; you can learn to do this. I closed my eyes, took a deep breath, and called in the tail. It coiled up and disappeared with a pop making me stagger a bit—I might actually miss the extra balance a tail provided, but the change wasn't so bad. Not nearly as painful as shrinking had been. I stretched my fingers and wiggled my toes. A streak of heat raced down my limbs. I grew nervous again, but shook my head. My ears didn't flap. Long hair tumbled around my shoulders. I stood on my feet, a bit shaky, but all seemed in order…except one thing. Unfortunately, clothes did not appear as my fur vanished.

Great. Well, at least I'm alone.

The sheer number of rolled up tapestries were a little overwhelming. I wound in between them, trying to see if there was any rhyme or reason to how they had been piled. Where do I even start? I grabbed the nearest one and lugged it. The tapestry made a thump as it hit the floor. Sparks lit up the room like a cloud of dust.

I got on my hands and knees and unrolled it. The tapestry was large—about eight feet long and as wide as I was tall. The scene glowed when I ran my hand over it. White capped mountains, a large river cutting through a flowering plain. It was pretty, but where would it lead? I shivered. It'd probably be cold—especially with no clothes. I dragged it toward the wall before pulling a second down and unrolling it.

This tapestry showed a small cottage covered in ivy at the edge of a forest. A fawn peered from the underbrush. Again, pretty, but not very helpful. I needed something I recognized. I dragged it toward the wall and dumped it, too.

The third tapestry I drew down was a port. Ships with slender masts and colorful sails were tied to docks. Small triangular flags atop the main mast fluttered in the wind. The last thing I needed was a bunch of pirates. I dragged it over and returned for the next tapestry, sweat beading on my forehead. The tapestries were heavy, but I was determined to find something that would help. As I prodded the fourth one open with my foot, I shrieked with excitement.

The tapestry was certainly worth the labor it took to get to it. It was a map of the kingdom—of Brindle. Perhaps it would transport me to a clothing shop. I smiled as I imagined the look on the owner's face when a naked girl walked out of his back room.

The castle was situated in the center with roads that led to it from each direction. The port was at the end of one of these roads. Concentric circles radiated from the castle. Houses and merchants were labeled in each section, but it was the black square that caught my attention. I ran my fingers over it but drew them away quickly. My fingers—I rubbed them together—they were covered in soot. The smell of wood burning wafted in the air. My heart ached for the tapestry that was burnt down with the cottage. Did that mean the tapestry in my room was destroyed as well? Did destroying one of the tapestries render its twin powerless?

I pulled more tapestries out of the heaping pile and dragged them to their respective sections. One pile for tapestries with actual buildings in them, and another for tapestries with only landscapes. I didn't find anything near as exciting as the map tapestry, and the muscles in my back ached from the effort. Intending to take a short break, I sat down, but the hair on the back of my neck stood up. Slowly, I slid off the tapestry I'd sat on and unrolled it.

It was black. Totally black. I leaned down and sniffed the loops of wool. They didn't smell charred. I ran my fingers over the surface. No sparks, no tingles of magic—nothing. It was like it was dead. Is this what happens to the tapestry when its twin is destroyed? If it was, what would Dad think when he saw the change in the tapestry hanging in my room?

I shuddered and started to pull it out of the way when I heard a noise. Stumbling to the small opening in the wall, I pressed my face against the rough surface and peered through. One of the guards was making a lot of racket at the tunnel entrance.

"Crap!" I turned my options over in my mind. There were too many tapestries left to unroll to finish now. I didn't want the guards to get suspicious of the lump in the cell…or realize I'd vanished. I'd have to come back tonight when no one would bother checking on me. I pictured my mousey self and after a handful of painful moments that made me hold my breath and pray for release, I squirmed through the hole again and dashed down the corridor.

chapter twenty

An involuntary squeak popped out of me as a heavy foot stomped just a hair's breadth from my tail. I squirmed under the cell door and scrambled for the corner where the toes of my shoes peeked from the edge of the cloak.

"Damn mice." One of the guards fumbled with the flap at the bottom of the cell door and the scrape of a plate being shoved through it echoed off the walls.

Diving under the cloak, I tunneled through the straw and hoped the guard wouldn't notice that my "body" wasn't moving.

The door banged on its hinges and made the walls quake as the guard shook the bars. "Wake up and eat if you want it warm."

I waited until the guard's footsteps faded then let out a pent-up breath. I turned, surprised at a shuffling in the straw behind me. My ears went erect. My whiskers stiffened. Then a little pink nose emerged, followed by two deep brown eyes in a gray head. The other mouse leapt toward me. I shoved out my paw, knocking him in the nose. He tumbled away, regained his feet, looked over his shoulder, and decided I wasn't worth pursuing. I stretched my arms and legs as he bounced through the straw and out between the bars. Good riddance.

The whiskers receding made my cheeks burn. As I shifted form, a shocking streak of pain ran up my spine and I yelped. I rubbed my hands together to warm them and pulled the blanket I'd stuffed with straw around my shoulders. I snatched up the stockings and pulled them over my knees. This "no clothes" thing would not work. I could almost hear Lawrence chuckling in my ear. I dropped the cloak, yanked the shift and kirtle on, and stepped into my shoes. The boxer shorts were crumpled in the straw. I really didn't want to put on dirty underwear. I'd have to go without. With my foot, I scooted them into the corner and covered them with straw.

Picking up the plate, I sniffed the roasted leg of chicken and scooped a few peas into my palm, letting them roll off and into my mouth. A delicious, sweet glaze over them made my mouth water. I picked the leg clean and actually licked the glaze off my fingers. It seemed my appetite was returning. That was good because I'd need my strength if I was going to find a way out of here.

I poured water into the mug Edward had given me and chugged it down as I rehashed the day. It'd gone okay. I'd found other tapestries, and with them, hope of going home. I just had to find the right tapestry—the twin of the one in Anna's birthing room—it suddenly hit me. Or the dragon tapestry in Gran's room. My chances of going home were suddenly doubled.

My thoughts wandered back to the black tapestry. I wondered if my first instinct about it was right. That its twin had been destroyed.

Tonight. Tonight I will go back.

I yawned and stretched my sore muscles. With hunger fading and thoughts of escape dancing in my mind, my eyelids fluttered. What seemed like a few minutes later, I was startled awake by keys rattling in the lock. My cell door protested against being opened. Two tall shadows loomed over me. The moonlight accommodated me by lighting their faces.

My heart jumped when I saw Lawrence, but then anger ripped through me. The other shadow was the king, a confident sneer plastered his face. He wiped his lips with his wrist and gave me a once-over. I made no attempt to rise, but swatted at that familiar pinch in my forehead that told me someone wanted in.

~Are you well?

~I'm tired and cold—isn't that what you'd expect when someone's been locked in a dungeon?

"You will come with me now, dear Sophinestra. I believe you've had enough mice for company." King Stuart's tone was sarcastic and jovial as if we shared a great joke. Little did he know that the joke was on him. If he only knew how close he was to the truth.

Lawrence's eyebrows arced over his amber eyes.

I turned my gaze away from him and settled it on the king. "I have a feeling the mice are better company than you two."

Stuart laughed. "Come, my little lark. Soon it will be time for you to sing for me."

I hugged my arms to my chest. If the king took me out of the dungeon how would I get back to the tapestries? There was one in that room that led home. I could feel it in my bones. I frowned and shook my head. "I won't."

~Please, Sophie, don't push him. You don't know what he's capable of.

I tossed my hair over my shoulder. *~I've seen his cruelty.*

"What shall I tell your mother?" The king leaned casually on the wall and stroked the patch of hair on his chin. His belt buckle gleamed in the moonlight; the two intertwined dragons seemed to leer at me. "That you'd rather rot in the dungeon than sing for the king? It would break her heart." He snapped his fingers at Lawrence who squatted and took my arm forcefully.

I glared at him, but he didn't loosen his grip. "I don't care."

Lawrence's eyes narrowed. I thought I saw the same narrowing of his pupils that I'd seen in Edward, but it was so quick, I could've imagined it. The king pushed away from the wall and snatched my other arm. The men pulled me up as if I was a child weighing nothing more than a sack of potatoes.

I yanked out of their grasp, then smoothed my skirts. I tossed my hair all the while willing my heart to stop racing. I couldn't think clearly when it was beating so loudly in my ears. "You won't be able to use her against me. I don't care one fig how my mother feels."

"I see…" The king's eyes bored into me. "And what about Jack? Do you care how he feels?"

I caught my lower lip between my teeth. Wilhelm had burned the cottage that held the twin of the tapestry in my room, but he must know there were others who would lead him to Jack.

The king's eyebrows rose and he nodded as if he was following the conversation I was having with myself. "So, you do understand. Not all of the portals into your world were destroyed when Wilhelm burned down the traitor's house. Do you think me ignorant?"

"What do you want from me?" I glanced at Lawrence, but he stood with his head bowed, arms crossed over his chest.

"I want you to rule beside me—a great commander of an army of dragons. We'll be unbeatable."

"I can't command an army of dragons!" Was he crazy?

"Then you will lose the people you love…one…by…one. Starting with Jack."

Tears welled up in my eyes. My chest burned with rage. The cell seemed to list under me. ~ *You betrayed me. You said you were always going to protect me.*

Lawrence furrowed his brows and swallowed hard.

The king stepped out of the cell. "Follow me. Now."

I darted my eyes from side to side in the low light as I stepped from the cell and into the main chamber. With sweat pooling in my underarms, I crossed the open area where the guards played cards at night. A dirty face suddenly appeared in the barred window of another cell. Wisps of ratted light-brown hair framed the woman's face. Her lips were cracked and dried. Blood crusted in the corners of her mouth. Her fingers wrapped around the iron bars, blue from cold but still I recognized her. Maria. She'd been so close and yet so far.

"You want a song, my king? I'll give you a song." Her voice was soft and husky.

"Huzzah to the queen, fair faced is she,
A delicate touch for bird and bee,
The dragons dance for her,
And the unicorns lay down once more,
When the vile king falls to the floor—"

The ring of a sword drawn from its scabbard echoed in the cavern as the head guard rushed to quell the singing.

The burning rage crouched in my stomach leapt forward.

~*No!* Lawrence's voice resonated in my head.

Too late. I flung out my hand. "Stop!"

The guard froze in place as his sword was ripped from his grip by an invisible force. It fell to the floor with a deafening clatter. Maria stopped singing. The air sizzled and cracked as strong fingers curled around my shoulder. Moist words were whispered in my ear. "I believe the wait was worth my while."

"Cut out the prisoner's tongue," he commanded the guard.

"No. I will sing for you. Please… don't hurt her."

"Take her hand instead." Stuart's chuckle filled the cavern as his arm circled my shoulders. The physical strength of his body sapped some of my courage as he led me up the spiral stairs.

Moments later, a spine-cracking scream resonated from the cavernous space below.

chapter twenty~one

I paced the uneven stone floor of my new cell, trying to rid myself of the sound loop of Maria's scream haunting my mind. I concentrated on the chamber I'd been locked into, hoping to distract myself. It was no bigger than my bedroom at Grandma's house, but there was a fire roaring in the hearth and colored glass in the windows. I grasped my skirt, pounded my feet on the floor, and screamed as long as I could. I needed to let out all the anger I'd bottled up, all the anxiety.

~*Relax.*

~*Shut up, Lawrence.* I plopped against the thick door and slid down to the floor in a heap. My fists were balled so tight I felt the pinch of fingernails digging into palms. I'd been so close.

~*So close to what?*

My throat tightened. I shook away the tears threatening to spill. ~*Nothing. Go away.*

~*You can trust me, Sophie.*

~ *Right now, I trust you about as far as I could throw you.* A rush of heat tingled into my fingers and toes. I wanted to trust him as I had back in Vermont, but he'd kept secrets from me—made me believe things that weren't true. Which was almost as bad as all those years of believing that things that actually were true weren't! It made me sick to think of his possible ulterior motives for gaining my trust. Did he really like me, or did he just use me to gain favor with the king? And if it was the latter, why did he want that favor?

The reflection of the flame flickering on the table by the bed danced in the colored windowpanes like fairies playing in a stream. I had to find a way to stall King Stuart. I had no idea how to call the dragons and no idea what to do with them once I did. Some feminine demands might be just the thing. *~Tell the king I want clean clothes and a hot bath before I do anything.*

~You really aren't in a position to make demands.

His disapproval of my request was like waves crashing into me. I brushed them off with a sweep of my hand. *~If he wants what I've got, he'll provide what I ask. I'm sure you can find a way to make it happen. You are, after all, part of his inner circle.*

A large sigh emanated from the other side of my door. "I'll see what I can do."

"See what you can do about what?" murmured another man in a deep voice. There must be two guards outside the door. Two guards for little ol' me. Well, that was just precious.

"Getting that crazy woman a bath—can't you smell her stench wafting from under the door?"

~Jerk.

The growl from Lawrence's throat reverberated through the chamber door. Almost as if the sound waves had been magnified. *Good.* I'm glad I caused him frustration. What did he think he'd done to me? My time in the dungeon had been no tea party.

As his footsteps faded, I slipped off my shoes and set them aside. The crackle of the fireplace drew me to the large hearth. A thick mantel that looked as if it had been sliced right out of a tree created a shelf above it. On the shelf, amongst other statuary, was a marble dragon holding a large, pale-blue glass ball. A white mist swirled inside the orb, like a snow globe. It beckoned me closer. I drew my fingers across the smooth surface and then, with slow movements, like Aladdin in the Cave of Wonders, I pulled it from the dragon's claws.

It was cold to the touch. The swirling mist changed into snowflakes. The top of a mountain appeared and then faded back into the whiteness. The snowflakes swirled again, and then the scene came back into focus. A large shadow loomed near a craggy ledge…a dragon… *The tapestry*. It couldn't be the same mountain I'd seen in the tapestry in the dungeon, could it? A loud scraping noise outside the door was followed by a knock. The intrusion encouraged me to place the sphere back in the statue's claws.

"Can we come in, *My Lady*?" Lawrence's voice traveled through the door, a slight sneer coloring his tone. "We have a tub and some hot water."

"For Heaven's sake. Bring them in!" I sighed, thankful that he'd managed to pull it off, but I wouldn't give him the satisfaction of saying so.

The lock rattled and the door opened with a creak. Two men hauling a four-foot long copper tub entered the room. Five boys carrying kettles of steaming water and a softly rounded, gray-haired woman followed them. Her arms were full of linens, soap, and what I prayed were clean clothes. The men centered the tub over a small floor drain in the corner of the room. The sound of hot water splashing in the tub actually made me giddy. What had it been, seven, eight days?

I wondered if someone had found my dad. I thought of him lying on the hard wood floor in the kitchen, dazed and confused. A small part of me hoped someone was telling him he'd imagined everything that had happened. It wasn't very charitable of me, I knew, but maybe he'd be more sympathetic if he knew how it felt. I pulled at the cuffs of my shirt and worried at my lip. How long had he lain on the kitchen floor, bound up?

I was brought out of my thoughts by the men's stares. I crossed my arms over my chest and tossed my head. "What are you gawking at?"

Lawrence cleared his throat and made a dismissive gesture. "Thank you for your help. Please, return to your duties." The men filed out of the room. More than one of them glanced back in my direction with a disbelieving look on his face.

"What was that all about?" I asked the woman holding the linens.

"Beg your pardon, miss, but your resemblance to the queen is remarkable," she said.

"Oh…right." I'd nearly forgotten how much I looked like my mot—the queen. I stuck out my hand. "You can call me Sophie. And your name?"

The woman juggled her linens into one arm and accepted my handshake. "Brunella, miss."

Brunella? Why did that sound so familiar? Oh, right. I looked at Lawrence. She was his *other* aunt.

The maid smiled. "I'm to help you with your bath this evening."

I scoffed. "I haven't had help bathing since I was seven. I can do it myself, thanks."

Lawrence scowled at me.

The woman blanched. She nodded and placed the stack of linens on the bed and next to it a crisp pair of white stockings, a shift, and a sea green overdress.

~This is not the modern world you are used to. Let her help you. It is her job and she takes pride in her work.

I sighed. I hated to admit that Lawrence was right, but when a man's right, he's right. I held my hand out to stop the maid from leaving. "Brunnella, while I don't need help bathing," I returned Lawrence's glare, and then looked back at the maid. "I could use your help afterward with my hair. Would you be willing?"

Crinkles framed the maid's dark eyes when she smiled. "Yes, miss. I'll be back in twenty minutes? Is that enough time?"

Twenty minutes in a hot bath sounded like a dream. I nodded, and she shuffled out of the chamber with Lawrence.

As soon as the door was latched, I stripped off my dirty clothes and stepped into the hot water. The reflection of the flames moved over the metallic surface of the tub like sands shifting in the desert. At once, the water soothed me and made me feel guilty at the same time.

I should be strategizing my way out of here, but how could I get away without Jack being hurt? Or possibly even killed. The king was not a negotiator. And what about Anna, Samantha, Henry, and little William? The king had hinted that he knew the location of another portal. Was he lying just to make me comply? Or did he really know how to get to them? Had Lawrence told him of the portal in his aunt's house? Or was Anna in league with the king, too?

I groaned and slid further into the water, letting its warmth flood over my head.

~Perhaps the key is getting everyone in, not getting you out.

I spluttered water and broke the surface. *~Stay out of my head!*

I pictured a heavy wooden door in my mind and slammed it shut. "That should keep you out," I muttered. Between my hands, I lathered up the cream-colored soap Brunella had left. It had a slight lavender fragrance. It reminded me of Anna and the night William was born... I swiped at the tears that stung my eyes and began the task of scrubbing the dungeon out of my hair.

Maybe Lawrence was right—but why would I want to bring everyone here? I'd just be putting more people in more danger.

~This is where they belong, too.

I grit my teeth. *~I said stay out.*

~You need to talk to someone.

~Not you. I hurled the words at him like poison darts. I wanted to talk to him, but how could I trust a man in the service of the king? Even if he made my insides ooze like melted caramel despite my brain's objections.

Then a sudden thought hit me. What if I went to the dragons instead of singing them to the castle? Could I beg for their help in removing Stuart from the throne? If only Bailean were here. I could trust him, and he'd know what to do. He'd know how to reach the other dragons too. I was sure of it.

I swirled my fingers on the surface of the water and relaxed as it grew warm again. I dunked my head under and rinsed the soap out of my hair. If I were to go to the mountain I'd seen in the glass orb, the mountain of dragons, I would need warmer clothes. I wrung out my hair as I emerged from the water. *~Lawrence, you said I could trust you.*

~And you can, My Lady.

~Don't call me that. I stood and stepped out of the tub, wrapped a towel around my body and stood close to the fire as I dried off.

~What should I call you then?

~Call me Sophie, like you always have. Can you get me a clean cloak, one that will keep me warm? And a pair of pants?

~I suppose I could, but what for?

~That's for me to know.

~If you're planning on leaving the castle, don't. Stuart has spies everywhere. You wouldn't last long.

~Then you'll have to come with me. You did say I could trust you.

~You can, but—

~But what?

~I'm a king's man, here at his pleasure. If I do anything to jeopardize that…

A wave of irritation washed over me—it wasn't the emotion I was feeling, though it was close. Lawrence had let down his guard. I was sensing him the way he'd sensed me when we first met. I didn't care if what I said upset him though; there was nothing to be done about the trust that he'd broken between us.

I towel dried my hair, slipped the stockings over my legs, and then the shift over my head. I still felt naked and wished

I'd brought that pair of boxers I'd abandoned in the dungeon with me. I could've scrubbed them clean in the bath water. Oh, well. Hindsight and all that.

Leaning over the tub, I pulled out the drain plug and watched the water swirl into the hole in the floor. "Brunella, please come in now."

The maid bustled into the chamber. Brunella walked to the bed and grabbed the dress she'd laid out previously, pulling the length of it over my arms so I could guide my head and arms through the fabric. She then spun me around and shifted my hair to tie up the lace at my neck. I sat in the chair in front of a small dressing table. An oval mirror in a gilded frame hung above it. I felt like Medieval Barbie.

Bluish-purple streaks stained the skin under my eyes and my hair was a tangled mess without conditioner. Okay, make that Gothic Barbie. The maid, undisturbed at the challenge before her, picked up a comb and commenced the chore of untangling my hair from the ends up. She used a bit of pomade in the particularly knotted spots and made quick work of it. Then she split my hair into sections and twisted it neatly.

The weight of the woman's stare on the scars covering my neck, nearly undid me, but Brunella said nothing. Her deft fingers manipulated the strands into compliance. "How long have you worked in the castle?"

The maid glanced at me before returning to her task. "Most of my life, miss."

"Do you know who I am?"

"Sure, I do. The whispers started a few years ago." She pulled up half of the braided sections and wrapped them into a bun above my ear, pinning them in place. If the maid knew who I was, how many others would recognize me? If everyone in the castle knew who I was, it wouldn't be easy to escape. On the other hand, Brunella might know what the king wanted from me.

"Do you know what the king wants me to do?"

Brunella shook her head. "I beg you, My Lady. Don't tell me anything. If he finds out you're confiding in me he'll torture me until I tell him every word."

I thought of Maria and my hands shook. I'd hate to see anyone else hurt because of me. "All right."

Brunella patted my shoulders. "I *can* tell you that the king is planning a ball to introduce you to the court. Tomorrow night in fact."

"Tomorrow night?" That didn't give me much time to figure something out. *~Did you know about the ball, Lawrence?*

~I was going to tell you, but you shut me out.

"Yes, My Lady." Brunella leaned forward and caught my gaze in the mirror. She lowered her voice to a whisper. "I know you question who to trust. You can trust your gut, but you can also trust Lawrence. He just looks as if he's on the wrong side."

I swiveled in the chair to face Brunella. "Did you know my father?"

Brunella turned me by my shoulders so that I was facing the mirror again. She twisted the other half of my braids up and over my shoulder, hiding the scars on my neck. Brunella had tact.

"My sister Hildar worked in your grandfather Edward's household as a ladies maid to your grandmother. Hildar was there when your dad, Ronan, was born. Saw the rare Golden Dragon, too. A rare dragon, a rare gift."

My stomach was in knots. I had no idea what was expected of me, or how to get out of it. If I displeased the king, would he kill me? I wanted to ask Brunella, but I couldn't make my mouth form the words.

Lawrence answered my unspoken question. *~Worse. He'd kill everyone you love first.*

Hot tears sprang to my eyes. I cleared my throat. I needed to go back to a safer subject before I gave myself away. "Gold dragons are rare?"

"Oh, yes. Dragons around here were mostly red, when you caught a glimpse of them anyway. I haven't seen one since I was very young, and even then it was a rare sighting."

"You said the dragon gave my father a rare gift? What was it?"

"His gift—Ronan was afraid of his gift. It—well, I've said too much already." Brunella patted my shoulder apologetically and turned to pick up the wet linens from my bath. My cheeks suddenly flushed with embarrassment. I'd just discarded my towels on the floor like a common motel guest.

"Now, I believe the king is expecting you." Brunella walked out of the chamber, smiling back at me before shutting the door behind her.

chapter twenty two

A breeze wafted through the corridor as Lawrence escorted me to the king's private chamber. I tried to walk tall, but my kneecaps were shaking. How I got into this whole situation was a jumbled mess in my head. Every touch from Lawrence scorched over my skin and made my nerves fray with unwanted attraction. I hated that my body betrayed me with even the smallest of touches. I put some extra mortar on the wall I was building against him in my mind.

The long hallway opened into a chamber; the vaulted ceiling soaring overhead. Lawrence led me to a blue door nestled into the far wall. He rapped on the thick wood panels. My heart raced.

Wilhelm opened the door and gestured me in with a leer. A monster wave of anxiety washed through me, but I swallowed, stuck my nose in the air, and pretended he didn't matter. As I passed him, I didn't even give him a glance.

The king turned from the blazing hearth, swirling a deep red beverage in a tall wineglass. It looked like blood. The reasonable part of my mind told me it must be wine because he wasn't Dracula, but the unreasonable part still held doubts. The king cleared his throat. "I've been waiting for you two."

"Can't hurry a woman's bath, can we, sire?" Lawrence said with a chuckle.

Stuart scowled. "No, no you can't."

I curled my arms around my torso as the king looked me over like a suckling pig on a platter. All I needed was an apple wedged in my mouth.

"Now, now, you mustn't hide yourself from your king." Stuart plucked my arms away one at a time with his free hand. He bid me turn with a wave of his finger.

I circled for his inspection, fists clenched at my sides. Anger and embarrassment boiled up my neck and filled my face.

~There is more than one way to win a war, Sophie.

I scowled at Lawrence. What did he know about war?

His expression darkened and his brow furrowed. *~Are you kidding me? I've been fighting this fight since I was barely out of nappies.*

~But you are the king's man. I narrowed my eyes at him, daring him to lie to me.

~Am I?

The certainty that had built up in me about Lawrence being on the wrong side began to crumble. Again, I found myself thinking that Lawrence was right. It was insufferable, but I should use whatever I had to my advantage. And right now, my sex appeal was to my advantage. Perhaps I should play the thankful fool, too—that's what the king wanted, what he expected—for me to be thankful to be out of the dungeon. To be thankful that he didn't torture me. I steeled my courage and said the first thing (that didn't have something to do with cutting his family gems loose) that came to mind. "Bru-Brunella did wonders with my hair," I stuttered, and patted the braided locks skillfully arranged to hide my scarring.

Stuart took in the intricate braids and swirled his wine. "Yes, it is very fetching. You are even more beautiful than your mother, I think. Don't you think, Lawrence?"

"Yes, sire, she is beautiful," Lawrence answered without letting his gaze drift from the king. I blushed in spite of myself. I wasn't used to being called beautiful. Cute. Attractive, maybe, but not beautiful.

Stuart smiled and raised his glass with a wink. He drained the last of the beverage and set his glass on the table next to a half-full decanter. He took my arm and offered me a chair. "Tomorrow we are having a ball in your honor, to introduce you to the court. You do know how to dance?"

"Um—a little." I could at least pretend enough to look like I knew what I was doing. Just follow the man's lead, right? Not step on his toes too much? I sat and folded my hands in my lap to keep from fidgeting.

"Ah. Well, then. Lawrence will tutor you. He's the best dancer in my guard."

My palms grew clammy at the thought of having to be so near Lawrence. How could I keep my distance if he was holding me in his arms?

"It is a masked ball, my favorite kind. When one can dance with any lady he wants without fear that tongues will wag." He chuckled. "Well, they'll wag, but without knowing for sure who is under the mask, it won't matter."

I nodded. "Will the queen be there?"

"Perhaps. But will you know her with her mask?" Stuart laughed. "You aren't allowed to reveal your true face, you know."

"Do we ever, my king?" I said.

Stuart's eyes narrowed. He shook his head and smirked.

I smoothed my skirt nervously, silently chastising myself. When would I learn to keep my mouth shut?

Lawrence scoffed from the corner where he lurked. ~*That's what I was just thinking.*

I glared at him while the king filled his goblet with more wine and swirled it in his hand before looking back at me. "After your session with Lawrence, Brunella will bring you a dress from the queen's wardrobe. The gods know she has plenty to spare."

He set down his goblet and tugged me to my feet. His hands were cold and his grip firm. He caught my gaze and wouldn't let it go. His thumb stroked my cheekbone sending pulses of disgust into my gut. "Abandoned by a mother, not just once, but twice in your short life. What sorrow."

I swallowed and looked away, tears stinging. He had a way of twisting the truth, of making every word sting, didn't he? "I try not to think of it much." *At least not like that. I blame you.*

The king clicked his tongue. "I do hope you know that *I* have never abandoned you, but searched both of our worlds until you were found. Your mother and her midwife tricked me into believing you were dead. It took me a little while to uncover the truth—but the truth will always wiggle its way out of even the tightest lips." A genuine smile softened his otherwise sharp visage. Did he really believe what he was saying? "I can be quite devoted to the right person…but you must understand your place." He stepped in close to me, his hand stroking my neck with the back of his fingers. "I'd hate to have to hurt you…"

I bowed my head. A tear tumbled onto the stone floor. My vocal chords were tight, face hot. I could barely release the words trapped in my thickened throat. "I understand."

I understood that I had to get out of here as fast as I could.

The king smiled and lifted my hand to brush a kiss atop my knuckles. "We shall make fine partners then. Prove your worth to me now. Show me that all the trouble I've gone through to rescue you was worth it. Sing."

My mouth went dry. I struggled not to extract my hand too quickly. When he released me, to bide some time, I strode to a pair of long windows in the tower room. I bit my tongue to get my mouth to water and nervously played with my hair. The sun was setting over the village below. Birds were finding their nests in trees and in the nooks and crannies of buildings. Far out on the horizon I could just make out the snowy peaks of a distant mountain range beyond a body of water. I trembled as if I was standing naked in Antarctica, but sweat beaded at my temples.

"I-I don't know the words," I lied.

"You know the words," the king purred. "You were born with them on your tongue, just like your silver-tongued father."

The comment pierced my heart, like the memory of my father's death; the smash of the scepter—my mother's hand raised in victory. I glanced over my shoulder. Lawrence was as still as a marble carving, his face unreadable, his mind closed. I bowed my head and took a deep breath. I couldn't see a way out of this. I had no choice. I must get back to the chamber where the tapestries were being held if I wanted to get back to my dad before Stuart got hold of him. If that meant singing for the king, then so be it. I opened my mouth, not knowing what would come out, but what sprang forth was surprising. It was the lullaby Bailean used to sing to me. The one I had sung to little William, yet the words were different, as if they'd formed on my tongue unbidden.

"Speed, bonnie lads,
like a bird on the wing,
Onward the dragons cry.
Speed to the child,
Who was born to sing,
Over the sea and sky.

The wind whistled outside of the tower room. In the corners, where the castle walls met outside the window, leaves danced in the swirling eddy. I startled as a fat drop of rain splattered against the colored windowpanes. Goosebumps rose all over my body.

"Louder!" the king ordered.

I took a breath, my conscious mind grasping for the words, but again, they were there, ready to be sung.

"Come to me lads, come to me now,
No longer will you refrain.

213

Come to the child—

A strong gust forced open the window; it stung my cheeks and howled into the room.

~Don't. Don't say it.

I faltered, my hands covering my ears as if a gunshot had gone off right next to me.

Lawrence's plea rang in my mind. *~Stop. You can't call the dragons to the king's aid.*

King Stuart charged forward, a nasty sneer marring his carefully composed expression. He raised his hand and struck me. Hard. Stars swam before my eyes, and the world spun. I crumpled to my knees, my hands clawing for the stones beneath me. I needed the safety of the stationary floor.

"You will not stop next time. I will have the dragons at the ball or I will force you to watch my guards torture that woman you tried to save in the dungeon. They are very good at it."

The world had stopped whirling, so I stared at the king with hatred in my heart. My hand hovered over my tender cheekbone. My belly roiled like a coiled snake preparing to strike. He turned on his heel, slammed the window, and then closed the latch. A breeze rattled the pane, but its force had waned.

"Why would I care if you tortured some stranger?" My voice came out as a harsh whisper. I found my feet again and stood, my shoulders rigid.

Stuart stepped into me. His breath was hot. His body laced with violent energy like a spring compressed to its limits. "She's no stranger to you and you know it. And for her, you shall sing again." The king's lips pressed into mine, stiff and demanding.

He pulled away and I tried to keep my expression plain even though I wanted to throw up. He snapped his fingers and the chamber door opened. Lawrence offered an arm, but I ignored it. I marched into the corridor and he fell into step behind me. Wilhelm chuckled as he shut the chamber door with a soft click. The sound raised the hairs on my neck. It was no wonder Bailean took me away from these people.

I turned abruptly on Lawrence. "That was Maria in the dungeon. My *mother.*"

Lawrence glared at me. "Not your mother...she's—"

"My mother." I started shaking. The horror of it all made my stomach feel like lead. I had to get her out of here, too. I couldn't leave her in the dungeon.

It seemed like Lawrence wanted to add something, but he looked away, swallowed and nodded. He led me around the corner and guided me onto a bench. I was in such shock that I didn't argue. I swiped tears away with the back of my hand. "He didn't kill her when she was taken from—"

He tried to press a finger over my lips, but I pushed his hand away, grasped his outstretched finger. I held it as his eyes held my gaze. Was it longing in those amber orbs? Or was he praying that I wouldn't try to break his finger?

I softened and switched my approach. *~Why did the dragons give us these gifts? Why make it possible for me to call them if I shouldn't? Why did you stop me?*

Lawrence curled his hand around mine and pulled me back up. His steps were brisk as he tugged me down the corridor. We trotted down a flight of stairs and turned down another long hallway. *~Long ago dragons and men worked together, until King Stuart's grandfather decided he didn't need the dragons to rule by his side. He abandoned the old ways for new and turned against those who clung to tradition. Men were sent by the king to kill the dragons, so the dragons withdrew. Some of them risk their lives to return and pass on special gifts. They hope that the old ways will return, that dragons will once again live by our side—be revered as they once were. But if you had called the dragons tonight, without fully understanding your gifts, they would have given their service to the king—for that is who they are ultimately pledged to—and we can't risk him having that kind of power.*

~How do you know all this?

~Obviously I haven't spent my whole life in Vermont.

The second guard was dozing by my chamber door as we approached. Lawrence shook him awake. "Go on to bed. I'll take the night watch."

"But Wilhelm said—"

Lawrence grabbed the front of his doublet and spoke through clenched teeth. "Wilhelm changed his mind. Told me to take the night watch from you because you can't seem to stay awake on the job. You are released from duty."

Servants passing in the hall gawked. Lawrence freed the sleepy guard. He glared and straightened his coat before he shuffled away. Lawrence yanked open the door, grabbed me by the arm and shoved me in.

"Hey! Watch it!" I growled, nearly tripping over the long skirt swishing under my feet. I rubbed the spot where his grip had practically given me a friction burn. *~What the hell?*

Lawrence slammed the door. *~I'm sorry. I lost my temper. But you'd be surprised how fast rumors spread through the servant hall. If word got to Stuart that I was showing you particular favor, we'd be in a lot of trouble, fast.*

I flipped him the bird and plopped on the bed. It was late, and I was tired. I kicked off my shoes and curled up on the blankets. I just needed a little sleep, a little break from this world. Then I'd have the energy to go back down to the dungeon, search the hidden room more. Lawrence shuffled just outside the door. *~Why didn't you tell me who you were earlier?*

~If I came out and told you the whole story that first day that I met you at the river—would you have believed me? Would you have ever talked to me again? No. You would've thought that I was some crazed lunatic. I had to know that you believed in yourself first. Only then could you believe in me.

I punched the pillow and then hugged it close, a stream of hot indignation flaring up in my core. He was so infuriating when he was right.

chapter twenty-three

the crackle of the fire woke me. As I became aware of my surroundings, I noticed a tall shadow leaning over the hearth, poking at the fire. My heart lurched into my throat, but then I realized that his back was curved as if he held the weight of the world. The king would never have an emotion like that. I tried to speak past the lump. "Lawrence?"

The shadow swiveled toward me, surprised at hearing his name. "Yes. I brought a pair of breeches and a thick cloak. I thought you might feel more comfortable in them than…" He gestured to the fancy dress that was now full of wrinkles from my nap.

I sat up and fingered the rough woolen cloak that lay over the foot of my bed. "Thank you."

Lawrence poked at the fire again and set the poker in its stand. "I wish you'd tell me what you're planning. I can't protect you if I don't know where you are."

I shook my head. "I can't. It would put both of us at risk. You might tell the king my plans—"

He turned on his heel, fury making his eyes spark as he marched over to the bed. "I said you could trust me!"

I tucked my feet under me and rose up on my knees. My hands grasped his shoulders. "Or the king might force you to tell him, even if you didn't want to."

His hair was a mess of tangles, as if he'd been running his hand through it all night with worry. Lawrence's shoulders slumped forward as he shook his head. "I don't know if I can let you go forward alone. Not again."

My grip tightened on his muscles. "What do you mean?"

"I heard you call me, Sophie. I saw in my mind the men in your kitchen. I knew who they were. My only hope was to get to Brindle before you and pray you would understand that I was still trying to protect you…in the only way I knew how."

The coiled ball of anger that had formed in my gut the moment Lawrence ordered me to stop talking to him in the cottage melted away. Tears sprang into my eyes. "How did you get here? Is the tapestry in your grandmother's house a portal, too?"

Lawrence nodded.

"Then we can go back the way you came in!" I grabbed his arm and practically leapt from the bed with excitement. "I don't have to go to the dungeon at all!"

With a sigh, Lawrence walked away. He leaned his head on the mantelpiece, the fire silhouetting his muscular frame. "We can't. Anna burned the tapestry as soon as I went through it."

I sank slowly back into the bedcovers. "Why? Why would she do that?"

"Because I told her to."

"Why would you do that? That tapestry was our way home. Now I have to find the other one."

Lawrence narrowed his eyes at me. "What other one?"

Too late, I realized that I'd never shown him Gran's room.

He shook his head. "You found another tapestry in the house? "I'm so sorry. I just wanted to keep it secret for a bit. To have something that just belonged to me—if only for a little while. I was going to share it with you. I was…"

Lawrence bit the inside of his lip. "Looks like I wasn't the only one keeping secrets. But the time for that is over between us. There's something you need to understand before we move forward. You have to know the whole truth."

"Okay." I drew the syllable out suspiciously. Heat flushed down my limbs. My stomach twisted into a knot.

He turned back toward me and licked his lips. His hands were clenched at his sides. The expressions crossing his face looked like he was arguing with himself.

~It's probably better if I just show you. But, don't freak out.

Bailean? I searched for the dragon in the dark corners of my room, but my gaze was quickly pulled back to Lawrence. A green haze grew over him. My heart picked up its rhythm. I'd experienced this sparkling haze before. I wiped my palms on the velvety coverlet. He stretched in ways no normal man could. He grew taller, and his face changed. His nose elongated, the tips of his ears grew long hairs. Wings burst from his back and he pitched forward, his hands searching for the floor. A crackling noise, like a tree falling in the woods, hung in the air as antlers protruded from his head and glimmered in the light. A long tail curled out from his body and around the room. As the haze cleared, I gaped.

~Sophie?

"L-Lawrence? You're a drag—you're *Bailean?*" My chest was tight, breath quick and shallow. My head spun. I considered the transformation I'd just seen. Words wouldn't form on my tongue. I managed to stammer out, "How?"

~I was born in the grasp of a dragon.

"So was I… that doesn't explain…"

But it did. It explained even more actually. Like why I could change into a mouse.

Lawrence lowered his head. He was so big that he couldn't even move his wings in the small chamber. He was like a jack-in-the-box ready to pop. Waves of heat emanated from his scales. Gold eyes peered down at me as I ran my hands over his muscled chest.

"You're…you're my dragon."

~Yes.

"So you knew. You know everything. You even know that the queen is my real mother and Maria—"

He winced, as if it hurt him to have the knowledge of these things. ~ *Maria isn't just the woman who raised you... She's my mother, too.*

The shock of the revelation knocked me flat. Maria was Lawrence's *mother*. Like, he spent nine months in her womb mother.

~*I can't leave her here any longer.*

My stomach cramped. I covered my mouth with my hand as a sudden, deep fear for the wellbeing of those I loved settled in. Maria's scream in the dungeon replayed in my head like a record skipping.

~*You were given the power to call the dragons when they witnessed what was done to your father and that's why you were taken away by them, too. The dragons made the portals when they brought the first Stuart here to this island so that his followers could travel between the two places with ease.*

"The first Stuart?"

~*The Bonnie Prince.*

"But he was taken to France."

~*That's what the historians want you to think. In reality, it was one of your great grandmothers who called the dragons. They opened the hidden way to the great island we call Brindle. You've heard of the isle of Avalon, haven't you?*"

"Of course I have. Are you saying this is Avalon? The island where Merlin took King Arthur?"

~*No, it's not Avalon, but it's the same idea. One of Anna's great grandmothers was a powerful dragonsinger. She believed that the Stuart line had the right to rule Scotland, but after the battle of Culloden, all hope was lost. They took a boat and sailed away. The rumors were they sailed to France, but that is not where they landed.*

"They came to Brindle."

~*Some of them. Others settled in a rural place named Vermont. Kept the secrets of the Bonnie Prince. This is an island full of magic and possibility. But over time, power corrupted the line. And here we are. To be safe from Stuart, you were taken away by the dragons until you were old enough to do what must be done.*

~*So, in killing my father, my enemy gave me the power to defeat him.*

~*Precisely. But you have to use the power at the right time and with the right intentions.*

"And last night, in the king's chambers, was not the right time."

~*Or the right intentions.*

I walked around Lawrence, my hand trailing over his lean body. I ran my fingers on his soft underbelly. He shuddered under my touch, muscles rippling under his emerald armor. The green haze returned and enveloped Lawrence. In a few moments, he returned to his human form. I found my mouth dropping open as the mist faded away. His clothes were still intact! "How did you do that?"

"I just showed you. It's one of the gifts the dragons gave me. I can shift form—and—"

"No." I waved my hands in his face. "*You* came back with your clothes on, I couldn't do—" I stopped mid-sentence, catching my lip under my front teeth.

Lawrence tipped his head, his lips slightly parted. "You couldn't do what?"

I hugged myself and looked away. My cheeks filled with heat. I collapsed on the edge of the mattress. "I've been experimenting."

Lawrence crouched at the edge of my bed. His fingers found my hand and curled around it. They were strong hands, calloused hands. Hands used to hard work.

"The tapestries that everyone believes were destroyed long ago…I found them in the dungeon, in a walled off chamber."

Lawrence grinned. "I knew it!" His forehead touched our clasped hands as if in prayer. "I knew he didn't destroy them. How did you find them?"

"You have to be very small to enter the chamber. As small as…" I grinned. "Well, a mouse."

"Wait." Lawrence stood abruptly and ran his hand through his hair. "You're telling me you can shift into a mouse form?"

I quirked an eyebrow and shrugged.

That cute grin lifted the corner of his mouth. He crossed his arms and lifted his chin. "Show me.

He wanted me to transform? "What? *Now?*"

Lawrence shrugged. "Why not?"

"No."

"You chicken?" He tucked his hands into his pits and started flapping his elbows. "Bock, bock, bock."

I sighed and flung the covers away, planting my knees on the soft mattress. "You're such a child."

He stood still, an irritating grin plastered on his face.

Teeth gritted against the pain, I transformed into the little black-patched mouse. It was easier this time, quicker, and more uncomfortable than painful. Thankfully.

Large hands moved away the gown that had pooled around me and scooped me up. I squeaked, surprised. Lawrence held me close to his face. My whiskers twitched with the smell of pine and cedar. He must have just put wood into the fire when the crackling woke me.

Lawrence shook his head. "I can't believe it…I thought you would be—"

~What? Thought I would be what?

"Well, something a little more fierce."

I bared my teeth. *~I'll show you fierce!*

He picked me up by my tail and I scrabbled at the air with my front paws. *~Put me down!*

"Not so fierce now, are you?" He chuckled as he put me back in his palm.

I rubbed a paw over my twitchy whiskers. *~That wasn't very nice. And now I have a problem. My clothes. They don't reappear when I transform back like yours did and it's awfully embar—Lawrence?*

Lawrence was still, as if suspended in time. I wriggled out of his grasp and crawled up his arm. He was staring off into the chamber; fingers of flame reflected in his eyes.

~*Lawrence? Lawrence!* I patted his cheek. He wasn't breathing. Panic made my heart squeeze in on itself. ~*Lawrence!*

He drew in a sudden breath and leaned forward, his hands grabbing for the side of the bed. I dug my claws into his shirt to keep from tumbling to the floor. ~*What's the matter? Are you all right? Are you sick?*

~*No…no.* He panted and drew his hand across his forehead. "I'm…I'm fine."

I jumped to the bed and circled to face him. ~*Are you sure? You don't look fine. You look like a zombie.*

Lawrence righted himself. "I saw…I saw two dragons—one green, one gold. I don't understand."

~*What else did you see?*

He shrugged. "Nothing… Swirls of color. People dancing."

~*Like a ball?*

"I know, it doesn't make sense. Why would you give the king what he wanted?"

~*Maybe I don't. Maybe it just looks like it—like you aren't seeing the whole picture.*

"I'm not sure." Lawrence gathered me in his shaky hand. "I can take you down to the entrance of the dungeon. It will be faster, and then we'll figure out how to get all of us out of here without the king knowing we've gone. Then we'll have to destroy any portals we can find so he won't follow us. We must go now, before too many in the castle wake." He turned on his heel and strode toward the door.

~*Wait!*

Lawrence came to an abrupt halt. ~*What is it?*

~*I-I don't have any clothes.*

"You're a mouse."

I gave an indignant squeak. ~*I won't be a mouse forever. Grab the cloak.*

Lawrence gathered the cloak he'd brought from the bedcovers. He mumbled something that sounded like *crazy woman*, but I didn't argue since he tucked the cloak under his arm. I clung to his shoulder as we entered the hallway. Lawrence looked right, left, and then dashed for the stairwell.

Air rushed past my ears and made my nose cold. My body bounced with each of Lawrence's steps, and I was weightless for a moment, before falling back to his shoulder. When we reached the stairs leading down into the dungeon, Lawrence slowed his pace and descended into the dank chamber.

~What are you going to say if someone asks why you are down here?

~Don't worry. I've got that covered. His boots rang out on the stone floor.

"Who's there?" called out a gruff voice. A shuffling figure holding a small torch approached.

"It is I, Lawrence Emberwing."

~Emberwing? That's your last name?

Lawrence's fingers curled around me and stuffed me into the bundle. Why was he hiding me? I wished I'd thought about biting him when I'd had the chance.

His conversation with the prison guard was muffled through the layers of cloth. I circled and stuck my head out.

"It was requested that I bring these clothes to Maria. Seems she is to have an audience with the king this morning."

The guard reached for the bundle, but Lawrence drew away. "No one is to deliver them but me."

"Well then." The guard ran a hand under his nose and sniffled. He pointed down the corridor. "If that's how it's to be, fourth door down on the left, after the bend. We 'ad to move her yesterday on account of her caterwauling driving us out of our skulls."

"Thank you." Lawrence nodded and moved swiftly away from the guard.

~You are a complete ass sometimes.

~And you can be thoughtless and headstrong.

His thoughts pricked my ire. I sniffed. ~*You have no idea what you are talking about.*

Lawrence chuckled. ~*And you are so easy to rile.*

~*Hmph.* I curled up and covered my nose with my tail.

Lightly, Lawrence rapped the wooden cell door. "Mom… it's—it's Lawrence. Are you awake?"

"Lawrence?" Maria's face appeared in the small barred window and I poked my head back out of the bundle.

I couldn't help but compare the woman in front of me with the mom I remembered. She was dirty, but if I looked past all the grime and years of imprisonment, she was the same woman. Her toffee brown eyes softened as she looked at Lawrence. I scurried out of the bundle and up his shoulder.

Maria held her arm close to her chest as she coughed. Dirty strips of linen were wrapped around the end. Dried blood laced the edges. My eyes burned at the sight. I didn't want to believe what I was seeing. I didn't want to believe that any of this was true.

Lawrence's face glowed with fury at the sight of her. "Are you okay?"

"He took my hand to force Sophie's." Pain and anger twisted her mouth. Streaks of clean skin showed the paths of tears. "That's all. I can live with the loss of a hand. At least he didn't take my life."

Lawrence's head and shoulders stiffened. "He'll pay for it. I swear I will make him pay."

"We've all had to make sacrifices, and we've all risked life… and limb." A small smile pulled at the corner of her mouth. She shivered and pulled into herself as if she had chills.

I stared at her face for telltale signs of fever. Her eyes were glassy.

"Keeping Sophie alive is the most important thing. She's our only hope." Maria pointed to his shoulder. "Who's this?"

"Her? Oh, a little *pet.*" He patted my head and I swiped at him. "If you see her crawling into your cell, don't hurt her."

~Try to pet me again and you'll get two very sharp little teeth stuck in you.

Lawrence's lips twitched into a half-smile.

~Give your mom the cloak. She needs it more than I do.

"I brought something to keep you warm." Lawrence pointed to the bundle under his arm.

Maria nodded. "Push it through the little door below."

As he knelt, I jumped to the floor and scampered toward the hidden room.

"We'll get you out soon, Mom," Lawrence said. "I promise."

His footsteps thumped behind me as I scampered down the corridor. *~Are you going to be okay?*

~ I'll be back.

~I'll wait for you. Be careful.

A sweet pang in my chest made my eyes sting. *~I don't know how long I'll be. I don't want you to be in danger if they find both of us missing.*

~We've got about an hour before the sun rises. I'll be back for you then.

My heart lurched and my stomach knotted. I was anxious to find the right tapestry and call the dragons, but I'd be worried sick the whole time I was gone. My paws slapped the cold stone floor. Ahead were the blinking golden lights. I scrambled up the wall to the small hole that led into the chamber full of tapestries and looked over my shoulder. Lawrence paced at the end of the tunnel. My heart tripped over itself. I shook my head; I didn't have time to think about him right now. I had to think of the bigger picture. I turned away and squeezed through.

If it was possible, the chamber seemed to glow even brighter than yesterday. I forced my body to change into my human form, a little grudgingly. I was starting to enjoy being a mouse. My whiskers curled up like springs and disappeared. The noises of the dungeon muted as my ears transformed. My hair fell around me, a cloak of sorts since my clothes were still in the chamber. The tapestries I'd unrolled were glowing like the lights in Times Square. The chamber was warm, too, like walking through the square in February. I can remember feeling the heat of the lights on my face, the tall buildings blocking the cold wind, and I always wondered for a brief moment if I'd stepped into another world. Funny how things in this world sparked memories of the old.

The dark tapestry I'd found yesterday was lit up now. At first it was just at the center, and very faint, but it increased the longer I stared at it. I was drawn to it like a tracking dog to a scent. I crawled over.

The wool loops were scratchy. I stroked the tapestry and a shower of sparks rose around me. There was something familiar in the growing light. A willowy, vague shape. Then someone sobbed. It sounded like my name. I put my ear to the tapestry.

There it was again—faint, like snowflakes gathering on eyelashes. I leaned into the wool loops. "Dad? Dad, it's me! Sophie!"

He was alive! Thank goodness, he was alive. I shoved at the tapestry. I didn't remember Wilhelm using any special words when he dumped me through the portal, but something prevented me from passing through. I screamed and punched the fabric. Why couldn't I go through? The shadow disappeared and a sudden jolt made me cringe. The air above the tapestry shivered and quaked. It wasn't like the stream of energy I'd experienced when I'd been transported into Brindle. It felt different. It felt wrong.

A loud crack filled the chamber. And another. The dark part of the tapestry looked as if it had been cut—no—chopped! Light was streaming through now. I could see more clearly to the other side. There was a second man. Henry. His voice resonated through the portal like a church bell echoes over the hills.

"This is how it must be. It's the only way."

"Dad!" I shrieked, my voice terrible even to my own ears. A splintering creak filled the chamber as my dad heaved the axe again.

"No!"

A haunting sound, like that of an oncoming train, took over my senses. I covered my ears to block out the blare. A maelstrom of wind and magic sucked the air from the room. Stuck in the center of it, I gasped for breath. Unable to draw enough air to fill my lungs, I dropped to the floor. Black spots appeared in my vision.

As suddenly as the air had been taken from the room, it returned in a shower of gold sparks. They faded like dying embers. I coughed and rolled to my side. I lay there watching the fading light and feeling my ribs move in and out with each breath. The tapestry beneath me was totally black again. I ran my hands over the wool loops. No sparks. No energy vibrating up my arm. The magic was gone. The portal destroyed.

Why would Henry tell my dad it was the only way? The only way to keep the king and his men from returning? The only way to force me to do the king's bidding? I didn't know. I liked Henry and Samantha, but did I know them well enough to trust them? Were they part of the king's plan? Or were they on my side? At least my dad would be safe from Stuart. I kept repeating that to myself: *at least Dad is safe.* I tried to make myself believe it, even as I curled ino a ball, hot tears spilling down my face. My chest heaved with sobs until my stomach muscles burned with fatigue. I cried for my dad, and the tapestry, and the day Maria was taken away from me. I even cried for Mrs. Ling.

I cried out the pain of the last fifteen years—for my lost childhood and the mother and father I never knew. The dragonsong pulled at me. It promised comfort and reassurance. It sang to me of wonders I've never seen. I was in the right place, doing the right thing. I yearned to sing—to step into the shoes destiny had cobbled for me. But that line, calling the dragons to the king's side… I couldn't give power to that line.

What would happen if I changed the words? Would it destroy the magic? What if the line didn't mean what everyone thought it meant? I recalled my earlier words to Lawrence: "perhaps you aren't seeing the whole picture."

My mind spun, but I drew a shaky breath, trusting my instincts.

"Speed, bonnie lads,
Like a bird on the wing,
"Onward the dragons cry."

A cold wind circled the room. My skin raised in goosebumps—but no. It was bigger than that…the bumps on my arms looked like scales. My voice caught, but I swallowed, cleared my throat and continued.

"Speed to the child,
Who was born to sing,
Over the sea and sky.
"Come to me lads, fly to me now,
No longer will you refrain.
Come to the child,
And for the king,

I stood, my voice gaining power as it echoed through the chamber. The wind rose as a storm brewed above. I raised my hands, a golden haze enveloping me.

"Order shall rule again."

The last note lingered in the air so crisp it crackled. There was another stanza dancing on the tip of my tongue. I held it there like a bit of cotton candy and let it get warm and syrupy.

Golden sparks hung in the room as if they were a string of Christmas lights. Time stopped. A sudden flood of pictures rushed into my head.

Anna's voice swirled into the chamber. "Push, my Lady. I can see her raven hair."

My lungs tightened around my heart. The cry of my infant self rang in my ears.

In a misty whirlwind of golden-laced magic, the golden dragon appeared. Like Lawrence this morning, she took up most of the room. The dragon curled the infant in her claws before trying to hand over the bundle.

Gwendolyn turned away, tears coursing down her cheeks.

My mother hadn't rejected me—it had just been too painful. I understood that now. To hold a baby that you must give to another and maybe never see again. I'd only held little William for a minute, and already he had a firm grip on my heartstrings. To have a baby live inside you for nine months and then hand it over? I couldn't imagine the pain. Hot tears splashed my cheeks as my heart broke for both of us. The truth of my birth resonated through me, made the hairs stand up on the back of my neck. The sight of my mother's tears washed away all the resentment that had bubbled up. A glint of silver peeked from the queen's hand as she pressed the locket into Maria's palm.

I curled my hand against the place where my locket used to lay. It had been the queen's locket.

A knock thundered on the door of the chamber.

~We must go now, My Lady, the golden dragon demanded. *~Give her to me. She will be safe until you can join us. Are you ready, Maria?*

Gwendolyn's heart-wrenching sobs filled the room as Maria gathered the baby and followed the dragon to the tapestry. Tears tracked down her pale face.

"Tell Lawrence I'm sorry." Maria's lip trembled.

The room swirled in a vortex of color. I closed my eyes until the spinning stopped. When the world stilled, I was in a little kitchen in a cottage. A group of people gathered in front of a fireplace. They were younger, but I recognized Anna and Edward. When the young boy looked up, I saw his amber-colored eyes—there was no mistaking Lawrence's eyes. Edward had his arms around him. Tears were streaming down both of their faces. In a hollow voice, Edward said, "Your mother has been taken to the dungeon. As soon as he finds Sophinestra, he will have no more need of her. We must prepare for that day. We must protect them both."

The echo of sobs filled my ears as the golden sparks in the tapestry room twinkled down to earth and winked out. The vivid memories faded from my vision, but were engraved on my heart. My grief-stricken soul draped like a heavy woolen coat, pulling at my shoulders. So many lives tainted by the king's cruelty and obsessive need for power. It had to end if I was ever going to find peace.

I unrolled the closest tapestry. It was smaller than the rest, but as I opened it my breath caught. The dragon seemed to blink in the bright morning light, as if I'd woken him from a deep sleep by yanking the curtains open. The wool threads he was worked from shimmered in a deep emerald hue. *The tapestry from Gran's locked room.*

Sudden homesickness threatened to blind me with tears. I stroked the colored loops, and bright golden lights leapt into the air from my touch. A desperate ache tightened my ribs. I wanted to go home.

A small voice in my mind whispered, *you are home.*

But I'd never known Brindle as home. My heart warred with my mind. I pushed on the tapestry, sensed the tug of the portal. A picture of Maria cradling her arm popped in my head and my stomach fell into the ground. I couldn't leave Lawrence and Maria to face the will of the king alone. Maria had already paid a heavy price.

Rage consumed me, and with a growl, I kicked open another tapestry. It unrolled. The end slapped the floor, creating a wave of air and a lot of golden sparks. A unicorn lay in the center of a wooden paddock and there were flowers all around. I crumpled to my knees and, with all of my will power, contorted the anger into a small ball in my stomach where I could hold it until it was needed. I stared at the unicorn, wracking my memory, trying to remember where I'd seen the tapestry beneath me before—my dad's textbook. I couldn't remember if it said where the tapestry was, but it must be in some museum if it was pictured in the book. I could use it to get home— in a round about way. I didn't know if the portals left any traces of those who passed through them. I risked everyone's lives if I used the dragon tapestry and the king could trace my movements. What if the king discovered my absence before I could get to my dad?

It seemed I was stuck playing the king's game until I could make a plan—one where everyone was safe from Stuart. But I wouldn't be safe from him no matter where I was until all the portals were destroyed. And I couldn't destroy all the portals or I wouldn't be able to get back home.

There were only two choices as far as I could see: destroy all the portals in Brindle and keep my dad and the others safe in Vermont, or destroy the king.

~*Lawrence?*

~*I'm here.*

I curled up, the change into my mouse form nearly instant and painless. I scrambled for the hole in the chamber wall. ~*I think it's time to sing for the king.*

chapter twenty-four

A few minutes later, Lawrence knocked on the chamber door where I was supposed to be imprisoned.

I rapped his skull with my little mouse hand. *~Hello? You know I'm not in there.*

~It has to look convincing. Lawrence glanced to the right and I followed his look. A maid was approaching, carrying a long dress in her arms. Brunella trotted behind her and managed to catch her arm.

"Oh, please let me catch my breath a moment," Brunella panted, holding the maid back.

The maid's expression was one of annoyance as she turned. Brunella, giving us a sly expression, quickly waved Lawrence forward while the impatient maid tapped her shoe on the stone floor.

"Uh, are you decent, My Lady? It's time for your dancing lesson." Lawrence opened the door. He curled his fist around me and flung me toward the bed.

I squealed as I flew through the air, the wind pummeling past my satellite shaped ears. I landed in the bedcovers with a loud poof. The air around the feathers in the down coverlet whooshed past me. I managed to wiggle under the covers and shift back into my human form as Brunella sing-sang her way into the room. "Rise and shine sleepyhead."

I pulled the covers off of my head, stretched, and half sat up—extremely conscious of Lawrence lingering by the door and my nakedness separated by only a thin linen sheet.

"Ach! Look at that hair. We'll have to do something with it." Brunella turned to the maid who'd entered the chamber behind her while I furiously patted down my wild hair. "Fetch another dress from the queen—a plainer day dress suitable for dancing lessons. And bring the lass some breakfast. An egg and a toasted slice."

"Can you make that two eggs?" I asked. Yeah, yeah, it wasn't lady-like, but I was starving. Plus, a girl hell-bent on revenge needed a good breakfast.

The maid's eyes rounded with disbelief, but she bobbed her blonde head and mumbled in compliance before disappearing from the chamber.

Brunella pushed Lawrence from the room. "Shoo, shoo. It'll be an hour before she's ready. Go to the kitchens and get yourself something to eat. You look like you could use a good meal."

"Yes, Ma'am." Lawrence pecked her on the cheek.

"Such a good boy." She patted his arm before pushing him out and shutting the door behind him.

"Well, the castle's all a-bustle today." Brunella poked at the coals in the fireplace and added a couple of logs. "There, now. That should catch and warm the chamber up in no time."

I smiled at the woman's infectious energy and then yawned.

"Now, now, no more of that." Brunella patted the chair by the fire. "Come on, big day with the ball and all. We'll just brush those tangles out for this morning. I'll come back after supper and put it up when we change your gown."

"I thought I was going to see the que—my mother today." I stretched my legs toward the floor, pulling the sheet up tight around me and dragging it from the bed.

"There's a note with the dress." Brunella pointed to the gauzy confection hanging in the wardrobe. Tied to the hanger was a small rolled up bit of parchment. I pulled the strings loose and sat in the chair in front of the vanity table.

Brunella brushed my hair, chattering away about the ball, and the strange wind the village had experienced last night, and again this morning. Her voice droned in my ear like a mosquito, except pleasant. I unrolled the parchment and read the scrawling hand.

Sophie,

My schedule does not allow a meeting with you this morning. Please know that you honor me in wearing my dress to the ball, and in this way I will know you.

Your loving mother,

G

What the hell? What on her schedule could be more important than seeing me? I crumpled the note and flung it into the fire. My hands clenched the armchair rests. My teeth ground together.

"Did you hear me, Sophie?" Brunella looked at me expectantly in the mirror, lines creasing her forehead.

I shook my head, fighting back a sob. "My mother can't see me this morning."

"Oh, dear." Brunella's expression clouded. She patted me on the shoulder with a warm hand. "I'm sure it's none of her doing, child."

Staring at my white-knuckled fingers, I removed my hands from the armrests and made myself relax. Was the note just another mind game of the king? Had he made it impossible for my mother to see me? Was he trying to get me to think that she didn't care about me? "She does *want* to see me, doesn't she, Brunella?"

The maid brushed the front of my hair away from my face and split the strands in three pieces. "Of course she does. What mother wouldn't want to hold their child after so many years apart?"

"Were you there?"

"Where?"

"At the town square. When she was…made queen." I swallowed. The memories of that day made bile rise in my throat. "Were you there?"

Brunella lifted her eyes to the mirror and met mine. "Unfortunately, I was."

"So you saw my mother command the crowd to hail her as the new queen of Brindle?" I asked.

"Well, yes, but that's not the full truth, is it?"

"What really happened then?"

Brunella shivered and shook her head.

Twisting in the chair, I grasped the maid's forearms. "I need to know. I need to know the truth from someone I trust."

She sighed, her eyes darting around the chamber as if there were spies in every corner. "All right."

I released her and Brunella perched on the edge of the mattress. She picked at the linen apron spread over her lap. "As I remember it, the king was not pleased with the girls he had to choose from. He picked your mother from the crowd and…" The maid wrung her hands.

"Yes, go on."

"The next thing I remember is a bloody scepter. Gwendolyn's screams still echo in my nightmares. There was so much blood. It filled the cracks of the cobblestones and soaked her dress." Her hand shook as she pushed an errant curl away from her forehead. "We were all stunned. We knew he was not a righteous ruler, but that…we never expected something like that. He paraded her around the crowd, commanding us to hail her as the new queen of Brindle, but no one could speak until she commanded it. I think she was afraid that the king would hurt others if we didn't obey.

"She was a mess, your mother. Wouldn't speak to no one for months—not even me. Until her belly grew round and the midwife started to visit. Then I would catch her smiling every once in a while. She would sing to you, too. She had a lovely voice."

Brunella shrugged. "That's all I can tell you. The king feared we were getting too close and he ordered a new handmaiden. No one is allowed to stay for long with your mother. It's like he's isolated her on purpose—to keep her from having a confidant, I suppose."

"Or a chance at escape," I mumbled.

A knock at the door made both of us jump.

"Oh, bless me." Brunella hopped off the bed. "Must be the maid with your breakfast."

The chamber door opened and the blonde maid walked in with a tray. Another maid followed her in, arms stuffed full of a pale lilac fabric. The maids were dressed in skirts that brushed the floor, waistlines pulled in tight, busts pushed out.

"Thank you, girls. I will handle it from here." Brunella waved them off.

Brunella put the plate of food in front of me. I attacked it with a vengeance. While I ate, she fussed over the wrinkled state of the lilac-colored day dress and laid out the other things that had been brought up: stockings, matching shoes, and a corset. Good Lord, I'd have to wear a corset.

I wiped my mouth with the back of my hand. Brunella plucked the corset off the bed. "Let's get you dressed. Lawrence will be back soon for your lesson."

Self-consciously, I stood and let the sheet fall away from the top part of my body. I held it up so Brunella could wrap the stiff garment around me and lace up the back. Immediately, I regretted having so much breakfast.

"Too tight," I gasped. I was convinced that men designed corsets so that women couldn't breathe well enough to run away. The laces relaxed and my lungs could move again. Brunella pulled the sheet off me and whisked a long skirt around my waist. The fabric tightened as the maid tied the drawstring.

"Arms up." Brunella drew the gauzy dress over my head. I pushed my arms through. A rap sounded on the chamber door.

Lawrence opened the door. "Are you ready, My Lady?"

I turned and my insides went all gooey at the sight of him. His shirt was crisp and white under his bright blue jacket, the cuffs slightly ruffled at his wrists. His tall boots had been polished to a shine, and his black hair swept gently across his brow. I smiled as my heart pounded at a fierce pace. "Let's go."

Brunella held up the stockings and a pair of shoes. "You'll need these."

"Oh, yes, of course." Flustered, I sat on the edge of the bed and pulled my skirt to my knee. Lawrence's face turned a bright pink. He cleared his throat and turned his back.

~Oh please…you're embarrassed? You've seen me in my underwear!

~In our world, it is unseemly for a woman to bare her legs in front of a man. I'm not turning away for my sake, but for yours. Plus, if Brunella knew I'd seen you in the flesh, she'd be scandalized.

~That's silly—it's just a leg for goodness sake. It's not like I'm flashing my—

~Stop. I get the picture loud and clear. Lawrence's face turned a scary shade of scarlet.

I giggled. Sometimes it was as if Lawrence were two different people. He was so good-looking and funny. He'd even been rather bold back in Vermont that day by the stream. Surely he'd had plenty of girlfriends, but the way he was acting… *~You aren't still a virgin, are you?*

Lawrence rubbed the back of his neck. *~I believe in waiting for the one. Don't you?*

A hot flood of pleasure made my cheeks flush. *~I never really had the chance to think about it.*

I stood and stepped into the flats Brunella placed on the floor. Lawrence turned and offered his arm.

"You two go on now. The east portico is probably best. Right then, I'm off." Brunella bustled down the hallway with

Lawrence and I gliding casually behind. My limbs were warm and relaxed for the first time in a week. Strolling down the hallway on Lawrence's arm seemed the most natural thing. It was almost easy to forget about what I had to do tonight. I was determined to live this day minute to minute. To enjoy every second I was with Lawrence. If my plan backfired, it may be the last day I spent with him. I pulled him closer and squeezed his arm.

He tipped his head and quirked his eyebrow. "Everything okay?"

I nodded. "I'm just happy. I haven't been this happy in… well…a long time." I laid my head on his upper arm. I knew the feeling wouldn't last.

The corridor to the east portico opened up into a sunny, window filled room. Lush green plants bearing lemons, oranges, and limes lined the perimeter. Beautiful melon-colored tiles made a smooth dance floor. A boy around thirteen stood by the entrance, his hands cradling a violin. He bowed as we entered.

Lawrence gestured to the boy. "This is Able. His father is the village baker."

I held out my hand. "It's nice to meet you, Able."

The boy looked at me as if confused. Then, in a flurry of motion, he tucked his bow under his arm, clasped my hand, and kissed my knuckles. "Yes, ma'am. You as well."

I pulled away and laughed. I'd meant for him to shake my hand.

Able nodded, his smile curling up to his ears.

"Thanks for helping me out today," Lawrence said.

"Anything for you, Lawrence." Able tucked the violin under his chin and drew the bow over the strings.

Lawrence twirled me under his arm and pulled me close. "Stand up straight. Shoulders back. Left hand on my shoulder, your other hand goes in mine."

He swayed to the rhythm and I desperately tried to mimic his motions. The dance was a bit like the waltz I'd been made to learn in fifth grade gym class when we were studying the pioneers, but that was so long ago. Lawrence was patient as I stepped on his toes and tripped over my own feet. Eventually I coordinated my limbs to work together, and we glided over the tiles with fewer bobbles. As Able played another song, I relaxed into the steps and hummed to the tune.

"Now you've got it," Lawrence whispered in my ear. He pulled me closer and turned in a tight circle. My skirt whirled around my legs, and I was giddy for a moment, dizzy from the sudden spin. I laid my forehead on Lawrence's shoulder and tried to catch my breath. If only I could make the world magically melt away, then I could stay here, safe and warm in his arms forever.

"Ever since we met, I can't stop thinking about you." Lawrence's breath tickled my earlobe and drew shivers down my neck.

My face grew warm. He held me tight, muscles taut beneath his fancy jacket. I bit my lip as electric pulses shot through my limbs. Those few words hit all the right spots. My brain went into overdrive. I thought of all the things that could go wrong. His desire for me put him in even more danger. I was letting myself get in too deep. "We-we need to slow down." Pushing my free hand against his chest, I broke away from him. I ran to open the door at the end of the portico, my shoes clicking on the tiles. I leaned my forehead on the sun kissed wooden frame. The music blundered to a stop.

"Take a break, Able. Run to the kitchen for a sweet bun," Lawrence whispered to the boy.

Able's quick footsteps pattered over the floor and the door squeaked as it opened and then shut behind him.

The tap of Lawrence's boots on the tiles mimicked my heartbeat. My back curved into his body when he stepped in close. His kisses moistened my neck and spread goose bumps over my shoulders. He reached for my hand, curling his fingers around mine while his other hand snaked around my waist. His cheekbone settled on the top of my head. The weight was comforting. He was comforting, and he smelled amazing. My breath caught as my mind wandered to places it shouldn't go. I reined in my imagination and focused on the tall hedges that walled off the garden growing just outside the door. I felt the sting of tears.

"I can't imagine life without you anymore, Lawrence. What happens if I lose you?"

His lips pressed against the nape of my neck sending tingles into my fingers and down my legs. "I'll be here, whatever you need me for." He turned me in his arms and lifted my chin. "Always."

The door banged open and we drew away from each other quickly, a blush in both of our cheeks. With confident strides King Stuart marched in, eyebrows raised. "How are the dancing lessons going?"

Lawrence stepped forward and bowed slightly. "Fine, My King. We were just taking a short break."

Able squeezed through the door, licking his fingers.

"Ah, there's our little musician again now." Lawrence turned to me and offered his hand. "Shall we show the king what you've learned this morning?"

Hesitant to show off my lack of skill, I nodded and took his hand; nervous, short breaths made me light-headed. I swallowed, knowing Lawrence would support my temporary weakness, but Stuart inserted himself between us. "I think I'll take this dance."

Forced to accept the king's arm, I tried to smile as Able drew out a new song. The king turned me under his arm and bowed. I curtsied in return, throwing a glance at Lawrence before reluctantly stepping into the king's embrace.

We twirled over the tiles. Thankfully, I only stepped on his toes once. The king whirled me past Lawrence. "She'll do for tomorrow night, but she'll need more practice."

I was relieved when the king stopped dancing. I made to return to Lawrence's side, but Stuart snatched me fast by the elbow. With a stare full of lust, he licked his lips and smoothed his hair. The movement wasn't necessary, as not a single hair was out of place. "I believe we need to take a walk. Lawrence, thank you for your tutelage this morning. Your help is now required at the scaffolds."

"The scaffolds, sire?"

The king raised two fingers and made a quick gesture. "Dismissed."

Lawrence's jaw set firm. He dipped his head, but not before a flash of anger lit his eyes. "Yes, sire." His shoulders were tense, his posture rigid as he left the room.

I missed him already. My body longed to press into his on the ballroom floor.

"Able, we will see you later at the ball." Stuart turned away and led me out of the open doors on the far end of the portico.

I risked a glance over my shoulder. Able was watching me walk out of the doors like a widow watches the casket of her lover pass.

Lawrence's last thoughts prickled down my spine. *~He didn't choose me to teach you because I'm the best dancer—he was testing my loyalty and saw it lacking. Be careful.*

chapter twenty-five

With Lawrence's warnings dancing like a devil on my shoulder, we ambled through the hedge maze in the garden. The hedge was at least fifteen feet high and four feet thick—a veritable fence, though the top was trimmed into fanciful animals. Topiary dragons charged along the perimeter. Long-tailed unicorns stood alert at the corners. With my nerves fraying, I expected even stranger creatures to pop out at every turn, like that old movie about the labyrinth.

The cloying fragrance of roses seeped through the thick shrubbery. The smell reminded me of the reindeeer from the tapestry. The scent of roses had filled my room when he'd visited me. Stuart hummed the tune of my dragon song and patted my hand. The touch felt almost consoling, which freaked me out. Of course, his consolation felt fake—like another mask he'd put on for the day. But what did he have to console me over besides the thing I already knew about? He wasn't truly sorry for any of his previous behavior—so, it must be something even worse. My imagination played around all the things he could've done that I hadn't learned of yet.

Finally, we entered a large open square. Rows of pink, red, and white roses grew in a clearing in the center. Yellow and orange lilies dotted the outer limits of the courtyard.

The king plucked a flower from a bush and tucked it behind my ear. "One must be careful of roses—for though they are beautiful, sometimes they draw blood."

A bright red bead glowed on his thumb. He sucked the crimson dot from his finger. I cringed. I could almost taste the metallic tinge. I swallowed the bile that threatened to rise. Slipping from his hold, I pretended to admire the blooms, my finger trailing along the soft petals. "Many flowers have thorns. It's all in the approach."

I stroked a rosebud and the thorns retracted. I was able to pull the bud from the stem without injury. I offered it to the king.

He plucked it from my fingers and inhaled its fragrance. A smile stretched his lips. He offered his arm. Reluctantly, I took it because I knew I must. He led me straight to a wall of hedge, and I briefly wondered what he was doing. Was he going to throw me into it? Back me against it and threaten my life? My fight or flight response turned on, but the hedge wall wasn't a wall at all. There was a path leading around another row of hedges that made it look like one solid wall from the square courtyard. We turned right; the world opened up before me, and my mind was relieved a bit. At least if I had to flee, I'd found an escape route.

A wide lawn stretched in all directions and the sun glittered off a small bay beyond that. About a dozen tall ships with colorful sails were secured to the docks. Sailors, their bodies browned from the sun and dressed in bright flowing pants, bustled below unloading wooden crates and casks. From my vantage point on the hill, I could clearly see the markings on the side; two bears painted in an emerald green. My grandfather's heraldic device.

We proceeded to a set of stone stairs built into the hill and started down. Tall stakes, stained a deep brownish-red, were driven into the ground at the bottom of the stairs. My stomach turned and dread engulfed me like a tidal wave. The stakes swayed with the weight of heads speared at the top. The closer I got, the more details I could make out. Some of the heads were dried and decaying, others were fresh, eyes still blindly staring, streaks of blood not yet washed away by the rain. My heart pounded so hard my ears throbbed. Was this what the consoling pats were for? Did he think the sight of so many beheaded men and women would disturb me to the point of acquiescing to his demands without question?

"Sometimes a ruler must lead with an iron fist," Stuart said. "Examples must be made for order to be restored." He took a deep breath and smiled. "This is my kingdom. Smell the clean ocean air—so much better than that nasty place of concrete and metal where you grew up. Maria and Gwendolyn deprived you of a childhood in Brindle. Grass to run in, forests to explore. You would've turned out much differently if you'd grown up here, where you belonged."

"It doesn't feel like home yet," I said.

Stuart patted my hand again. "It will." He pulled me forward and we started down the stairs. Guards dressed in bright blue waited for us in the courtyard. They held back a rowdy crowd from the steps and some kind of wooden stage. They seemed to be over-excited, anxiously waiting for something to happen. What did Stuart have planned?

King Stuart ignored the staked decaying heads as if it were a normal, everyday occurrence. However, those two eggs I'd had for breakfast were trying to worm their way back up my throat.

He gestured to the ships in the port. "I'm very proud of the trade my men have been able to secure this season. We've received casks of wine from the Elven Valley just this morning, rare unicorn ivory last week, and the finest silks and satins from the west."

I searched every bloodied face as we descended. for one I recognized. No one looked familiar. The sheer number of people who had been killed frightened me, but the fact that I knew none of them was a little bit of a relief. I straightened my shoulders and steeled my resolve. I would not let Stuart frighten me like a child watching a horror movie. I would just pretend I was on a movie set.

But then, near the bottom, long dark hair streamed from one of the staked heads…

A cry caught in my throat and my knees went weak. Gwendolyn? I covered my mouth as the king led me past. I didn't dare blink but searched the vacant eyes, the slack mouth.

"You won't find who you're looking for here," King Stuart purred. He pulled me down the final steps and the guard encircled us. We forced our way into the crowd. "I always like to be in the midst of my people when they least expect it. Keeps them on their toes."

One of the king's men climbed the stairs of the stage and stood in one corner. I drew a sharp breath. It was Lawrence, hands clasped in front of him and an expression of calm indifference on his face. I pointed, trying with all my might to keep the shaking that was working its way through my body out of my hands. "What's Law-Lawrence doing on that stage?"

He laughed. "Stage? Haven't you ever seen a scaffold?"

Shocked confusion must have shown on my face because Stuart laughed again. The head guard shouted, "Make way for your king!"

The crowd parted slowly and he pulled me to the front of the stage where there was a small box, like a dugout at a baseball field. Within it were two chairs upholstered in blue velvet. My knees shook so hard, I was glad to sit down as Stuart bid. The guards surrounded us, weapons at the ready.

Stuart slapped the wooden planks of the floor of the scaffold before taking his seat next to me. "This is no stage. It's a gallows—where criminals are executed."

"Executed?" The word stuck to the roof of my mouth, making it hard to draw a breath. Stuart pointed to six hooded figures being led up the back stairs. The hoods were withdrawn from the "criminals" one by one as they passed the guard standing next to the top of the stairs. The last hood was removed and I gasped. Edward's eyes met mine.

"No!" My voice barely made a noise in the crowd. I stood, wanting to propel into action. "You can't do this!" I cried louder. I tried to go to the old man but Stuart swept me up and held me like a vise. My feet dangled in the air, useless. I turned my head away. I couldn't bear to watch. A familiar sensation pinched in my forehead.

~Be smart, sweet granddaughter. You can beat him at his own game. My only regret in this life is that I did not know you well. Still, I loved you with all my heart.

I stopped struggling. My eyes filled with tears.

"Look at me." King Stuart set me down and dug his fingers into my chin, prying my face toward his. "I told you what would happen if you didn't do what I asked. You've forced me to hurt you."

I glared at him. His steel blue, hard as flint eyes, returned the look. Hatred burned in my chest. Tears rolled down my face. My shoulder muscles bunched.

"I can, *and I will*, make you watch," Stuart said through clenched teeth. "Even if I have to carve your eyelids off."

I blinked furiously, willing the tears to recede. The knowledge of what would happen to Edward and the other men crushed the air from my lungs. I hadn't even gotten to know my grandfather, and Stuart was taking him away.

"I'll sing for you. I'll call the dragons like you want. Anything…please."

The king sneered. "It's too late to save these men. They've been inflaming a rebellion for years. They *will* swing. Today." He loosened his grip and shrugged his shoulders to straighten his coat, the oily-sweet smile returning to his face. His fingers trailed down my neck and over my collarbone. His bottom lip pouted out. "Besides, I promised a spectacle today, and a spectacle my people will receive."

Stuart's eyes roved over my exposed skin, following the path his fingers had just blazed. He grabbed my arm in a fierce grip.

"Dougal!" the king cried, shifting his attention reluctantly from me.

Dougal approached the front of the gallows. Arms crossed, he waited the king's order, eyes shining.

The king pointed to Lawrence. "String him up with the others."

"No! No!" I struggled to release myself from the king's grasp. His fingers dug into my skin like a pinch collar; my physical strength wasn't enough to pry them off. I gave up and watched in horror as Dougal led Lawrence to the front and tightened a rope around his neck. He bound Lawrence's wrists. I screamed his name but he refused to look at me. The crowd burst into a loud murmur.

~Why aren't you fighting back?! Panic lodged in my throat.

~There are many who cheer to hide their true feelings. They will rise up to fight beside you.

~I don't care about them! I need you!

~We all knew we were playing a dangerous game. I've done my part. I love you, Sophie. I'll always be with you. Remember that.

I turned on Stuart and hissed. "How can you do this? He's one of your guards." Fear clawed like a cat inside my brain.

"He's a traitor, just like the rest of them." Stuart spit on the ground and then waved his hand in a bored gesture. "Get on with it."

A third guard leered at the crowd as he walked to the side of the gallows where a large pulley held the ropes taut. His hand lingered over a lever.

~Please. You said you'd always be here for me... I begged, but there was no answer. Had he shut me out? *~I need you, Lawrence.* I shoved the thought at him so hard he jerked.

"Look," the king chuckled. "He's already going into fits and the lever hasn't even been pulled yet."

I glared at Stuart. "I won't sing if you kill them. I will cut my own tongue out first."

The king glared back at me. "Oh, you'll sing, because if you don't, I'll kill every last soul in this kingdom…starting with your mother. Haven't enough people suffered because of you?"

I swallowed the bile searing my throat. My hands trembled. He was right. In some perverted way this was all my fault. If it weren't for me, no one would've died. A drum roll echoed over the harbor. Reluctantly my gaze returned to the guard at the lever as my heart disintegrated into ashes.

A loud clang of moving gears rang out. The floor beneath the men fell away.

"No!" I keened and reached out to Lawrence. A blinding light flashed over the crowd. Shading my eyes, I peered up at the gallows, praying for a miracle. Six bodies hung from their rope necklaces still twitching, but Lawrence was splayed on the ground, beneath the trap door. My heart skipped. A tug heaved at my core. Had his rope broken?

Dougal rushed forward and jumped from the stage. He yanked Lawrence out from under the wooden platform and rolled him over. Dougal tilted his head, waited for the rush of air on his cheek that would tell him if Lawrence were still alive. Tears built up on the fringe of my eyelashes. I held my breath.

Dougal's head whipped up to find me in the crowd…no, not me, his hazel gaze shifted to the king. When their eyes met, he nodded. Stuart rubbed his hands together and chuckled as if he'd just succeeded in pulling a grand prank. Tightness grew in my chest. My neck ached from holding in the sob as Stuart shuttled me forward with quick steps.

A jaunty tune from a trumpet echoed over the roar of people. It was all I could do to keep my feet moving beneath me. My thoughts swirled and tangled in my mind and though I wanted to dissolve into a miserable puddle, Lawrence would have wanted me to go on, to continue playing the king's game until I was victorious…but how could I go on without him?

I prayed that Dougal was wrong, that Lawrence was simply knocked unconscious. I looked over my shoulder. His body was no longer lying in the dirt. My heart jumped into my throat. Frantically I searched the crowd for him.

He was flung over Dougal's shoulder like a sack of grain. Stuart yanked on my arm, and I turned, catching my balance. The look of pure joy on Stuart's face, the way the crowd celebrated the death of those men—it was despicable. Blood rushed through my veins, and the scarring on my neck constricted tighter over my muscles. I spread the fingers of one hand out in front of me—they were shining in the sunlight like I'd been rolled in glitter. A sharp pain in my back made me gasp; the world titled off kilter. What was happening to me?

Stuart pushed me through the edges of the encroaching crowd. The sky seemed to spin above me. I scolded myself. It was no time to lose control. The king nearly dragged me back up the stairs to the castle. "My father told me a king controls his kingdom in one of two ways: fear or love. If you are to be queen, you will learn that fear is a far better, and more expedient, tool."

"Queen?" I stopped abruptly. "Brindle already has a queen."

Stuart circled me like a cat stalking wounded prey. "Don't you understand yet? Is your head full of wool? Gwendolyn has never produced an heir—not for want of trying."

I cringed at the thought of his touch, his hands roaming over my body, his mouth hot on my breasts.

"I've kept her around because she was my link to you. Now that I have you, I don't need her. We will be married in three days." Stuart stalked up a few steps. When he realized I wasn't following, he turned. "Are you coming?"

I glared at him. "Do I have a choice?"

Stuart laughed and turned away, ascending the stairs. "One always has a choice. But can you live with the consequences?"

I reined in the hatred that boiled up through my pores. I counted the next ten stairs and took a deep breath with every step. I couldn't put my plan into action if I didn't have control of my emotions.

He waited for me at the top of the stairs. Calmly, I placed my hand on his outstretched arm. If I were to beat him at his own game, I would have to play by his rules. Stuart grinned as he escorted me through the hedge wall. "A divorce is so boring, don't you think? Not enough scandal in that, is there?"

I refused to give him the satisfaction of a reaction. My voice was flat and emotionless when I spoke. "Whatever you deem necessary for the occasion, My King."

The king gripped my arm and pulled me close. He kissed me deeply, and then his moist breath was in my ear. "Now that's the answer of a queen."

I leaned into him. "I've just realized that I don't have to worry about how my actions will affect anyone anymore. You've taken care of that little problem for me. Honestly, it's a bit…freeing." I pulled away and managed a small smile. I wove thoughts of lust through the space between us. I didn't have much to lose—Lawrence and Edward were both dead. My dad was in Vermont; Maria was relatively safe in the dungeon, and my mother…well, I'd never really known her, had I? My heart lurched in its cage. The lies I was telling myself buried deep into my gut and made me sick, like a parasite that sucks the life from its host.

The lustful gleam in Stuart's eyes grew. He drew me close to him and kissed my neck. His hands slid under my hair and pulled at the neckline of my dress. I didn't pretend to enjoy his touch, but I didn't tell him to stop either. Then he sank his teeth into my shoulder, his hand covering the cry that rang out over the hedges. I pushed him away, but he reeled me back.

The king's kiss was hard, demanding. He lingered as if wanting to say something, but he refrained and peered at me through his eyelashes. "Until tonight, then, when I will truly make you my queen."

"Yes, tonight." I turned on my heel and marched through the portico where just an hour ago Lawrence had held me in his arms and twirled me. I glanced over my shoulder. The king remained motionless in the courtyard, but his gaze stalked me like a tiger shadowing its prey.

chapter twenty~six

"Hush now, Sophie." Brunella rubbed my back in soothing circles. Her whisper was soft in my ear. "Your tears will not do your complexion any justice."

Didn't she understand? Didn't she care that the king had just killed her nephew? My blood boiled at her response.

"I don't care if my face is blotchy and red! I don't care if snot runs down my face and stains this dress." I gripped the yards of fabric in my hands, wanting to tear it from my body. "He *killed* him." I choked out the sobbed words. *I need him*, my mind echoed. How could Brunella be so calm? Why wasn't she upset?

Brunella handed me a handkerchief. Tears clung to her eyelashes, sparkling like dew on a spider's web. She met my eyes as I took the handkerchief and mopped my face. For a moment, I thought she was going to break down, but she stiffened up and set her shoulders.

"He knew what he was doing. Lawrence knew the danger— we all do."

I stared at my hands, tried to control the flow of tears. The handkerchief was already soaked. My hands were no longer glittery, though my rage still dwelt just beneath the surface like a sea monster stalking a sailing ship. It was just waiting for the right time to rear its spiny head. So far, I'd been able to control my emotional overreactions, but that was when Lawrence was by my side.

I grabbed Brunella's hands. "We must do something—it's not fair."

"Life is never fair and revenge is a never ending circle. It's best if it isn't drawn." Brunella wiped her tears away.

She pulled a blue candle and a rolled up parchment from her pocket. "He asked me this morning to give these to you when the time was right. I think he must've seen it—his future. It was one of his dragon gifts."

A tingling traveled up my spine and made my brain light up like fireworks. He must have seen it… If he knew, why didn't he tell me? Why didn't he try to escape?

With a shaking hand, I took the candle and settled it in my lap. I unrolled the parchment after Brunella left the room. My locket slithered out and into my lap. Sobs burst out as I slid the locket over my head and tucked it into my dress bodice. I wiped the tears from my eyes and read the tiny script.

As flame lights shadow and truth ends fear,
Open locked thoughts to my minds' willing ear.
May the smoke from this candle into everywhere seep,
Bringing innermost voices to my mind in speech.

The air in the chamber shifted and the parchment fluttered in my hand. It was a spell.

A hissing filled the room. The candlewick burst into flame. I scrambled to pick it up off my lap. A small dark ring had appeared. The heat had blistered the delicate fabric, but it hadn't burned through. I took a calming breath and repeated the spell, the candle wavering before me. "As flame lights shadow and truth ends fear, open locked thoughts to my mind's willing ear. May the smoke from this candle into everywhere seep, bringing innermost voices to my mind in speech."

I closed my eyes, focusing all my energy on hearing some voice inside my head. But the only innermost voice I could hear was my own nagging at me that I must have done something wrong.

Somewhere in my brain, that little voice reminded me of the rule of three. All the fairytales had three—three blind mice, three little pigs, three fairy gifts, three times to make something right. I took a breath. Then I spoke the words a third time.

On the mantle, the glass ball rocked between the dragon's paws. With a blast of cold air, a flurry of muffled voices swept into my head.

…I shouldn't put the table there… The king will have my head for this… I hope I can sneak a dance in with Liddy… I wonder what the masks will look like…

My heart fell when I didn't recognize any of the speakers.

No matter what happens, give these bottles of whiskey to the dungeon guards tonight. Be sure they are good and drunk…

I sat up straighter at the sound of the queen—my mother's voice. Another gust circled the room, carrying more broken thoughts. *…I hope infection isn't setting in… These pups will have to be kept secret or he'll drown them for being mutts…*

More randomness. Errant thoughts from people I didn't know. What was I doing wrong? Surely Lawrence meant for me to hear someone or something specific.

She doesn't know what will happen when she sings…

That was the king's voice! What did he mean by that? I tried to focus in on the clamor of voices, to pick out Stuart's thoughts again. The candle flickered, and I heard another voice I recognized, one that broke my heart.

Sophie…

I could barely breathe. Lawrence? Was this his final thought? Unspoken words that sat lingering on the earth waiting for me to hear them?

It's not over.

I twirled in my seat and frantically scanned the room. My heart swelled and emptied so fast I felt light headed. His voice had been so clear—as if he was standing right next to me. Tears sprang to my eyes again. I shook. The candle flame disappeared, like someone had dropped a snuffer on it. A knock at the door made me jerk out of my skin. Literally. My nose twitched. My ears went loose and flappy. I felt the sting of whiskers. I couldn't transform right now, though I wanted nothing more than to hide away from the world. I shook my head, touched my ears. They shrank back to normal. I ran my hands down my face to make sure there weren't any whiskers protruding.

"C-come in…" Quickly I rolled the parchment around the candle and stashed it under the pillows on the bed.

The door opened and Brunella entered. "I'm so sorry to disturb you, My Lady. The king requests that you wear this tonight."

She held out a thick leather collar bulging with dark emeralds in the shape of tears. Each gem was nestled in gold filigree. I fingered the gems. They were beautiful. Cool to the touch and smooth, like glass. I shivered. No way was I wearing it.

"It will look beautiful on you, but then again, you'd be beautiful in anything—even mouse fur." Brunella chuckled tearfully and placed the necklace on the vanity. "I never understood what Lawrence meant by that. Ah, well, I suppose that's between you two."

Lawrence told his aunt I was beautiful? Even in mouse fur? Tears pricked my eyes again. I dabbed at my face with the back of my wrist.

Brunella's fingers hovered over the collar, but her training didn't allow her to linger. She turned quickly and strode from the room, only pausing at the door to tell me that she'd be back in an hour to help me dress.

I nodded in understanding as the door was closed, kicked off my shoes, and tumbled into bed. I wanted to close my eyes, to drift out of this world, and wake up from this horrible dream. I wanted Lawrence's arms around me, his body under mine like that day in my bedroom. Those memories seemed so far away. I didn't understand why he didn't tell me that the king suspected him earlier. Together we could've come up with something—something that could've saved his life. I didn't want to go on without him, but I knew I must. King Stuart would expect me to cower now, to give in to his demands, but I wouldn't do it.

The glint of the glass globe on the mantel caught my eyes before I could close them.

I raised my hand and the globe lifted into the air. I beckoned it closer with a flick of my fingers. It floated toward me. A spark of excitement made my heart race. I hadn't really expected that to happen. The orb settled gently into my palm. Misty white swirls opened into a blue sky. A rush of frigid air made my nose run. I dropped the orb on the bed and the coldness dissipated. I picked it up again. My stomach suddenly dropped, like the sensation when an airplane flies into turbulence.

I rolled on my side and watched the clouds swirl until my eyelids grew heavy. I fell asleep with one comforting thought in my head: The dragons had heard me singing. They were on the move.

chapter twenty seven

Brunella laid a plait of hair across my shoulder. She'd attached long peacock feathers down the length of the glossy black braid, adding a metallic shine to it and a bit of creative coverage. She clasped my upper arms, her hands warm on my bare skin. "You'll take their breath away."

"At least the king's breath," I said. I *literally* wanted to take his breath away.

Brunella released me and fingered the emerald choker lying on the top of the vanity. "Just one final touch."

I stopped her from picking it up with a gentle hand. "No. I will wear my mother's locket and nothing else." I looked up into the mirror and smiled at her. Brunella's face shone with a mixture of fear and awe.

"Are you certain, My Lady? The king will be angry if you disobey his request."

"I don't care." I fingered the locket hanging around my neck and fixed her with a stare. "Now promise me that once I go downstairs, you'll walk out of this castle. Stay away tonight."

Brunella's hand fidgeted at the base of her throat. "What if you need me?"

A loud rapping on the door announced the arrival of my escort.

I stood and clasped her hands. I gave her a reassuring squeeze. "I know you take your job seriously, but please be with your family tonight." The door opened. I turned.

A masked guard filled the doorway. He bowed. He was tall with strawberry blond hair. It was slicked back on his head in smooth waves. A short curving beak protruded from the mask perched on his nose. The bird-like mask was made in such a way that his eyes could not be seen, but he seemed familiar. Perhaps I'd just seen him around the castle, but he was too broad to be Stuart, too blond to be Wilhelm, and too skinny to be Dougal. I glanced back at Brunella. My own mask was clenched in the maid's hands. I gestured to it. "I think I'll need that."

Brunella shook herself as if waking from a dream, and hurried over. "Yes, of course. Let me put it on for you."

I turned so Brunella could tie the small golden mask in place. I nodded in thanks and took the guard's offered arm. His touch was stiff, but tense energy danced just beneath his cool façade. He didn't speak to me as we strode through the corridors buzzing with servants and guests. When we reached the top of the stairs that led into the Great Hall, the guard paused.

We stood there for a moment while people streamed around us. It was like one of those moments in a movie where time stops for the main characters and a stream of color winds around them. I looked for the ticking clock that was always the next camera shot.

"What are you waiting for?" I asked. My anxiety was rising by the minute. I just wanted to get this over with. To get my mother, and Maria, and go home.

My guard didn't answer, but he kept his grip tight on my arm as if I might fly away if he relaxed.

The deep notes of a cello thrummed under the higher notes of violins and flutes. A few moments later, a fanfare trumpeted and two of the king's servants appeared at the head of the stairs. A loud voice announced the couple, the Earl of Palomino and his filly. The couple wore large horse headdresses with gold cording draping over their shoulders like reins.

"Is that their real title?" I asked.

Again, the guard stayed silent, but shook his head.

The couple bowed and descended the stairs to the dance floor. Another guest moved forward and was pronounced as "The Muffin Man." I rolled my eyes at the absurdity. How were they going to announce me? Little Bo Peep? Why were there so many people to announce anyway? The waiting was making me fidget. I wished I had spent more time planning my escape, making the details more concrete in my mind.

Creeping fingers of anxiety crawled up my torso. The guard silently reprimanded me with a subtle clearing of his throat. I took a deep breath, pressed the anxiety into a little box in the back of my mind, and gathered my composure. At long last, the landing was clear of guests.

My escort stepped to the crest of the stairs, pulling me along. A new rush of panic swept through me. Goosebumps crested over my body and my hands shook. What had I been thinking? Why did I think I could go through with this? I wasn't sure if I could even make it down the stairs without fainting. But the dragons were on their way. I had already set the plan in motion when I sang in the dungeon room. It was too late to stop it now…or was it? Could I somehow get Gwendolyn and Maria into the tapestry room? Even if I did, I'd have to keep the king and his men from following us. I'd have to find all the portals in my world and destroy them. Was it possible? What would happen to the innocent people of Brindle?

I scanned the hall below for my mom. The guests were a blur of color, feathers, and masked faces. A small stage had been set up to the left of the dais where the king sat on his throne, his hair slicked back. He wore a black mask encrusted with jewels, but there was no mistaking his smug expression and confident air. It made me want to vomit. At the king's feet lay a lumpy velvet sack. To his right stood Wilhelm, his white porcupine hair making him obvious. Just behind Stuart I recognized the blocky build of Dougal. Even not in his guard's uniform, his massive form stuck out of the crowd. The chair next to the king was empty. My muscles tensed as if I had just caught the gaze of Medusa, my own gaze moving back to the velvet sack by the king's feet. "Where's the queen?"

The guard's shoulders stiffened. He scanned the room, but he remained as silent and still as the guards outside of Buckingham Palace.

I scowled. Why wouldn't he answer me?

The trumpets played a longer fanfare. The music softened. The whole crowd turned toward the stairs, murmuring. All eyes were on me. My escort pulled me forward. I swallowed and cleared my throat, fighting the urge to flee. My arrival was broadcast across the grand hall.

"Sophinestra, the Duchess of Wirth…and the future queen of Brindle."

In those few words, my anxiety turned to fury. The edges of my self-control already frayed, adrenaline gushed into my veins. What did the king do to Gwendolyn? Where was she? Did he hurt her? My escort tightened his grip.

"He needs an heir," he said in a low voice. "That sick bastard."

"He's not getting one from me," I said through gritted teeth.

The man nodded, his mouth a grim line.

I lifted my chin and stared straight ahead as we descended the stairs. If I had the power of lighting fires bigger than a candle flame with my mind, the king would be dancing around in smoldering pants about now. *Liar, liar.*

My escort, who'd finally loosened his vise-like grip on my arm, marched across the ballroom floor toward the dais. We halted about ten paces from the king. He released me and bowed to Stuart before stepping away, but not too far away. He could still grab me if I tried to flee, though I was pretty sure he was on my side.

King Stuart rose and swung out his arm toward the crowd "Sing for me, my Dragonsinger!"

I opened my mouth to reject the suggestion, but felt the dragonsong filling me. It made my limbs fiery warm. Sweat beaded up on my forehead. I trembled from the effort of keeping my mouth shut, but finally I had to let go of my control.

"Speed, bonnie lads,
Like a bird on the wing,
Onward the dragons cry.
Speed to the child,
Who was born to sing,
Over the sea and sky."

King Stuart closed his eyes and swayed with the melody. I longed to wipe that smug smile off his face with my fist. I could feel the scales rising again and my confidence grew.

"Come to me lads, come to me now,
No longer will you refrain.
Come to the girl,
And the true king,
Order shall rule again."

The words formed on my tongue without thought, and yet, they had changed. King Stuart narrowed his eyes at me and rolled back on his heels. His arms crossed over his chest, and there was a contemplative expression on his face. His jaw worked at chewing the inside of his cheek. High, plaintive notes of a violin swept in, threading through the haunting melody. A young boy drew his bow over the strings of a highly polished instrument—Able. Lawrence said I would have friends in the crowd. My voice gained power as it echoed through the hall.

"Speed, bonnie lads,
Like a bird on the wing,
Onward your children cry."

A gust circled the Great Hall—mussing hair, catching skirts, and drawing feathers from masks. The feathers swept through the chamber like autumn leaves. A sparkling golden haze enveloped me. I raised my hands to the ceiling. Lightning streaked past the windows and thunder added a drumroll. The stained glass windows in the hall burst from the frames and scattered over the floor like spilled gems.

The king flinched. The smug expression had turned into one of dismay. "Guards! Guards!"

As the rain pelted into the hall through the broken windows, I drew a last breath and sang even louder.

"Speed to the child,
Who is heir to the king,
Over the sea
And sky."

The last note lingered, hovering above the crowd. As it faded, the air was drawn from the room. Everything went still, like we had all suddenly been enchanted, yet no one was falling asleep. Then, all at once, the world around me seemed to fly in reverse—as if I was traveling back in time.

chapter twenty eight

The guests retreated, the tables of food vanished, the staging for the musicians broke down. The sun rose in the west and traveled to the top of the sky. The scaffold by the harbor appeared and time shifted again. I relived the terrible moment the lever was pulled, dropping the men from the gallows. The memory zoomed in on me. My hand stretched out. I screamed. A white-hot streak of light leaping from my mouth and flashing over the crowd as ropes were pulled taut around necks—except one. The rope around Lawrence's neck was black… as if the blinding flash of light had singed it. The light that had come from me! The rope frayed and uncoiled, dropping Lawrence's body to the ground under the stage.

The memory zoomed in over Dougal's shoulder. I was staring at Lawrence's face. His eyelids fluttered as Dougal lowered his head to check for signs of life. "I'll take it from here, my friend." Dougal's voice caught in his throat.

The memory swirled into a mist and opened into a chamber in the dungeon. Gwendolyn was curled into a ball in the corner. Hair mussed, skirts streaked with dirt. There were manacles around her ankles. She looked up and her eyes brightened with recognition. "Sophie." A smile wavered through her tears. "I've always loved you, Sophie. Be strong."

I reached for her, but the image was swept away. A cry of anguish caught in my throat, but the memory swirled and I was back in our apartment in New York, in my small bedroom. The curtains billowed gently at the open window. The soft glow of lights from the street below filtered in. A younger version of myself slept in the bed, one hand under my cheek the other curled on top of my blankets as if holding something—the leg of a bear, or more likely, the tail of a dragon.

From the only dark corner in the room, a cloaked shadow separated itself. A low growl rumbled across the room and then a green glow appeared on the bed next to my sleeping form. Bailean! He was little, the size of a Great Dane, and he was curled up like a dog at the end of my bed, his tail disappearing in my tiny grip.

"At ease, dragon. It's me." Gwendolyn pulled back the hood of her cloak. A shower of golden sparks lit up the tapestry behind her. It was the same dragon tapestry in Gran's locked room. "I just want to see her."

The green misty glow grew again, and uncurling, the dragon transformed into a little boy. His golden eyes gleamed in the low light before he threw his arms around my mother. His soft sobs echoed off the bedroom walls. "They took her...Mother. They took her back to Brindle, but I hid us in the wardrobe. It was all I could do to keep us from being discovered."

Gwendolyn picked him up and patted his back. "Shh, hush now, you don't want to wake Sophie up." After rocking him for a moment, she set his feet back on the floor and held him at arm's length. Her eyes held his. "You did very well protecting her. Better than anyone would've expected."

The boy wiped his eyes and nodded his head. His lower lip quivered. "Can we come home now?"

Deep sadness grew in the crinkles of Gwendolyn's eyes. "I'm afraid not. The kingdom has become very dangerous. This is the last time I'll be able to visit until she is ready."

The boy fidgeted with the edge of his tattered tunic. "But everyone keeps telling Sophie that I'm not real. What happens if she starts to believe it?"

The question hung heavy in the air like the pressure you feel just before the clouds burst open and rain pours down.

Gwendolyn stroked a length of hair from the pale face of my smaller form, tucking it behind my little ear. Tears sparkled like jewels on her cheekbones. "If she loses the ability to believe, then all is lost. You must not let that happen."

The room faded. I longed for the comfort of my mother's arms. To hold Lawrence and tell him that I was grateful for his protection all these years, even if I hadn't known it was him. I wanted to return to that moment, but I was jerked into another darkened room.

It was cold. A tense fear was palpable in the chamber. I strained in the dim light, trying to see what had caused a scuffle in the chamber. In the center of the room stood a large rock. A v-shaped notch was carved into one edge. Below the rock was a slab of stone with a carved groove, like the routered edge of a cutting board. I followed the groove with my eyes. It ended at a hole that emptied into a pit dug into the ground. My stomach tightened and broke out into cold sweats. My mother, bound and gagged, was forced to lie down onto the large stone, her wrists strapped to each side.

Gwendolyn struggled and cried out. I ran toward her, but found myself on the other side of the table. I was like a ghost. A cold dread chilled my soul. I wheeled on my heel just in time to see the blade flash.

My chest squeezed so hard that it felt like my heart shattered into a million pieces. A deep chuckle reverberated in the chamber. The king picked my mother's head off the floor by her hair. He dropped it into a velvet bag like he was dropping an apple into a sack. There was no regard for the life he'd just ended. For the mother I would never know.

Rage flooded my veins. The bones in my back crackled. I screamed and curled into a ball. Golden scales rose on my arms, like armor. My hands extended and my fingers curled. I stretched my neck and screamed again—but it sounded like the roar of a monster. Blinding pain seared my brain.

chapter twenty-nine

~*Let go. Just let your body take over.*

It was a voice I'd never heard in my head before though it seemed familiar. A deep, commanding tone. One that bade me to follow orders. I clapped my clawed hands over my ears to block out the voice. I tried to fight the change, but that only caused more agony. The abrasive laugh of King Stuart reverberated through the chamber. Another wash of fiery pain rendered me mute.

The world had returned from its slumber.

~*Stop fighting, Sophie.* The deep voice ordered. *Henry*—it was Henry. I searched the room for him. It was his fault I couldn't get back home. He'd made my dad destroy the tapestry.

As my gaze swept over the hall in search of my quarry, a large gold eye blinked by one of the pillars. A dragon's face appeared, followed by his body. His expression pleaded with me to let go—to stop trying to control the change my body was undergoing. That all was as it must be.

I rejected that idea and felt the rise of panic taking hold. My gaze slid to the cowering guests. I searched for Henry's face in the crowd, but they all were wearing masks. Some crumpled to the floor in fear while others backed away in jerky steps. Was it me that was scaring them?

With all my willpower, I drew a breath and let it out slowly, counting to seven. I didn't want to scare everyone. I just wanted to go home. I just wanted things to be as they were before I ever knew about Brindle. I unclenched my hands and let my arms drop, the weight of them pulling me forward, down on hands and knees. Waves of pain washed over me, but now that I wasn't fighting it, it was bearable. My mother's locket dangled from my neck, the long chain accommodating my neck as it grew thicker. It swung like a pendulum. I concentrated on the swing instead of the fear. Back and forth, a steady rhythm I could follow. Once I stopped letting the fear control me, I recognized what was happening. I was changing into something new.

A sudden spurt of growth let me see over every head in the room. The counterbalance of a long tail set me firmly in place. I flexed my shoulders. The bunch and pull of new muscles was strange. Turning my long neck, I tested those muscles and unfurled pale gold wings. A dragon. My dragon song had brought on the change, and the rage at the injustice of my mother's murder propelled it. A sudden rush of new thoughts made my heart race. What would I be capable of as a dragon? Knocking down a brick wall perhaps? Burning a scaffold to ashes? Biting off the head of a tyrant?

I blinked my new eyes. The world was sharp and clear. I could zoom in on the tiniest details: the worn threads of the curtains hanging behind the dais, the flaking gold leaf on the king's throne, the wrinkles on his forehead.

I flexed my fingers, sensed the strength contained within my talon-like grip. If there was one person in the room I'd like to test my new skills on, it was Stuart. I crept forward, pinning the king in his throne with my stare. He shifted uncomfortably. A growl rose in my throat and pushed past my clenched teeth. The sound reverberated through the high ceilinged room. I turned in a circle, beat my wings, and swept my tail. Many of the guests cowered tight along the walls, but the young violinist stepped forward and kneeled before me.

That must have been too much for Stuart. He seemed to gather his courage as he bent to pick up the velvet bag at his feet. He pushed Dougal away from him and burst through the guards that had gathered in a protective circle.

"You still have much to lose, Sophinestra, if you don't obey my orders." He dumped the contents of the bag. I braced myself for the sight of my mother's head. Then, it thumped onto the marble floor and rolled to a stop at my feet. Her dead eyes blindly stared up at me. My chest and throat grew tight. I'd seen it in the dragon memory, but nothing would've prepared me for seeing it now.

I roared, pouring out my heartache. He'd never even given me the chance to know her. All I had was the memories of the dragons, the few moments we'd shared in the dungeon. I'd never have anything else.

"She is just the beginning." Stuart pointed to the back of the room as he crept down the dais stairs. The cry of an infant carried across the hall.

My heartstrings tugged as I turned toward the familiar sound. Guards pulled heavy velvet coverings away from two large cages hanging from the balcony. I hadn't seen them when I was escorted in; I had been too focused on the king in his decrepit throne. In one cage, Maria stood defiantly. In the other was Samantha with little William cradled in her arms. But…my dad and Henry destroyed the tapestry. I'd seen them. I closed my eyes as my thoughts spun. My wings fluttered against my back. They must have come through the tapestry in Anna's house…or maybe Jack had found the key to Gran's locked room—but that meant that they'd portaled into the dungeon. How did they get through the wall? Was my dad here, too?

"Now!" yelled the king.

The sudden shock of a cold heavy metal net brought me to me knees. I was trapped under its weight, my wings pinned to my back. Wrath crackled in my gut. I gasped for air as the leather collar with the beautiful emerald was fastened around my neck. It was tight. Constricting. I fought the panic and concentrated on just breathing.

Stuart strutted toward me, kicking my mother's head like a soccer ball so that it rolled closer. The dead flesh making a dull thud against the cold stone floor. "Everyone you love will be separated from their heads if you don't obey."

I couldn't bear to look at my mother's beautiful face. Those flat eyes—no spark of light reflected in them. I stared at the discarded velvet bag instead, the bottom soaked with blood. The king pulled the locket from my neck, breaking the chain. After pocketing the piece of jewelry, he leaned in close. His voice was low and rough as gravel, "You see, the emerald collar you now wear contains a spell. I gave the necklace to Brunella so that she could do that little job for me…but alas, it all worked out in the end. As long as it's around your neck, you won't be able to change back into your human form."

My guts boiled. Stuart didn't really think he could make me a slave, did he? I narrowed my eyes. The king prattled on. I curled my lips and growled deep in my throat.

"I must confess, I will miss those lovely curves, but your dragon form is more useful for my purposes. If you are good, I'll think about letting you be human at night, for your *other* duties."

The king opened his arms and gestured to the guests in the room. "Does anyone have any objections?"

The crowd was silent.

"No?" Stuart laughed. "Dougal, I don't think I'll need you tonight after all. Seems our little dragonsinger understands the predicament she's in well enough."

The thought of having to endure his mouth on mine again, his hands groping my body, his desperate touches. He was mad. This was madness. My gut boiled as I tried to think of a way out.

~*We are in* your *service*, a dragon's voice whispered in my mind.

One by one winking eyes appeared and long, padded claws curled around smooth pillars in the great hall. Red, bronze, blue, white, green. They'd come. The dragons of Brindle had come to me, called by the magic in my song. Their wings rustled like the wind in the trees. The dragons whispered their names— names that rang of a long ago time: Raynorak, Greindhide, Baltashar…and it went on. They told me they were old, but still strong. As their minds touched mine, colors bloomed at the edge of my vision. They filled me with strength, resolve, and a history that belonged to Brindle—that belonged to me. They only awaited my orders.

My voice was raspy, but I was able to give form to the words I longed to spit out. "It will be a cold day in Hell when you touch me again."

Stuart laughed and cradled his hand to his ear, making a show of not being able to hear me. "What did you say, my little dragon?"

I gathered my courage and anger. I crushed it into a bullet that could be hurled at my enemy. It lodged itself in my chest. I roared. "I object!"

The metal nets dug into my plated skin as the guards pulled it tighter against me. The king tried to crush my skull into the smooth tile floor with his boot. I played along. Instinct would tell me the right time to act.

Stuart's voice rang over the crowd. "The age of the dragon is over! Those few born Grasped will be executed, starting tonight." He pointed at me, pinned under his boot. "Now that I have her, there will be nowhere to run and nowhere to hide where I can't sniff you out. No one will challenge my right to rule ever again."

The guard who had escorted me into the hall stepped forward. His jerky movement caught my eye and I strained to turn my head just enough so that I could see him clearly. He tore his mask from his face.

My breath caught in my throat.

"Henry?" I whispered. My heart picked up its pace. Henry! I growled at the traitor.

The king's boot scraped off of my face as he turned. He pointed and stuttered. "Y-you! You were banished. I knew I should've killed you."

Henry laughed. "I've been waiting for this moment for a very long time, Stuart."

"Guards! Arrest him!"

Stuart's guards circled Henry, hands on swords.

Henry put up his hands as if he was going to surrender. "Now, now gentlemen. We are all on the same side." His voice made a funny, echoey sound.

My brain was fuzzy at the edges, like when you wake up unexpectedly, and you can't quite remember if the dream you were having was an actual dream, or if it was real.

"Get up and be *my* dragonsinger, Sophie, as your father should have been!" Henry commanded.

I struggled under the weight of the metal netting, but finally I found my footing. I didn't understand—how should my dad have been *Henry's* dragonsinger? Unless…was Henry the true heir to Brindle?

Lawrence's voice rang in my mind. ~*Those born Grasped knew the danger. Too many have died to bring about this day. Let their deaths count for something.*

I fought the netting, straining my new muscles. I couldn't let Lawrence down. I had to trust that there was a reason Henry told my dad to destroy the tapestry. The other dragons glided down from the pillars, and made themselves visible to the crowd. The guards surrounding Henry shifted from foot to foot as if trying to decide if they had a better chance at life defending the king or defying him. One by one they backed down and turned on Stuart.

"Where is your courage now, brother?" Henry chided the king.

Stuart balled his fists and reached to his side for a sword that had not been strapped on this evening.

Henry pulled the sword hanging on his hip from its scabbard. He hefted the weight in his hand. "Dear *brother*, our father taught us that there were two ways a king ruled a kingdom—fear and love. What you never understood was that one will do anything for love."

"Love," the king scoffed. "Those who love are weak. They can be broken. Our father loved you best and look how that turned out. *I'm* the king of Brindle—not you. I was first born, it is my right." Stuart thrust his finger at Henry. "Banishment obviously wasn't a big enough warning for you to stay away. Dougal, kill this imposter!"

Dougal pulled his sword and stalked toward the men. His eyes flashed dangerously. *~Prepare yourself, Sophie.*

All of my nerve endings sprang to life when Dougal's baritone voice echoed in my head. I remembered him leaning over Lawrence's body, listening for his breath. His hazel eyes searched for me in the crowd. He *had* been nodding to me, not the king. My grief had blocked the message he was sending.

Dougal hacked at the netting. A surge of renewed energy helped me scramble to my feet. I shook off the metal net. The guards still loyal to Stuart swarmed Dougal; he wheeled round to fight them. Henry joined, metal clashing into metal. Stuart's face turned purple when he realized his right hand man wasn't fighting for him, but against him.

~Have no mercy. I flung the thought at the dragons.

When the dragons leapt into the fray, King Stuart ran.

"Coward!" I roared. A stream of fiery liquid erupted from my mouth. The heat steared my nostrils. The metal netting sizzled and evaporated leaving only black flecks of ash to float around me like gnats. I lurched forward but was grabbed by the neck.

I roared and rolled, and my attacker rolled with me. My claws caught the dragon's underbelly. Did Stuart have a dragon on his side? My talons pierced the dragon's soft skin. If he did, he wouldn't for long. I narrowed my eyes, working up another fiery blast when the dragon's voice ripped through my hazy red anger.

~*Be still, so I can get this thing off of you!*

I froze. ~*Lawrence?*

My eyes stung with hot tears.

~*I had to play the game as Stuart was playing it. I had to make him think he'd killed me.*

I retracted my claws. ~*I thought I'd lost you.*

~*I gave you the spell. I tried to tell you.*

~*You said it wasn't over! That doesn't translate as* I'm alive. I thought you wanted me to keep fighting. To not give up.

His gold eyes crinkled. ~ *I'm sorry. And I'm sorry for this, too.* He dug his teeth into the collar around my neck and a loud hissing sputtered in my ear.

I roared as acid dripped down my scales. I tore away from Lawrence and the collar shredded. I growled and spit at him, small flames charging toward his face.

~*Settle now, Sophie. Don't let the beast inside take over. I haven't spent my life watching over you to lose you now.* A thin membrane flicked across his eyes and then Lawrence launched himself at me. I ducked but his wing still clipped the side of my face as he rose into the air. His claws clamped down on a spear spiraling in my direction. He broke it in two and flung away the pieces before tearing after the guard who'd thrown it. ~*Don't just stand there! Fight!*

The large doors beneath the balcony burst open. Hooves thundered into the hall as a mob of unicorns charged through. They herded some of the king's guard into a quivering mass, using their horns like swords. Horse-like screams fused with the sounds of battle. I turned away as two of the dragons engulfed the corralled men in an instant inferno.

I tightened my ears to my head to block out the horrifying screams and scanned the room for Stuart. My sharpened vision caught him stumbling down a low-lit passageway, the spiky, white-haired Wilhelm close on his heels. I dashed through the crowd spitting fire.

Wilhelm looked back, stumbled and fell, spilling forward and catching Stuart in a tangled mass of limbs. My flames stalked the king and his man down the corridor like hellhounds on the hunt.

chapter thirty

The ragged breathing of the king hitched as I growled and released a small wisp of smoke. Sweat beaded on Stuart's forehead. Wilhelm crab-crawled away, his leather-clad feet shushing on the stone floor, his breath coming out in quivering little gasps.

"How does it feel to be hunted?" My soft voice carried to the far end of the hallway. The scrape of my talons echoed off the corridor walls.

I raised a talon to Stuart's throat. It shone with a metallic gleam like the glint on the edge of a knife. He scrambled back, but only managed to trap himself between the shaking Wilhelm and the unrelenting wall.

"Please…" He held up his hands, as if declaring innocence. "I've done nothing to harm you." His words made my blood boil.

"You made a young girl a prisoner of your cruelty."

"No." Stuart shook his head. "I would have loved you if you'd let me."

I put pressure on the tip of my talon, pressing into the hollow above his collarbone. Blood beaded onto the razor-sharp claw and dripped, staining his jacket. "I was already loved. But you took them all away."

Stuart's eyes sharpened. "Do it then. Take your revenge!"

My eyes narrowed and I growled in his face, fangs inches from his nose. What was he playing at? Stuart squeezed his eyes shut. His lip trembled. I released the pressure on his neck and his expression changed instantly. He smirked, sidling away. "I knew you couldn't do it. Face it. Deep down, you're weak... just like your mother."

Stuart opened his mouth to continue, but I lunged forward, fangs slicing into the side of his neck.

Wilhelm shrieked as Stuart's blood spurted over him. Even though I wanted to shake Stuart violently, he didn't deserve a fast death. I released him and he crumpled against the wall. His trembling fingers pressed the wound. He held the bloody digits in front of him and stared in astonishment.

"I will take pleasure in your death," I growled. "I will watch your life drain away as you have drained the lives of this kingdom."

I swiped at his jacket, ripping off the pocket. My stashed locket slid onto the floor. I curled a claw around it and picked it up.

Footsteps pounded down the corridor. I spun, fire boiling in my throat, prepared to spew flames. Weapons clattered to the floor. Hands flew up in the air.

Henry and Dougal stopped abruptly.

Lawrence, no longer in dragon form, skidded to a halt behind them.

"Relax, Sophie." Henry held one hand held in front of him to halt my charge.

I snarled, imagining my fangs glistening with liquid fire.

Henry kneeled. "I was not commanding. I was simply suggesting that you calm down before you roast your friends by mistake."

I swallowed and blinked rapidly. *~Jack destroyed the tapestry. The one that would've taken me home. I saw him do it. I heard you tell him to. So how did you get here? What did you do to him?*

Henry's eyes were bright as he pleaded with me. "I was afraid after the guards took you that King Stuart would find the second portal. I was protecting your father, Anna, Samantha, and the baby. Everything we'd built in your world! You wouldn't have wanted the king's guards to take little William away from us, would you?"

He'd heard her plead with Lawrence!

"It's true, Sophie." Samantha pushed through the crowd, William cradled in her arms.

I pointed at Samantha and the baby and thrust my thoughts into Henry's head. ~ *Your little plan obviously didn't work if they were caged up and held as ransom!*

Henry held an arm out to stop Samantha from approaching. "She's dangerous right now. Take William and go back into the hall."

"I will not." Samantha brushed past her husband.

His brows furrowed. "I said—"

Samantha whirled on her husband, her finger in the air in a threatening manner. "Don't take that tone with me, Henry."

Abashed, Henry clamped his mouth shut as Samantha turned back to me.

"She won't harm the baby." With that said, Samantha placed the baby in my claws and palmed my locket.

The crowded corridor held a collective breath.

The sweet smell of lavender permeated my senses. A wisp of damp red curls framed William's face. He blinked up at me and smiled, his chubby hand reaching out. His tiny hand curled on my snout and the rage and fear filling my heart melted.

"William and I were the bait, Sophie," Samantha said. She reached up, ready to slide the locket over my head. I lowered my head and felt the warm metal slide down my neck. "Dougal helped us," she whispered.

I stared at Dougal over her shoulder. How could I have been so wrong about him? He nodded and smiled. "I told the king that I found a new tapestry hidden in a peasant girl's cottage. Then I told him I went through it, captured Samantha, and lured Henry back to Brindle so he could be rid of him once and for all."

I cradled William close to my chest. His soft noises were comforting. The tenseness in my body withered. I shrank as my anger faded.

"You know Stuart couldn't pass up the opportunity to get rid of Henry for good," Lawrence said.

~*You believe them?* I stared hard into his amber eyes.

~*Can you think of a reason they would lie to us?*

I wracked my brain, but came up with none. Lawrence stepped forward, hands extended, but I shook my head and pulled away.

"Please, Sophie. You must believe us. We love you."

~*None of that explains how you all got here.*

"This might." Henry gestured to the back of the crowd.

My father stepped sheepishly forward with Maria in tow. They were hand in hand.

I stumbled forward. "I've been so worried." I thrust the baby into Henry's arms then hung my head over my dad's shoulder. I wanted to choke him and hug him at the same time. He stumbled under my weight, but squeezed me back, arms around my long neck, his grip fierce.

"Not as worried as I was, I'll wager." He chuckled nervously.

"How did you all get here?" I asked.

"There is a special tapestry on loan from France at the Cloisters," Jack said. "It's a scene of a lady and a unicorn."

"The Lady and the Unicorn—your notes in the textbook…" I drew away so I could look at him. "You made a note about the mirror in the tapestry being a portal to another world."

Dad nodded. "I'm sorry—I should have told you that I believed you a long time ago, but I felt crazy for believing in it myself."

"But, if you all went through that tapestry in New York, you came through its twin," I said. "And that's in a walled up room you can't access unless you're the size of a mouse."

"You can if you have a lot of magic on your side." A clear voice rang out of the crowd. Anna stepped forward and my wings grew lighter. "We pulled down the wall, Henry and I, stone by stone. I knew the chamber well from my younger days at the castle. It used to be a storage room for the kitchens. Oh, the stairs had been torn down long ago, but I still recognized it."

"And I saw them as they passed my cell. I knew Anna at once," Maria added. "Just as I knew Lawrence was mine the first time he was sent to me in the dungeon."

My legs returned to their soft curves. My fingers uncurled. Lawrence left my side to embrace Maria. When he straightened, he extended his hand to Jack who shoved it aside and pulled him into a bear hug.

Maria stepped forward and clasped my hand with her good one. Her grip was warm and firm. "We've lost many in this fight, but those who are left are true and just friends. I'm so sorry, Sophie. I recognized the king's men at the Cloisters when you were little. I thought the sheer number of people in New York would keep us safe."

I shivered as I fully returned to my human form.

"Give us your cloak then, son," Maria said.

Lawrence removed his cloak and wrapped it around me. He pulled the folds tight and his warm lips closed over mine. "I've been waiting for a long time to do that again."

A different kind of heat rose inside me. I pulled away before he embarrassed me in front of my dad. I buried my head in the crook of his shoulder. He held me, stroking my hair until I realized the nastiness of the day wasn't over.

I pulled away and gestured to Stuart lying in a sticky pool of crimson. I'd told him that I was going to watch his life drain away, but I'd missed it. Conflicting emotions swelled inside of me. I'd meant every word I said to him, but I was kind of glad he'd left this world with no one to give him comfort. He was dead now and couldn't hurt anyone else. However, his right hand man, Wilhelm—the one who'd found us at the Renaissance faire, the man who'd taken my mom from me and destroyed our apartment—was still alive. Alive, but unconscious. "What are we going to do with them?"

Henry sighed. "We are going to lock Wilhelm in the dungeon, give Stuart a king's burial, and then try to put this kingdom back to rights."

"Does he deserve that?" I asked. The ceremony of a king's burial for Stuart left a bad taste in my mouth.

Henry frowned. "Deserve it or not, he was my brother. We will build a funeral pyre in the courtyard, but not before we bury your mother."

Everyone held their breath and watched me like I might engulf myself in flames, but I smiled sadly as I took in Henry's words. "She'll be buried with the full honors of a Queen of Brindle, for that's what she was. A true queen any kingdom would've been happy to call their own."

"I couldn't have said it any better." Lawrence took my hand and rubbed his thumb along the top of mine. He spoke the words I couldn't get past the lump in my throat. "Thank you, Henry."

Henry nodded and gestured to Dougal. "Take my brother's man to the dungeon."

Dougal pressed forward through the crowd, a smile lighting up his face. "With pleasure." He grabbed Wilhelm's arm and tossed the unconscious man over his shoulder.

Henry put his arm around Samantha, and they strode down the corridor back to the great hall.

chapter thirty~one

Lawrence and I followed the king. Maria and my dad fell in behind us. The corridor opened into the hall. Henry paused, his eyes scanning the crowd. Scattered along the floor were the shattered remains of the stained glass windows and pools of rain. The colorful pennants that hung from the arched roof braces were scorched. Through the broken windows, thousands of birds had entered, perching in the nooks and crannies and along the arches. A smoking pile of blackened bones and ash were all that was left of the guards the unicorns had rounded up. They were now circled around one of their fallen. The unicorn's silver blood made a shimmering path across the stone floor. Disheveled and ashen guests huddled into corners. Dragons and gryphons held sentry at the doors. Able, the young violin player, was the first to notice our entrance. He scrambled forward and knelt.

A hush fell over the crowd. One by one, each man, woman, and child knelt for their new king.

Henry clasped his hands behind his back and rocked on his heels, building up the anticipation. He looked comfortable and practiced in front of a crowd. "When the king has more than one son, he may choose the eldest to rule after him, or the child born in the grasp of a dragon. It was just as much my right to rule as Stuart's, but our father knew his heart was fragile. My brother was a jealous creature, even as a child. That's why I was chosen to inherit the crown—not because I was special, but because my father knew I wouldn't misuse my power or compel others for my own gain. Unfortunately, Stuart plotted against me. He lured Samantha and me to the harbor for a picnic by the singing caves. We were abducted and thrown in the dungeon. If it wasn't for Anna Emberwing's brother, Gafford, we would've died there. He was the one who talked Stuart into exiling us to the old world instead. Please, rise. We are all friends here."

With Samantha on his arm, Henry entered the crowd. Masks were disposed of, names and hands given freely. Castle servants bustled into the room with brooms to sweep away the glass. The musicians re-formed and a soft melody filled the chamber. The dragons took to roosting in the arched braces above, shoving out the birds that had taken up residence earlier. The birds they displaced soared above like living streamers.

A warm arm encircled my waist. "The show must go on, I guess."

I turned to Lawrence, draping my arms over his shoulders and reveling in his embrace.

Red ringed his neck where the noose had rubbed his skin raw. A patch of hair by his ear was scorched. My eyes stung with tears. "I thought I'd lost you."

His hand stroked my hair. "I'm sorry. I had to make Stuart think he'd won. He suspected me even before he saw us in the solar dancing. That's why I gave Brunella the spell."

Dougal grinned like a Cheshire cat who'd just swallowed a canary.

I pointed my finger accusingly at him. "You were in on this the entire time?"

He nodded and bowed slightly. "From the very beginning, My Lady."

"But he was so…so…*nefarious*." I whispered to Lawrence.

"He played his part a little too well, I'll admit." Lawrence chuckled.

Dougal rubbed the back of his neck with his hand. "So, you can turn into a dragon, huh? That's pretty awesome. Look, Sophie. I'm so sorry that you thought I was…evil."

I squeezed his hands and searched for the right words to put him at ease. "You've proven yourself good. It's…it's just going to take me a little bit to get it all sorted out in my head. Okay?"

He nodded. "That's fair. I suppose you've seen enough betrayal to fill a lifetime."

Lawrence pulled me back into his embrace. I had a feeling he might not ever let me out of it again. I was okay with that. His hold was strong and comforting, his muscles taut and lean. He kissed my forehead and brushed my cheekbone with his thumb, careful not to touch the cut his wing had given me. It stung like the devil.

I searched his amber eyes. There were green flecks shining back at me, like the magic that rose and sparkled from the tapestries. I leaned in closer, my lips finding his easily. Lawrence's hand crept over the bare skin under my cloak. His fingers trailed lightly down my side, following the curves of my body.

Energy shivered through me. The dragon inside rose to the surface; my skin rippled like waves. The pleasure of heightened sensation as a dragon tingled at the edges of my being. I let the feeling float between us.

"Whoa." Lawrence pulled away, cheeks flushed. He cleared his throat and shifted uncomfortably in my embrace.

"Did I hurt you?" I lifted my hand to touch the wound on his neck but pulled back—my touch might hurt him even more.

He couldn't meet my gaze, so he lowered his head to whisper in my ear. "All I can think about is the fact that you're naked under my cloak."

"Oh." I drew away and pulled the folds close. He wasn't thinking about his injuries at all. My face burned. "I really need to learn to keep my clothes when I transform. Can you teach me?"

His eyes twinkled with mischief. "Sorry. Don't know how to do that, love."

"What?" I whacked him in the chest. "That's not true. C'mon, how do you do it?"

He quirked his eyebrow in amusement. "Wouldn't you like to know? You know there's always a consequence for using magic..."

A throat cleared near us. "Mind if I interrupt?"

I laid my forehead on Lawrence's shoulder and giggled a little. "Sure, Henry." I gathered the cloak even tighter around me and straightened, trying to look more formal. It was hard knowing that only a cloak separated me and my birthday suit from the king of the land. "Or should I call you *King* Henry now?"

Henry clasped his hands behind his back. "It will always be just plain Henry to you, Sophie, but we must decide what we shall do with you."

"What do you mean?" My thoughts swirled. My old friend, anxiety, fluttered to life. Now that he was king, would he want me around? Would he want to use my gifts the way his brother had?

"He means whether you return home, with me." My dad sidled up, his glance sliding over the charred remains in the hall behind me.

"Or if you stay here," Henry added. "In Brindle, where you belong."

I looked from my dad to Henry to Lawrence and back. "What are you going to do, Dad?"

"I have a good job, co-workers I like." Dad adjusted his glasses. "Maria doesn't want to stay here..."

"But her son is here," I said.

My father rubbed the back of his neck and glanced at Lawrence. "Henry has promised to find us a matching set of tapestries so that you both can come visit us anytime you want…and…vice-versa."

I looked away, my eyes prickling with tears. "Sounds like you've got it all planned out then."

His warm hand gathered mine. "Sophie, I love you. Stay for a while. Get to know the kingdom, the people. Learn what you can about your mother and father from those who knew them. If you don't feel that Brindle is the right place for you after that, you can always come home."

Home.

I turned and tucked an arm around my dad. "There's a tapestry in Grandma's locked room. The key is in my bedroom. In the silver chalice that sits on my dresser."

"And its twin?" Henry asked.

I nodded. "I saw it in the dungeon."

Henry nodded. "I will have someone gather it right away and put it in your chamber."

I turned back to my Dad. "The tapestry is of a dragon. I didn't tell you I'd found the key because I didn't want you to be mad."

He gave me a squeeze. When I pulled away, his eyes were wet and glassy. Our separation would be just as hard for him as it was for me.

"You promise I can come and go as I please?" I asked Henry.

"Of course," Henry answered.

"Any time, any day, no reservations needed." Dad stroked my hair and smiled. "You got your dragons, and I got back my daughter, my wife, and gained a son. Never in a million years did I think that dream would ever come true."

I smiled. "It just took a little faith, Dad. All you needed to do was believe in a bit of magic."

Henry's booming laugh filled the chamber. "Listen to her—no longer the skeptic, is she, Lawrence?"

My dad turned and shook Henry's hand. "I do believe you've all changed her mind."

Henry waved a dismissive hand. "Nah. She did that herself. She's got plenty of courage, that daughter of yours."

Dad drew his hand through his hair. "Well, you've certainly changed mine."

"Will you and Maria stay for the coronation?" Henry threw his arm around my dad's shoulders, subtly leading him away.

"Yes, we will."

Henry looked over his shoulder and winked at me. "We'll see you two in the family solar in twenty minutes."

"Is that an order, King Henry?" I smirked.

Henry cleared his throat and blushed. "Yes, but not because I'm your King. It's because I'm starving."

I giggled, then turned to Lawrence with a wicked grin. "Your aunt isn't here, so you'll have to help me dress."

"Oh, no he won't." Brunella puffed toward us arm in arm with Anna. "Let's go!"

"Brunella! You're supposed to be at home," I exclaimed. Damn it. Now it would be hours before I could get Lawrence alone again.

"You can all try to get rid of me, but the work of a lady's maid is never done." She and Anna gathered Lawrence in their arms. "I can't tell you how relieved I was when Dougal told me you were not dead." Brunella patted his cheek, eyes glistening. "Now, shoo! Shoo boy, so we can help our Sophie get dressed again."

She prattled on about the gown she had already laid out in my chamber as they dragged me out of the ballroom. I turned to look at Lawrence with a pleading look on my face. He smiled and shrugged. There was no changing his aunt's mind once it was made up, but I was in no hurry to leave him behind.

~*Lawrence, wait for me.*

~*Always.*

Acknowledgements

No book is written by a single person. I have been working on this story since 2003 or 2004. It has been a long journey, but one that was full of rewarding friendships. I'd like to thank the following people for their love and encouragment throughout this wild ride.

A big thank you to my first writing group: Laura Handy (AKA as Laura Ellen—check out her book *Blind Spot*, it's an amazing story!) Katena Presutti, Diane Telgen, and Tressa Parmann. Thank you for giving me the courage to write.

Another big thank you goes to my fellow writers, beta readers, editors, and emotional support group: Laura Pauling, Simon Brooks, Dee Currier, Cindy Davis, Tom Greenlaw, Jennifer Allis-Provost, April Wood, Wendy Brotherlin, and Trisha Wooldridge. These guys write some amazing things-- check them out too!

And I would be remiss if I did not thank my friends who found all those pesky typos: Jody Sharrow, Linda Ford, Elizabeth Gerrity, Doc Kia McCullen, and Jean Githrie Hiller. Thanks for reading!

Also a big thank you (with sloppy kisses) goes to my husband, Chris, who always helps me out with plot issues on long drives. I love you always.

Other books by Jennifer Carson

Hapenny Magick
ISBN: 978-1937053918

Carson has created a delightful story of joy and wonder and courage. I'm looking forward to sharing this one with my children.
—Jim Hines, author of the Jig the Goblin series

Also available as an audio book and musical stage play.

Tangled Magick
ISBN: 978-1633920002

Jennifer Carson's book is full of whimsy and a gentle humor, but it also includes peril and a satisfying adventure.
—Kate Coombs, author of Runaway Princess

Coming soon as an audio book!

Ducky's New Ball
ISBN:978-1622510344-
hardcover

Whent Spike's spines pop Ducky's new ball. The two friends try everything to fix it. Nothing works until Ducky's creative thinking, and Spike's "spikes", save the day.

About the Author

photo credit: Mary Bortmas ©2018

Jennifer Carson lives in Michigan with her husband, four sons, and many four legged friends. She grew up on a steady diet of Muppet movies and renaissance faires. Occasionally her parents would catch her reading under the blankets with a flashlight, but most of the time she got away with it!

Besides telling tales, Jennifer creates fantasy creatures and characters and publishes her own sewing patterns. She is also a playwright and is currently working on selling a movie script.

Visit Jennifer on the web at:

thedragoncharmer.com